Robert Muchamore was born in 1972 and spent thirteen years working as a private investigator. *CHERUB: The General* is his tenth novel.

The CHERUB series has won numerous awards, including the 2005 Red House Children's Book Award. For more information on Robert and his work, visit **www.cherubcampus.com**.

Praise for the CHERUB series:

'If you can't bear to read another story about elves, princesses or spoiled rich kids who never go to the toilet, try this. You won't regret it.' *The Ultimate Teen Book Guide*

'My sixteen-year-old son read *The Recruit* in one sitting, then went out the next day and got the sequel.' Sophie Smiley, teacher and children's author

'So good I forced my friends to read it, and they're glad I did!' Helen, age 14

'CHERUB is the first book I ever read cover to cover. It was amazing.' Scott, age 13

'The best book ever.' Madeline, age 12

'CHERUB is a must for Alex Rider lovers.' Travis, age 14

Coming in 2009:

A major new CHERUB series from
Robert Muchamore:

Henderson's Boys: The Escape
Henderson's Boys: Eagle Day

The original CHERUB series continues:

1. The Recruit
2. Class A
3. Maximum Security
4. The Killing
5. Divine Madness
6. Man vs Beast
7. The Fall
8. Mad Dogs
9. The Sleepwalker
10. The General

and coming soon . . .

11. Brigands M.C.

THE GENERAL

Robert Muchamore

A division of Hachette Children's Books

First published in Great Britain in 2008
by Hodder Children's Books

7

A Catalogue record for this book is available
from the British Library

ISBN-13: 978 0 340 93184 4

Typeset in Goudy by Avon DataSet Ltd,
Bidford-on-Avon, Warwickshire

Printed and bound in Great Britain by
CPI Bookmarque, Croydon, CR0 4TD

The paper and board used in this paperback by
Hodder Children's Books are natural recyclable products
made from wood grown in sustainable forests.
The manufacturing processes conform to the
environmental regulations of the country of origin.

Hodder Children's Books
A division of Hachette Children's Books
338 Euston Road, London NW1 3BH
An Hachette Livre UK Company

WHAT IS CHERUB?

CHERUB is a branch of British Intelligence. Its agents are aged between ten and seventeen years. Cherubs are mainly orphans who have been taken out of care homes and trained to work undercover. They live on CHERUB campus, a secret facility hidden in the English countryside.

WHAT USE ARE KIDS?

Quite a lot. Nobody realises kids do undercover missions, which means they can get away with all kinds of stuff that adults can't.

WHO ARE THEY?

About three hundred children live on CHERUB campus. JAMES ADAMS is our sixteen-year-old hero. He's a well-respected CHERUB agent with several successful missions under his belt. Australian-born Dana Smith is James' girlfriend. His other close friends include BRUCE NORRIS, KERRY CHANG and SHAKEEL DAJANI.

James' sister, LAUREN ADAMS, is thirteen and already regarded as an outstanding CHERUB agent. Her best friends are BETHANY PARKER and GREG 'RAT' RATHBONE.

CHERUB STAFF

With its large grounds, specialist training facilities and combined role as a boarding school and intelligence operation, CHERUB actually has more staff than pupils. They range from cooks and gardeners to teachers, training instructors, nurses, psychiatrists and mission specialists. CHERUB is run by its chairwoman, ZARA ASKER.

CHERUB T-SHIRTS

Cherubs are ranked according to the colour of the T-shirts they wear on campus. ORANGE is for visitors. RED is for kids who live on CHERUB campus but are too young to qualify as agents (the minimum age is ten). BLUE is for kids undergoing CHERUB's tough one-hundred-day basic training regime. A GREY T-shirt means you're qualified for missions. NAVY is a reward for outstanding performance on a single mission. Lauren and James wear the BLACK T-shirt, the ultimate recognition for outstanding achievement over a number of missions. When you retire, you get the WHITE T-shirt, which is also worn by some staff.

1. DEMO

The anarchist organisation known as Street Action Group (SAG) first came to light in summer 2003 when its leader Chris Bradford hijacked the rostrum at an anti-Iraq-war demonstration in London's Hyde Park. Bradford urged a peaceful crowd to attack police officers, before setting light to straw-filled effigies of Prime Minister Tony Blair and US President George W. Bush.

By 2006 SAG had built a cult following and was strong enough to begin staging its own anti-government protests. These culminated in July with the Summer Mayhem March *through central Birmingham. Dozens of cars were vandalised, windows were broken, more than thirty protestors were arrested and a police officer was stabbed.*

In the months that followed, prison sentences were handed down to several senior SAG members involved in the rioting. Heavy police presence wherever SAG planned to appear made staging violent protests increasingly difficult.

Chris Bradford became bitter at what he called 'state oppression' and an MI5 agent sent to infiltrate SAG made a shocking discovery: Bradford was trying to acquire guns and bomb-making equipment in order to transform SAG into a terrorist organisation.

(Excerpt from a CHERUB mission briefing for James Adams, October 2007)

It was December 21st, the last Friday before Christmas. The sky was purple and strings of lights dangled between Victorian lampposts on the pedestrianised London street. The pubs around Covent Garden tube station were crammed and office workers huddled in doorways smoking cigarettes. Teens gawped into shops well out of their price range and The Body Shop was full of miserable-looking men buying last-minute gifts.

Shoppers and drinkers ignored a rectangular pen made from metal crowd barriers as they shuffled past, though some noted the irony that two dozen police officers in fluorescent jackets lined up to face thirteen protestors inside the barriers.

James Adams was one of the thirteen. Sixteen years old, he was dressed in a bulky army surplus jacket and twenty-four-hole Doc Marten boots. His hair was shaved down to a number one on the sides and a shaggy, green-tinted Mohican ran from his forehead down to the collar of his jacket. He banged his gloved hands together to fight the cold as cops gave him stern looks.

Chris Bradford stood three metres away. Well built, Bradford had scruffy ginger hair, a baggy hoodie worn with the fluffy lining on the outside and two cameras filming him. One was held by a cop, who walked the perimeter with a titchy camcorder. The other was a more impressive beast. It sat on the shoulder of a BBC cameraman and a lamp mounted on top shone its light in Bradford's face.

'So, Mr Bradford,' BBC correspondent Simon Jett said. He had a silk scarf tucked into his overcoat and a microphone in hand. 'Today's turnout must be a disappointment. Many people are saying that the Street Action Group is on its last legs.'

Bradford's green eyes bulged and his shovel-sized hands shifted towards the correspondent's lapels. 'Who's been saying that?' he growled. 'Gimme names and addresses. It's always *certain sources*, but who are they? I'll tell you who – it's people who are running scared of us.'

Jett was delighted. Bradford's combo of slight menace and fruit-and-veg-seller cockney accent always made good TV.

'So how many protestors were you expecting to see here today?'

Bradford snatched a glance at his watch and bared his teeth. 'Trouble is, most of our crew are still in bed three o'clock in the afternoon. I guess I set the kick-off time a little too early.'

Jett nodded with fake sincerity. 'You sound like you're taking this lightly, but you *must* feel that the wind has been taken out of SAG's sails. Especially when you compare the turnout here with the thousand-plus people on the streets of Birmingham last summer?'

Bradford batted the plastic hood over the camera lens. 'You wait and see, Mr BBC,' he snarled, sticking his face right up to the camera. 'Inequality breeds hatred. There's more poverty and inequality in Britain today than ever before. If you're sitting at home in your nice house watching the likes of me on your thirty-two-inch LCD, you might not see the revolution rising up from the streets. But you mark my words: we're coming to get you.'

Jett could barely contain his smile. 'Do you have a timescale? When can we expect this revolution?'

'Next month, next year, who knows?' Bradford shrugged. 'Things *will* change radically before the end of this decade, but if you only watch the biased rubbish the BBC churns out, the first you'll know it is when my boys kick your front door down.'

The correspondent nodded. 'Chris Bradford, thank you very much for talking to me.'

'Cram it,' Bradford sneered, as the cameraman turned off the light and moved the weight of the big camera off his shoulder.

Bradford refused Jett's offer of a handshake and skulked towards a lonely-looking woman on the opposite side of the pen.

James overheard Jett telling his cameraman to take some footage from outside of the pen before they left. The policemen lifting up the barriers to let the BBC crew out asked when the story was likely to be on the news.

'Don't hold your breath,' Jett said drearily. 'I'm down here in case something kicks off, but I told my editor before I left: SAG is yesterday's news.'

'Hope so,' the policeman said. 'That officer up in Brum lost a lot of blood. She was lucky not to be killed.'

Jett nodded sympathetically. 'You take care of yourself, officer, and have a great Christmas.'

'You too,' the officer smiled.

As the cameraman filmed the barriers and lines of police, James raised the hood of his jacket and pulled the drawstring tight so that it covered most of his face. CHERUB agents are trained to keep away from the media and he gained further anonymity by taking out his mobile and staring down at the screen, typing a message to his girlfriend, Dana.

HOPE YOU'RE FEELING BETTER. TEXT ME I'M A LONELY BOY!

James pressed send and regretted it straight away. Dana hadn't replied to his last message and *I'm lonely* made him sound weak. He couldn't work out what he'd done to piss her off, but she'd been acting weird for days.

Two metal barriers were lifted away, opening up one end of the steel pen. The petite inspector in charge of crowd control bawled out, 'It's three-thirty, people. Time to march on Downing Street.'

The inspector knew she'd been heard, but the protestors ignored her. She grabbed a megaphone from a colleague before repeating herself.

'This demonstration was scheduled for three-fifteen,' she blared. 'You've already been allowed an extra fifteen minutes for assembly. Anyone not leaving the assembly point now will be arrested for a breach of the peace. Now MOVE IT!'

Bradford stepped towards the officer and glanced at his watch. A lone press photographer snapped a photo as the big man faced the squat officer with her fluorescent jacket and megaphone.

'Come on, sweetheart,' Bradford said, turning on the charm and tapping the face of his watch. 'We're waiting for a few more chaps to arrive. I've sent my man up to the station. The underground trains must be delayed, or something.'

'You've had your time,' the inspector said, shaking her

head resolutely. 'My men want to get home. So you can march, you can disperse peacefully, or you can take a ride in the back of a police van. What you can't do is waste any more of our time.'

Bradford spat on the pavement, before turning towards his pathetic gathering. 'You heard the nice lady. Let's roll, people.'

The photographer's flash popped as thirteen protestors filed out of the pen with fluorescent police jackets surrounding them. The cops exchanged grins, amused by SAG's pathetic showing.

Shoppers watched curiously as the march filed past and kids gawped as if it was a continuation of the street entertainment and human statues in the covered market a hundred metres away. As the police led the protestors briskly over the cobbles around Covent Garden market, James began eyeballing clumps of people in the uniform of rebellion: a mixture of punk, Goth and army surplus similar to his own. Some joined the back of the march, quickly doubling its strength, while others tracked its progress from a distance.

Bradford sidled up to the inspector as they turned out of the market and on to a side road leading downhill towards the Strand, a broad avenue of shops, theatres and hotels less than fifty metres from the north bank of the River Thames. James was near the head of the march and Bradford gave him a wink as two dozen youths dressed in sportswear emerged from a side street.

'Looks like someone turned up after all,' Bradford said to the inspector. 'Someone must have written the wrong address on our invitation cards.'

The inspector didn't give Bradford the satisfaction of an answer, but James could tell she was on edge. She grabbed her radio and ordered backup as she realised that the protestors had made a mockery of the police's attempt to assemble all the demonstrators in one place.

'SAG!' Bradford shouted, punching his fist in the air as the tracksuits and trainers merged with the dreadlocks and donkey jackets of SAG activists.

'SAG!' the crowd of close to a hundred chanted back.

James' heart sped as a fellow protestor caught the heel of his boot.

'Sorry mate.'

The crowd was tight and the cops now had bodies swarming around them. SAG had assembled the same toxic combination of hardcore anarchists and local youths looking for aggro that had kicked off the riot in Birmingham seventeen months earlier.

'Oggy, oggy, oggy,' Bradford shouted.

'SAG, SAG, SAG!' the crowd shouted back.

Another fifty marchers had joined the fray by the time James stepped on to the Strand and turned right. A huge drum was booming across the street and the shaven-headed drummer was leading a crowd of protestors out of an alleyway that ran up from the riverbank.

The cop nearest to James had spit running down his back. His baton was drawn but the officers were afraid to break formation and lash out because they were heavily outnumbered.

An amplified chant went up through the police megaphone. 'We've just nicked your megaphone; we've just nicked your megaphone, la-la-la-la.'

Everyone laughed as the drummer and his crew cut through snarled traffic and moved to the front of the march, but the next chant had a nastier edge.

'Let's stab all the coppers; let's stab all the coppers, la-la-la-la.'

A vast roar blew up as James glanced around and saw that the cops had changed tactics and dropped behind the protestors. Sirens wailed in the surrounding roads as the march merged with another large group of SAG sympathisers pouring out of a bendy bus.

There were more protestors than pavement and bodies spilled into the road and mingled with the crawling traffic. Horns blared and an impatient cab driver lost his door mirror and got his side window kicked in.

A gap between the buses enabled James to see across the street where more protestors were coming up from the riverbank, as the front of the march headed for Trafalgar Square.

James had lost track of Chris Bradford and all the other SAG members he'd got to know over the last seven weeks. He felt disorientated and was surrounded by a bunch of thuggish lads not much older than himself. They cheered, chanted and egged each other on, as the BBC cameraman balanced precariously on a concrete bollard, trying to film the chanting crowd from a high vantage point.

'Told you it was worth coming down here,' the lad next to James grinned, swigging from a can of beer as more glass smashed in the distance.

'Bloody 'ell,' his mate laughed. 'That was a big one. Someone's done a shop.'

His friends nodded. 'It's kicking off, man,' one said, before another chant of 'SAG, SAG, SAG!' ripped through the crowd.

Less than five metres from James, two Goth girls – who looked like the last people on earth to start a riot – pulled the metal liner out of a litter bin and hurled it through the front window of a sandwich bar. The crowd started clapping and a shout of 'Down with sandwiches,' went through the stolen megaphone.

The action of the two women embarrassed several testosterone-fuelled males into action. Four more shop windows caved within seconds and a man in a flash suit was dragged out the back of a taxi and given a slap before being relieved of a wallet and a Rolex.

James couldn't see over the crowd, but could hear hundreds of triumphant voices and the crunch of broken glass under his boot. Things were about to kick off, big time.

2. TWINKLE

'Will you all stop jabbering and shut the hell up!' Lauren Adams yelled, as the thirteen-year-old wrapped her hands over her ears.

She was in her eighth-floor room on CHERUB campus. Her bed had been tipped on its side to make space for the maps and diagrams spread across the carpet and she sat studying them with six fellow CHERUB agents: her boyfriend Rat, her best friend Bethany, Bethany's eleven-year-old brother Jake, Rat's best friend Andy Lagan and two eleven-year-old cherubs she barely knew called Ronan Walsh and Kevin Sumner.

'If we're gonna get picked to go to Las Vegas next month, we've *got* to get our plan straight and pull off this security test,' Lauren continued firmly. 'The ATCC is a new facility with state of the art security. We've got to get into the heart of the building and cause damage in the main control room.'

Kevin was the smallest kid in the room and he looked at the maps nervously. 'Which bit is the ATCC?'

'The whole building, doofus,' Jake Parker sighed noisily. 'ATCC: Air Traffic Control Centre.'

'Oh,' Kevin said. 'I thought it was one of the alarm thingies.'

Bethany cuffed her brother Jake around the head. 'Don't bite Kevin's head off, he's only little.'

Jake gave his sister the finger. 'He's less than a year younger than me, dog breath.'

Rat sighed. 'Don't start fighting again you two . . . Christ, what's that stink?'

They all turned towards Ronan. He was a stocky lad, mad on rugby and combat training but less keen on showering afterwards. He'd just pulled off one of his muddy boots.

'Put it back on,' Bethany gasped as she wafted her hand. 'How long have you been wearing those socks?'

'My eyes are watering,' Andy complained.

'Only about a week,' Ronan said as he buried his nose between his toes and took a long sniff.

'Don't!' Bethany yelled. 'Dirty animal.'

'It's harmless,' Ronan grinned, as he swung his foot towards Bethany. 'It's just my natural bodily juices.'

A couple of the lads laughed, but Lauren stepped over the maps and loomed above Ronan. 'If you don't put that boot back on, me and Bethany will drag you into the bathroom, strip you butt naked and scrub you with my toilet brush.'

'Kinky,' Andy laughed. 'Stripped and scrubbed by two hot chicks . . .'

'Two repugnant walruses, more like,' Jake said.

But Lauren shot the lads evil eyes and they both shut up. Ronan reluctantly pulled his boot back on and even though it was freezing outside, Bethany got up and flung open the balcony doors to clear the air.

Lauren went back to squatting in front of the maps before speaking again. 'I've got a good reputation and my black shirt,' she said, stretching out her T-shirt to emphasise the point. 'It won't make much difference to me if we mess this up, but we need to pull it off if you three younger lads want a sniff of some decent missions any time soon. So you guys choose: screw around, or calm down and start taking this plan seriously.'

Kevin, Ronan and Jake didn't like admitting that Lauren was right, but she glowered until they all nodded.

'OK,' Lauren said. 'I'm the only black shirt here, so I'm making myself Chairwoman. Any objections?'

Lauren half expected a mutiny. But they all knew someone had to take charge if their plan was going to work.

Rat raised his hand and waited for Lauren's nod before he spoke. 'Here's where I see the problem with our plan right now,' he said. 'Bethany and Lauren do their bit at the front of the air traffic control centre, but me, Andy and the three little dudes are gonna end up at the back facing six adult security guards with no weapons.'

'We need guns,' Jake blurted. 'Tranquilliser darts or stun guns at the least.'

'Why don't you read the mission briefing?' Lauren sighed. 'Our job is to test the security arrangements put in place by the private company at the new ATCC. If the government wanted people with Balaclavas and machine guns, they'd have sent in the army. We've got to dress and act like ordinary kids on a pre-Christmas rampage. We can use our mobiles, but no walkie-talkies. We can't take listening devices, explosives, lock guns or anything else that your average thirteen-year-old doesn't carry in the pocket of his hoodie.'

Bethany raised her hand and waved her mission briefing in the air. 'But Lauren, it does also say that the security guards are backed up by a team of military police.'

'With guns,' Jake added.

'Read it properly,' Lauren said. 'It's a rapid response team stationed on an RAF base eight kilometres away. As long as we don't give the regular security team at the ATCC time to sound the alarm, we'll only be up against private security guards with batons and pepper spray.'

'If only we knew *exactly* who these guards are,' Bethany said. 'I mean, they could be anything from doddery little old men to retired Special Forces.'

Lauren shrugged. 'When that control centre opens in the new year it's gonna be in charge of every civilian and military flight from the Midlands right the way up to the Scottish highlands. Planes could drop out of the sky if it was blown up.'

Ronan nodded solemnly. 'So unless the security has been set up by total idiots, we won't be facing a team of boy scouts.'

'Why don't we go over to Dennis King in Mission Preparation and say that we need more information on the security team?' Andy asked.

Lauren shook her head. 'Security tests like this one are part mission, part training exercise. King *might* give us more information if we ask, but we're supposed to devise our plan based on what they've given us. We'd get marked down in our assessment for sure.'

'I know,' Rat yelped triumphantly, as he smacked his fist into his palm. 'Slingshots.'

'What about them?' Lauren asked.

'Kids carry slingshots,' Rat explained. 'When I lived at the Ark in Australia I was always bored. One of the few toys I had was a slingshot. I used to fill it with rocks, pop out of a tunnel or a manhole, aim it at someone's head and dive for cover before they knew what had hit 'em. I caused at least a dozen concussions before Georgie caught me and had my butt paddled.'

'Sounds like a plan,' Lauren smiled, before Jake butted in.

'I'm a good aim with a slingshot – we used to massacre squirrels with them over the back of campus.'

Lauren didn't like Jake and as an animal lover and vegetarian she was even less impressed than usual. 'Excuse me?' she said ferociously. 'What have campus squirrels ever done to you?'

'Not recently,' Jake squirmed. 'I'm talking about when I was a little red shirt, camping out in tents in the summer.'

'Boys,' Bethany said, shaking her head. 'They all seem to go through a stage where all they want to do is kill stuff or set fire to it.'

Rat tutted, 'That's completely sexist, Bethany. If I went around making generalisations like that about girls you'd–'

Ronan spoke at the same time as Rat. 'I love setting fire to stuff–'

'All right,' Lauren interrupted, clapping her hands together. 'Let's focus on the security test, shall we? There are definitely slingshots downstairs in the weapons storeroom and if you think they'll help our cause, go and get some by all means.'

'It's been a while since I fired a slingshot,' Rat said, glancing at his watch. 'We've got a couple of hours before we leave, so I wouldn't mind getting a bit of practice in.'

Jake smirked, 'We could shoot up the ducks on the lake.'

'You're *not* funny, Jake,' Lauren said. 'If I see you or anyone else hurting animals on campus I'll pick you up and body-slam you so hard that you'll piss blood for a month.'

'Empty Coke cans make good targets,' Kevin said, trying to be constructive.

Jake nodded. 'Especially if you paint squirrels on them.'

'All *right*,' Lauren nodded, gritting her teeth and fighting the urge to jump on top of Jake and beat the crap out of him. 'You boys can go off and play with your slingshots. But before you do, I reckon we should go through the whole plan one last time from the top. I want all of you to know your jobs off by heart. Bethany, why don't you start?'

3. SURGE

After the Birmingham demo had turned violent the previous year Chris Bradford had found the police blocking every move the Street Action Group made. A hundred demonstrators would be met by two hundred cops. Bigger SAG events would be outlawed by local councils and anyone defying the ban found train stations closed, roads barricaded and lines of police eager to arrest anyone who stepped out of line.

These tough police tactics had crushed dozens of strikes and anti-government groups since they were first used during the miners' strike in the mid-1980s. To get around them Chris Bradford had created the impression that SAG was imploding by staging ever smaller actions that drew tiny crowds and an ever smaller number of police officers to keep them in line.

Once the police guard was down, Bradford organised the most ambitious anti-government SAG demo ever and Christmas was the perfect time to pull it off. If you want mayhem on the streets you need lots of bored young men, and school and university holidays are the time to find them. The cops would be at full stretch dealing with drunken revellers, while at the same time lots of officers would be taking leave. Most importantly, the run-up to Christmas is a quiet time for newspapers and TV, so you're guaranteed top spot on the news if you pull off something spectacular.

James Adams had successfully infiltrated SAG and he knew Bradford's plan. He'd told his mission controller John Jones, but John chose not to pass the information to the police. James was investigating the more serious possibility of SAG turning into a terrorist group and Bradford would have suspected a mole inside his organisation if he'd emerged from Covent Garden underground station and discovered hundreds of cops waiting for him.

It's a problem with all kinds of intelligence work: agents go undercover and get information, but you can't make use of it without compromising their safety. James couldn't help wondering if they'd made the right decision as hundreds of protestors steamed down the Strand towards Trafalgar Square.

The noise was deafening and although James was nervous, he got a buzz from being part of such a powerful group. Missiles flew overhead and glass was shattering on both sides of the street. Diners in festive hats screamed as a paving slab crashed through the window of a Japanese restaurant. Seconds later the leaded glass frontage of a Georgian theatre was kicked in, the box office was shattered and posters of the cast were ripped off the awnings and flung into the air.

Office workers and shoppers sheltered in doorways. Shop staff rushed to lock doors as the throbbing chant of 'SAG, SAG, SAG!' roared down the street.

SAG had sympathisers in some of London's roughest neighbourhoods and James was impressed that they'd pulled together a diverse crowd of activists and troublemakers without the cops getting wind. Chris Bradford said he'd be happy with a hundred and fifty protestors, but the crowd was now three times that. They divided evenly between the pavements on opposite sides of the road, with the overflow wading between four lanes of gridlocked traffic.

Two minutes after they entered the Strand the pavements ahead of the marchers were bare. Pedestrians were either locked inside shops or had cut up one of the many side streets to avoid the chanting mob.

Most of those who didn't get out of the way in time were ignored and a few homeless who sheltered in the area found protestors showering them with coins and wishing them Merry Christmas. It wasn't such a good day if you were a drunken office worker, returning from a liquid lunch in a pinstripe suit and expensive watch. While the majority of the crowd was happy to chant and trash property, one especially intimidating group of youths grabbed anyone who looked like they had a bit of money and ordered them to hand it over.

'SAG, SAG, SAG!' James chanted, repeatedly punching the air as the crowd jostled on all sides and broken glass crunched under his boots. He had to live up to his green Mohican and his role as a young anarchist so he took an enthusiastic kick, ripping the door mirror off a chauffeur-driven Mercedes trapped in the traffic between two buses. He grabbed the mirror out of the gutter and looked around, but couldn't find anything to throw it at.

A second later, James found himself bundling into the person in front. The crowd behind squashed up and stopped moving. Everyone was surprised and the chanting died down as James leaned into the road to see what was going on.

Charing Cross railway station was less than fifty metres ahead and Nelson's Column was lit up in the distance, but flashing blue lights and a line of police cars stretched across the road ahead.

'Nazis,' spat a bloke who was practically breathing down James' neck. 'How'd they get here so bloody fast?'

James didn't speak, but he knew there was a flaw in Bradford's plan: one of London's largest police stations was less than fifty metres from the route of the planned march. When the superintendent in charge of the Charing Cross police station heard that the march was getting out of control, he'd ordered several vehicles to drive out of a basement garage and blockade the entire width of the Strand.

Every officer inside the station – including plenty who hadn't been away from a desk in years – was ordered to kit up in full riot gear. More than fifty cops now stood behind the barricade with some less mobile officers jogging out clumsily to join them.

'Please disperse immediately,' a tannoy inside one of the police cars blurted. 'We're expecting more reinforcements shortly. You will be arrested and could face serious charges.'

After the announcement the cops tried to psyche the crowd out by drumming their batons on their plastic riot shields, and it seemed to work.

There was an eerie stillness as the crowd sought direction. James watched hundreds of plumes of warm breath wafting up into the darkening sky. The police lights mingled with Christmas lights and it felt like a break between hymns at an outdoor carol service. But menace hung in the air and James noticed that some of the protestors on the edge of the crowd were filtering away into the side streets.

As the number of people disappearing up the side streets grew, the mood deflated and it appeared the march was going to fizzle. But everything changed when an orange streak shot down from a third-storey window and exploded into a ball of flame between two of the parked police cars.

Beyond James' line of sight, several activists had forced a glass door and climbed a flight of steps into an office suite above the shops. They'd opened a window and thrown out a petrol bomb.

As the crowd cheered and whistled, more bombs rained down, spewing burning petrol over the road and setting light to the police cars as the officers scrambled from their barricade in total panic.

The big drum started banging again and the whole crowd was jumping into the air and shouting at the top of its voice, 'SAG, SAG, SAG!'

James thought he'd known everything about Bradford's plan. But he hadn't known about the petrol bombs, and the way they'd been expertly aimed at the police lines made it seem more like a planned operation than a spur of the moment thing.

'SAG, SAG, SAG!'

Anyone who wasn't shouting was whistling and it made James' ears hurt. But even though the police officers had backed off there was no way forward through the line of flaming cars.

The man holding the stolen megaphone came to the rescue, giving the crowd their orders: 'Trash the Savoy, trash the Savoy!'

'Bloody good idea,' someone shouted, as the mob turned on its heels and began heading back the way it had come, towards one of London's largest and fanciest hotels. James was much nearer the back of the mob than the front and it was almost a minute before he was back on the move.

'We just burned the coppers, we just burned the coppers. La-la, la-la, la-la, hey!'

Amidst the chaos and the sound of more breaking glass, James felt his phone vibrating inside his pocket. There was too much noise to hold a conversation, so he was relieved to see a text message from Dana:

HAVE YOU SEEN MY GREEN TRACKSUIT TOP?

James was pleased to hear from his girl, but disappointed that she'd ignored his message about missing her. It was a struggle tapping out the reply with bodies jostling on all sides, and one bloke almost knocked the phone from his hand.

THINK I SAW IT UNDER MY BED, he replied.

As James pocketed the phone he bumped into the person in front and looked up. The noise of the crowd had dipped again and he could hear the distinctive sound of cops whacking batons on their plastic riot shields.

With police blocking the road ahead and a flaming barricade behind, James was just one of three hundred heads that turned towards the side streets looking for a way out, but they'd all been blocked off by white cars with blue flashing lights.

*

Back on campus, Rat, Andy, Jake, Kevin and Ronan were charging down the main staircase, heading from Lauren's eighth-floor room to the weapons storage cupboard on the ground floor.

'Who the hell does Lauren Adams think she is?' Jake moaned as he swung around the end of a banister. 'Stuck up little troll . . .'

'You're talking about my girlfriend,' Rat warned.

Andy knew they had to work as a team and tried smoothing things over. 'Lauren might be full of it, but she knows her stuff, Jake. She's got one of the best mission records of anyone on campus and she's still only thirteen . . .'

Ronan giggled. 'If she had massive jugs like Bethany she'd be perfect.'

Andy and Rat both laughed. 'I swear they get bigger every time I see her,' Rat said.

'You're talking about my *sister*,' Jake said bitterly.

'Give over, Jake,' Andy said. 'You two hate each other.'

'Andy's in love with Bethany,' Rat teased, as Ronan jumped half a flight of stairs on to the sixth-floor landing, making a massive thud. 'But he's too much of a shitter to ask her out.'

'You talk rubbish, Rat,' Andy said, aghast. 'I said I liked her *one* time and you've been going on about it ever since.'

'Shitter,' Rat repeated.

By this time they'd all reached the sixth-floor landing, but Kevin peeled off into the corridor.

‘Where you going?’ Rat asked. ‘We’re all supposed to be going down for slingshot practice.’

‘I don’t want to get these muddy,’ Kevin explained, as he looked down at his glowing white Nikes. ‘I’ll nip to my room and change.’

Ronan shook his head. ‘Change your trainers! How much of a girl are you, Kevin?’

‘At least I don’t stink of piss,’ Kevin yelled back.

Ronan was half-way down to the fifth floor, but he spun around and squared up to Kevin. ‘Say that again and I’ll stomp on your head.’

‘Leave it out,’ Rat sighed. He was one of the strongest thirteen-year-olds on campus so he had no problem pulling the two eleven-year-olds apart. He shoved Kevin down the hallway towards his room before grabbing Ronan by his collar. ‘We’re gonna be stuck in a minibus for two hours on the way to the ATCC. If you smell like anything other than soap or deodorant, you’re riding on the roof rack.’

‘Yeah,’ Kevin smirked as he walked backwards down the hallway towards his room. ‘Take a bath, loser.’

‘See you down in the weapons room, Kev,’ Rat said, as Andy and Jake resumed the charge downstairs.

Kevin’s room was like all the others in the main building: small sofa by the door, double bed, desk with a laptop near the window, wardrobes along the length of one wall and a bathroom off to the side. But he was surprised to see a rusted toolbox in his bathroom doorway.

Karen, the campus plumber, leaned out of the bathroom. She wore battered denim dungarees over a white CHERUB shirt and held a toilet seat in her gloved hand. ‘Hello,’ she said warmly. 'Just fitting your new toilet.'

All the toilets on campus were being replaced with water saving units. It had been announced in morning assembly that Monday but Kevin had forgotten all about it.

'I'll be done in ten minutes, but if you need to go, you can christen the one I've just fitted across the hall.'

'No probs,' Kevin nodded. He sat on the edge of his bed and leaned forward to grab an old pair of trainers from underneath.

After lacing his shoes Kevin wished the plumber a merry Christmas before running back to the corridor. He reckoned it was a good idea to take a leak before heading out into the December cold to shoot slingshots, so he grabbed the handle of the door directly across the hallway and stepped into James Adams' bedroom.

4. BLAG

James ducked in fright as heat from the flames popped a tyre on one of the burning cop cars. Sirens wailed in the surrounding streets, while the crowd pushed and shoved. James was tall enough to breathe, but some of those lower down were getting crushed and starting to panic.

'Please remain calm,' a police tannoy announced. 'You will be dispersed in an orderly fashion.'

Eighty demonstrators had leaked up the side streets before the petrol bombs had gone off, leaving a rump of three hundred protestors trapped between the police lines.

Fifty officers blocked the crowd into place at the eastern end of the Strand and dozens more cut off side streets, but while the cops were outnumbered five to one, none of the protestors fancied their chances against shields, helmets and extendible batons.

A veteran protestor standing close to James explained police tactics to his girlfriend. 'Bastards will keep us here for hours, letting us out two or three at a time. They'll take all our photos and details before letting us go.'

'SAG, SAG, SAG!' someone shouted, but the reply from

the crowd was half-hearted and people were being blinded by the spotlight on a police helicopter sweeping overhead. James suspected they were prowling for Chris Bradford and other senior SAG members, but a lot of high-profile SAG members had been imprisoned after Birmingham and those who remained on the outside had slipped away before the protest reached its peak.

A bigger explosion ripped off behind James as the fuel tank of a police car exploded. On the side of the street away from the fire, the police had rolled a couple of lightly damaged cars out of the blockade and begun marching through the gap to block the crowd from the rear. The cops drumming on their riot shields panicked the crowd into an even tighter formation and a woman standing close to James screamed out that she couldn't breathe.

The crush wasn't caused by a lack of space, but by the fact that none of the protestors wanted to be on the edge of the crowd when the police closed them down completely. They were huddling from police batons the same way emperor penguins huddle from the cold.

'I've got to get out,' the woman screamed. 'Let me out of here.'

The crush seemed pointless to James and unlike the slender female, he had the muscle to make headway through the crowd. As he pushed past bodies he grabbed the panicking woman and put his arm around her back.

'Calm down,' James said firmly as they reached open space and found themselves in no man's land between the protestors and a line of riot shields thirty metres away. Across the street, the eastbound traffic that had been trapped between the two police lines was being allowed out one car at a time.

As the girl – who looked like she was in her early twenties – rummaged inside her shoulder bag and grabbed an asthma inhaler, James took a bottle of water out of his backpack and offered her a drink.

'Thank you,' she said, speaking with a heavy French accent before pausing to down some of the water. 'I got so scared in there.'

'No worries,' James smiled.

Once the traffic on one side of the road was clear, the crowd moved into the extra space and tensions eased as it dawned that the riot cops weren't going to charge in and start whacking people.

James and his new friend backed up to a column between closed shutters in front of a jewellery store and an electrical store.

'Smoke?' the girl asked, as she pulled a packet of ten and a lighter out of her bag.

James shook his head and laughed. 'Cigarettes and asthma. Nice combo!'

But his smile vanished when he glanced at his watch. He was supposed to be covering Chris Bradford's back at a meeting on the other side of London in less than three hours' time. It was important for the mission, but James didn't have a hope of making it if the police were planning to disperse the protestors by releasing them two or three at a time over the space of several hours.

'I need to be somewhere else,' James said.

The French girl smiled. 'If you 'ave a plan I'm all ears.'

James studied her clothing for the first time. Her black stockings and expensive-looking striped coat didn't fit the mould of a SAG activist or an urban yob.

'How'd you find out about the demo?'

'I'm studying journalism,' the girl explained. 'I'm working three months at the London bureaux of a Paris newspaper. I was at a party last night, I heard some guys talking about the possibility of trouble.'

'Looking for a scoop,' James said, before smiling absent-mindedly.

He usually paid attention to what pretty girls said, but his eyes had strayed towards the metal shutters at the front of the electrical store. Each shutter had metal clasps that were designed to be padlocked from the outside, but they'd been pulled down in a hurry and he wondered if there was any way to lock them from the inside.

'Where are you going?' the French girl asked, as James moved two paces to his left and peered between the slats of the roll-down shutters.

All the lights were on inside the store. There was a display area at either end of the shop's frontage, and in between them a recessed area behind which were six glass doors, all locked.

'There must be a way out of the back,' James said.

He kept a wary eye on the line of policemen before squatting down, lifting the shutter quickly and ducking beneath it.

'Where are you going?' the French girl asked.

'Don't stare,' James said anxiously.

He stood up slowly in the recessed area between the

shutters and the door. It was a relief to see that everyone had left the store except the manager, who stood at the rear playing *Pro Evo Soccer* on an X-box.

James stepped gingerly across the tiles and pushed each of the six glass doors, but wasn't surprised to find them locked. Cherubs are trained in lock picking using a mechanical lock gun, but it wasn't something James carried routinely so he'd have to rely on his multitool to get inside.

A quick glance up towards the door handles provided some relief. The shop's main security was provided by tough padlocks on the shutters. The doors also had deadlocks, but as with the shutters they were designed to be operated from the outside when the shop was closed up for the night. The two outer sets of doors were bolted from the inside, but the pair in the middle was designed to open electronically by swinging inwards. The current had been switched off, but there was no obvious physical barrier preventing them from being forced open.

James would be able to force them open as long as he could get his fingers between the two doors. The French girl blew cigarette smoke through the shutters as James crouched low and prepared to try.

'Are you OK? Can you get inside?'

'Don't stare, for *Christ's* sake,' James said irritably.

There were hundreds of protestors and dozens of cops nearby and it was a minor miracle that he'd got this far without being spotted.

He pushed the toe of his boot against the bottom of one door, opening a small gap into which he hoped to wedge his fingers; but they were too chunky. To get around this James pushed the saw-toothed blade of his multitool into the gap between the two halves of the electronic door, then used it as a lever until the gap was big enough to squeeze in four fingers of his right hand.

The whole weight of the door pressed on his fingertips as he pulled and he couldn't help making a noisy grunt. When the door had moved another centimetre he was able to get the fingers of his other hand into the gap, but it only budged when he shifted his whole bodyweight backwards.

The hydraulic pistons that usually operated the doors hissed in unison, but James' sense of triumph only lasted for the half-second between the doors breaking open and the loud clattering sound as his fingers lost their grip and his entire body slammed the grille behind him.

As James recovered his balance and stood up, the French girl clambered under the shutter. Fellow protestors who'd heard the rattling shutters saw the whole thing.

Inside the store, the manager had dropped the X-box controller and vaulted over the cashier's counter where he pressed the emergency alarm button.

'Get out of my store,' he shouted defiantly.

Unfortunately, sounding the alarm was the worst move he could have made. A couple of protestors were already following the French girl under one shutter, but everyone heard the alarm and the protestors were rejuvenated.

'Oggy, oggy, oggy,' someone shouted through a megaphone.

'SAG, SAG, SAG!' the protestors shouted back, as the remaining shutters opened and a scrum formed around the automatic doors.

Inside, James dragged the French girl by her arm and they

ran together towards a door at the back of the shop.

'It's zee storeroom!' she shouted, her French accent thickening as panic set in.

As James spun to exit, the manager blocked his path. If he'd known how much combat training James had done he wouldn't have dared and James effortlessly grabbed the squat salesman by his company tie and bundled him sideways into a rack of battery chargers and mains adaptors.

'Stay back or I'll hurt you properly,' James ordered, before setting off towards a fire exit sign on the opposite side of the store.

They were no longer alone. More than fifty protestors had made it through the double doors and were now fighting over access to a single fire door at the back of the store. While most wanted to escape, others couldn't resist thousands of pounds' worth of electrical equipment.

Dozens more alarms were set off as laptops and DVD recorders got ripped off their display stands. The youths who'd mugged several bystanders earlicr on were standing behind the photography counter stuffing boxed cameras and iPods into the biggest carrier bags they could find.

Out on the Strand, the police at both ends had rushed in to stop the getaway, but this spooked some sections of the crowd who feared that the police would lash out when they got close. Others were emboldened. The formations of police drumming on riot shields had been intimidating, but the cops' lack of numbers was plain to see once the lines were broken.

About seventy protestors made it into the electrical store before six officers with riot shields blocked it off, but none of them risked following the crazed mob inside. The remaining demonstrators divided between a charge through police lines towards the Savoy Hotel and a smaller breakaway group that forced its way past a pair of officers blocking one of the alleyways leading towards the river.

Outnumbered and out of formation, the cops made the situation worse by lashing out with batons and swooping into the crowd to randomly arrest anyone they could get their hands on.

Back inside the store James and the French girl made it through the crush around the fire door, down three steps and into a second, larger stockroom. Double doors at the back opened directly on to a narrow alleyway, but you had to fight through looters ripping off electrical goods to get there.

James wouldn't be allowed to keep anything he stole on a mission, so he wasn't interested. But the French girl couldn't resist cutting between two racks of stock and grabbing a pair of small boxes.

'Toshiba laptop!' she beamed, as she handed one to James. '*Très cher!* Lightweight, ideal for journalist.'

They exited nervously into fresh air and a single-lane road. There were dozens of looters heading off in either direction, but it was the kind of space that could easily be blocked off by a pair of police cars, so James grabbed his companion's skinny arm and began running at full pelt.

After a two-hundred-metre sprint they found themselves at a Y-shaped junction with two wider roads and despite there being no officers in sight, James was shocked by the distinctive blue lanterns hanging on the front of Charing Cross police station.

'This way,' he gasped.

'I'm so breathless,' the girl protested.

By some miracle a black cab hurtled around a corner and deposited a newspaper photographer on to the pavement less than twenty metres away. James harried the driver as he fiddled with some change.

'Take us to Islington,' James said. 'Caledonian Road.'

'Keep your green hair on, sonny!' the taxi driver said. 'I'm just writing this gentleman's receipt.'

James' heart leaped as he saw a police officer in riot gear staggering around a corner towards the station, but he was in no state to arrest anyone: limping badly and with a huge crack in one side of his helmet, like he'd been hit by a paving slab or something.

As the photographer made a dash towards the scene of the rioting James was horrified to see three huge looters in tracksuits and bling jewellery running towards the taxi.

'That's our cab, man,' they shouted.

The one leading the way held carrier bags stuffed with cameras, while his two mates had stacked one of the electrical store's trolleys with boxes containing PCs and laptops.

'I said, that's our cab,' the big man repeated, giving James a mean look as he grabbed him by his shoulder.

James was pumped from all the action. He grabbed the hand and twisted the giant thumb until it dislocated. Meantime, the French girl had climbed into the taxi and was banging on the glass partition inside.

'Just drive me,' she said.

James reached for the door handle but the cab driver pulled away without him. James couldn't believe it.

‘I saved your skinny butt,’ James yelled after her.

As he stepped back on to the kerb a clumsy fist swung towards him. He grabbed the arm out of the air and used the giant’s momentum to roll him over his back. The big man’s skeleton crunched as he landed hard in the gutter.

His two mates thought about moving in, but each held a three-wheeled trolley stacked with thousands of pounds’ worth of computer equipment and they were reluctant to let it topple into the road.

James was pissed off at the way the French girl had ditched him, but he knew he had to swallow his pride and concentrate on the mission. After giving the bag of iPods and camera stuff an almighty kick that scattered half its contents over the road he started running again with the Toshiba box swinging in his hand.

James didn’t know exactly where he was, but he’d kept his sense of direction and knew that if he headed north-west he’d reach Oxford Street within ten minutes. Once there he’d blend into the thousands of Christmas shoppers for a kilometre or so before going down the Underground and riding a train home.

5. FLUSH

Kevin's pee disappeared with a slight gurgle and a whoosh of air from James' newly installed eco-toilet. He'd been in James' room a few times, but he'd never used the bathroom. It felt awkward being in James' private space, but he was also curious about all his stuff.

As Kevin rinsed his hands, he reckoned that the big difference between being eleven and sixteen was the amount of stuff you needed to maintain yourself. His bathroom across the hall had shampoo, soap, toothpaste and a tub of hair gel he'd only used twice. James had around fifty bottles, ranging from shaving mousse and zit cream to expensive aftershaves and hair dye. There was also loads of Dana's stuff around and much to Kevin's amusement a box containing '48 Assorted Condoms'.

Kevin wasn't into girls yet, but he knew that would change pretty soon and he was intrigued by the whole idea of sex and girlfriends. He'd only ever seen a condom in a picture, so after drying his hands on a grubby towel he cast a wary eye towards the unlocked bathroom door before picking one of the little foil-wrapped packets out of the box. The foil felt cold as he turned it over between his fingers and he was tempted to rip it open.

But Kevin needed to hurry downstairs to catch up with Rat and the other lads. He briefly considered pocketing the condom to examine in his room later, but he'd never stolen anything in his life and had no intention of starting.

James' bedroom door slammed as Kevin dropped the condom back into the box. It made him jump and his thumb caught the edge of the cardboard and sent the box tumbling off the narrow shelf. Half a dozen shiny foil packets poured into the sink, while the remainder spilled across the floor.

Two people had entered the bedroom and now stood on the other side of the wall, less than three paces away. Kevin recognised the deep tone of sixteen-year-old Michael Hendry.

'Where'd James say your tracksuit was?'

'Under the bed,' James' girlfriend Dana replied.

As they spoke, Kevin moved quietly but quickly on his knees, throwing spilled condoms back into their box. His face burned red at the prospect of being discovered, because while he could act innocent and say that he'd knocked them on the floor while washing his hands it was the kind of story that might lead to all kinds of wild rumours and mickey-taking.

'Here we go,' Dana said, ripping her tracksuit top from under James' bed as Kevin scooped the last of the condoms out of the sink.

Kevin looked in the mirror when he'd finished. His cheeks were flushed and he thought he looked guilty about something.

'Where are you going now?' Dana asked.

'Shoulder still aches from the dojo yesterday,' Michael replied. 'I might go over to the pool. Half an hour in the hot tub might ease it off.'

Dana's voice became gentler. 'Maybe if you took your shirt off I could kiss it better,' she teased.

Kevin was shocked. He wanted to leave, but now felt that he'd been in the bathroom too long and had heard too much to reveal his presence.

'You sick puppy!' Michael said, before breaking into a deep laugh. 'You want to make out here, in your man's bedroom?'

'Screw James Adams,' Dana said. 'You think he's never cheated on me? He's probably bouncing around on top of some scabies-infested anarchist as I speak.'

'You're harsh,' Michael laughed. 'I can't help feeling bad for my Gabrielle though. She ain't done nothing but good things for me.'

'Yeah,' Dana said. 'But we're sixteen. If we can't have some fun at our age . . .'

Kevin heard a couple of grunts followed by a creak of bedsprings. His heart thumped as he crept up to the bathroom door and peeked. Michael was kicking off his trainers, while Dana sat on James' bed peeling her black CHERUB T-shirt over her head.

'You're *bloody* sexy!' Michael said, pulling his CHERUB shirt over his head and giving Kevin an eyeful of some nasty looking acne on his back.

As the shock wore off Kevin started to see the funny side and realised that he had a great story to tell his mates. The only trouble was, nobody would believe him. He patted the front pocket of his combat trousers and was pleased to feel the bulge of his camera phone.

Kevin cycled through the menus making absolutely sure that the flash and the little shutter noise the phone made were switched off before crouching down low and poking the phone around the edge of the door frame.

Michael and Dana now sprawled over James' bed, snogging, topless and apparently about to go much further. Kevin nervously snapped two pictures and checked the end result on the screen. They were grainy shots, but clear enough to see who they were and what was going on.

As Kevin slid the phone back into his pocket it started to ring. He gasped as he saw Rat's name on the display and realised Rat was calling to ask where he'd got to.

'Is that your phone?' Dana asked, as she pulled away from Michael.

'Sounds like it's coming from the bathroom. It can't be James', it would have gone flat by now if he'd left it on.'

Michael headed towards the bathroom as Kevin backed up desperately towards the toilet. He pressed the flush with one hand while answering his phone with the other.

'Hey, Rat,' Kevin said, trying to sound casual as Michael came through the doorway.

'What the hell, kid?' Michael boomed.

Michael's bare torso was bulked out with huge muscles, but Kevin had made it through CHERUB basic training so it wasn't enough to faze him. He gave Michael a *with you in a second* wave and carried on talking into the phone.

'. . . Sorry Rat. I changed my shoes, but I had to take a

crap as well. I'll meet you down by the back entrance in two minutes.'

Kevin pocketed the phone before explaining to Michael, 'Plumber's across the hall fitting me a new toilet.'

'Right,' Michael said uneasily. He was clearly worried that Kevin had heard something he shouldn't have.

The eleven-year-old struggled to keep a straight face. 'So what are *you* doing in James' room?'

'Oh . . . Yeah . . . Just, changing my shirt, you know? James said I could borrow one of his.'

'Cool,' Kevin said.

'You should lock the door next time,' Michael said.

Kevin shrugged. 'James is on his mission so I didn't expect company.'

He wanted Michael to think he'd been on the toilet the whole time, so he went to the sink and quickly rewashed his hands.

'Anyway, I've gotta get downstairs for some slingshot practice with the boys.'

Kevin breezed out of the bathroom, drying wet hands on his trousers and casually saying 'Hey' to Dana as he walked back to the hallway. She'd pulled her T-shirt back on but her bra strap dangled out where she'd hurriedly stuffed it under James' duvet.

6. JONES

Mission Controller John Jones sat on a ripped sofa with his socked feet on a coffee table and his reading glasses on a chain around his neck. The TV was on and the news cut to a live shot of the Strand, strewn with broken glass and strands of *do not enter* tape.

'James, they're showing it now,' he shouted.

James jogged through from the flat's tiny kitchen, with a meal tray holding a plate of microwave macaroni and a can of Coke Zero. John budged up so that James could sit next to him.

'Trashed!' James said excitedly, before hissing as hot cheese sauce burned the roof of his mouth. 'There must have been another wrecking spree after I legged it. There's broken glass all the way down to Waterloo Bridge.'

John nodded. 'They did a load of shops in Covent Garden as they ran off. Sixty arrested, couple of cops got a kicking and one burned by a petrol bomb, but it doesn't look like anyone was badly hurt.'

'Good,' James said. 'Wouldn't have felt happy about not passing the information on to the cops if someone had got done in. So how is the BBC playing it?'

'Hysterical, like you'd expect,' John smiled. 'The chief constable of the Met was in the studio a minute ago, getting a grilling about intelligence and why there weren't more cops there from the start. I saw a quick flash of you in the holding pen by the tube station, but your hood was up so you won't be recognised.'

'I didn't think it would get so big,' James said. 'A couple of hundred maybe, but it was easily double that.'

'Bradford's played the police for suckers,' John sighed.

'And he did everything by the book,' James said. 'Got permission for the march, stayed in the assembly area until the police told them to move out and vanished in a puff of smoke the second the trouble started. They'll have a job pinning anything on him.'

'Chris Bradford is a sharp cookie,' John said, holding his back as he stood up to grab a bunch of folders from the lower shelf of the coffee table. 'The last thing we want is someone like that getting his hands on a bundle of plastic explosive and a few hand guns . . .'

'Maybe after this he'll put the terrorist thing off,' James suggested. 'It was born out of frustration at the lack of media coverage SAG've been getting lately, but they're gonna be the centre of attention again after the riot.'

John shook his head. 'From now on the cops are gonna have three hundred officers on the street every time Bradford takes his dog for a walk. That's where he's so clever. The media are bound to force the cops into a knee-jerk reaction and they'll do all they can to make sure there are no more riots. Meantime, Bradford's running a completely different play.'

James had been starving, and bolting down the plastic dish of macaroni hadn't done much to help. 'I might have a couple of those cream doughnuts from the fridge.'

John nodded. 'I'll make a pot of tea. But I've been speaking with MI5 and first we need to go through the final plan for tonight's meeting.'

James nodded and placed his tray on the carpet as John pulled a black and white mugshot out of the folder.

'This is our man,' John explained. 'Or at least, the MI5 sound lab got a ninety-six per cent probability of a voice match on the person who phoned Chris Bradford's mobile last night.'

'Is he the kind of character we were expecting?'

'More or less,' John nodded. 'This picture's twenty years old. His name is Richard Davis, usually known as Rich. He's former IRA. Convicted on three counts of terrorism and murder, but he only served twelve years before being released under the Good Friday peace agreement. Most interestingly, he's thought to have organised the IRA's supply of Soviet weapons during the cold war.'

James' eyes opened wider. 'I never knew the Soviets supplied the IRA.'

'Oh yes,' John nodded. 'A lot of people think the communists only supplied left-wing groups, but they'd supply anyone who could help to undermine western governments. At times the Soviets supplied so many guns that the IRA had major problems hiding them all.

'A few years back they found a dozen Soviet-era grenade launchers and twenty crates of AK-47 rifles buried on the site of a new housing development near Dublin. It was all useless – rusted up – but we suspect that quite a lot of Russian gear in serviceable condition is still around.'

'Bradford doesn't have a lot of men though,' James said. 'And he's into the whole anarchist thing of riots and bombs for their own sake, so I don't think they're gonna set up an organised, military-style group. I reckon he'll be looking for something spectacular instead, like an RPG launcher or plastic explosives.'

'You could be right,' John said warily. 'Some of the people Davis would have negotiated with years back now run the Russian armaments industry and for all we know he's still in touch. He might be offloading old IRA kit, but he might also have the ability to bring newly manufactured stuff out of Russia or the Ukraine.'

'So what's my strategy for the meeting?' James asked.

'Bradford knows you can fight and wants you there as a bodyguard, but do whatever you can to stay out of trouble. Bradford is new to this game. He might have a brain but he's out of his league with these people. We're going to let this thing play out until we can learn some more about this Davis character. Take a couple of tracking devices. If you get a chance, try planting them somewhere that will enable us to trace his movements. Once MI5 know Davis' car registration, or his real address, they'll be able to start proper surveillance on him.'

'So we're not planning to make any move on Bradford or Davis tonight?'

'If we did, what would we have?' John asked. 'Two guys in a room talking. If we're lucky we'd get them on a conspiracy charge and they'd be out in two years. We need to find out more about Davis and we don't want to arrest anyone until we can catch them red-handed with a roomful of guns and a bunch of surveillance tapes and voice recordings to back up our story. That way we'll be able to bang them up for a good long time.'

'Could take months,' James smiled. 'And I'm not sure how long I can live with this dodgy hairstyle.'

John smiled back. 'Well, we set up the excuse about your going home to your auntie, so at least you'll be on campus for Christmas.'

'What about you?' James asked.

John looked a touch wounded. 'My daughter spends Christmas with my ex and her new bloke, so I'll probably head back to campus too. If we're not working on the twenty-seventh I'll take her out to the sales and let her spend my money.'

'Sounds good,' James laughed, before glancing at his watch. 'Six-fifteen. I'd better start sorting my equipment out for this meeting.'

'Yeah,' John said, stifling a yawn as he put the TV into standby. 'I'll go put the kettle on and then I'll give my liaison at MI5 a quick call. Davis will make you ditch your mobiles before he tells you his location, so make sure you use the boots with the tracking device inside. I'll be driving about half a kilometre behind you.'

*

Senior Mission Controller Dennis King sat at the wheel of a shabby minibus, rattling down an A-road at sixty miles an hour. His young assistant Maureen Evans was next to him, while seven cherubs sat in the back singing along to the over the top version of *Jingle Bells* playing on the radio.

Rat and Lauren sat together, hamming it up, playing air guitars and stamping their feet. Andy and Bethany sang at high pitch and Ronan was in the back row, droning half-heartedly with his fat check pressed against the window.

Jake and Kevin were the only ones not joining in. Jake was a popular kid with loads of mates. Kevin was slightly younger and eager to impress Jake and become part of his cool group.

'I swear this is good,' Kevin whispered as he slid his phone out of his jacket. 'But don't let Lauren see.'

Jake squinted at the blurry picture on the rectangular screen. The top half of the picture showed a Harley-Davidson motorbike.

'I know that poster,' Jake said, thoroughly unimpressed. 'It's James Adams' room. So what? I've seen James and Dana make out a million times.'

Kevin smirked. 'If that's James, he's got one *hell* of a sun tan.'

Jake looked again and realised it was a black person. 'Holy crap!' Jake giggled. 'So *that's* why you took so long to come down for slingshot practice.'

Jake snatched Kevin's phone and started pressing numbers. 'What are you doing?'

'Picture messaging,' Jake explained. 'I want a copy on my phone.'

'You *can't* spread that around,' Kevin said nervously. 'Michael Hendry will know I took it. Have you seen the size of that guy's muscles? He'll pluck me like a chicken!'

'I only want it on my phone,' Jake said reassuringly, as *Jingle Bells* ended and Dennis King told them not to start singing the next song because it was getting on his nerves. 'I won't send it to anyone else.'

Kevin wasn't convinced, but Jake gave him a look that seemed to say *Are you a cool guy or not?*

'Just be careful,' Kevin warned, as Ronan's head loomed between them.

'What are you girls whispering about?' he asked.

Ronan was hard to get on with. One day he'd be knocking on your bedroom door giving you free stuff and desperately wanting to be your best mate. The next he'd shove you down the stairs or stick your bag under the showers in the changing rooms to try getting a cheap laugh. He was as bright as any other kid on campus but the basic rules of friendship eluded him.

'Mind your business, Ronan,' Jake said. 'You're such an idiot.'

'Sticks and stones . . .' Ronan sneered. He tried acting like he wasn't interested, before snatching Kevin's phone as Jake passed it back.

'Give us,' Kevin shouted, grabbing at Ronan's arm.

'Ronan,' Jake moaned, before putting on a serious voice and speaking like a newsreader. 'In today's headlines, a campus poll has shown that ninety-six per cent of CHERUB agents said that they'd prefer a bout of violent explosive diarrhoea to a minibus ride with Ronan "The Dickhead" Walsh.'

Kevin undid his seatbelt and jumped up. He wrapped his arms around Ronan's waist and started driving him towards the back of the van.

'Gimmmmmmme my bloody phone,' Kevin shouted.

'Cut that out,' Maureen shouted angrily from up front. 'You two sit your arses down or I'll be dishing out punishment laps.'

Ronan was stocky and gave Kevin a shove that sent him sprawling down the aisle between the seats. He took a quick glance at the picture on Kevin's phone, before hurling it through the air towards Lauren.

'Here, Little Miss Black Shirt,' Ronan snorted. 'I've got a great Christmas present for your brother. Maybe you can print it out and frame it for him.'

Lauren disliked Ronan and didn't want to give him any satisfaction, but her jaw dropped as she picked Kevin's phone off the carpet and saw what was on the screen.

7. BOOZE

'You sure nobody followed?' Chris Bradford asked, as James clambered into the front passenger seat of a Volkswagen Sirocco and slammed the door. The two-seat sports car was heading for its twentieth birthday, with 150,000 miles on the clock and a vague smell of mould. It was a quarter to seven, bitter cold and drizzle in the air.

'I got two buses and a black cab hailed in the street,' James lied. 'Nobody's following me.'

'Good lad,' Bradford nodded. 'We've got some good men, but you're the only one I'd want covering my back and at your age I can be sure you're not an undercover cop.'

James nodded as the engine clattered. Cogs ground nastily as Bradford put the car in gear and pulled out from the kerb.

'Who's this box of bolts belong to?'

'Lady friend,' Bradford explained.

He flipped on the windscreen wipers, but only the one on the driver's side worked. A dilapidated car like this was an open invite to get pulled by the police, but James couldn't warn Bradford without sounding suspiciously knowledgeable.

'How'd you slip away from the demo so easily?' James

asked. 'One minute you were walking along beside the inspector, next you'd vanished off the face of the earth.'

'I looked for you,' Bradford said. 'I knew I'd need you out here tonight and I didn't want you getting nicked.'

James nodded. 'That crowd surged out of nowhere. It was a bloody good rumble.'

'Last hurrah for the old SAG,' Bradford smiled, sounding like he was making a toast. 'If this meeting comes off, it's a whole new ball game. I fancy doing a Guy Fawkes . . .'

'Yeah,' James laughed. 'Shame security round the Houses of Parliament is stiffer these days.'

'But the explosives are a lot more powerful,' Bradford said, before breaking into a laugh and thumping euphorically on the dashboard. 'Imagine all those fat crooks running down Westminster with the arses burned out of their three-grand suits!'

James half smiled and looked out of the window at a woman fighting her umbrella in the wind.

SAG was supposed to be an anarchist group which opposed all forms of organised government and authority, so it was ironic that its notoriety came about through a single charismatic figure.

Serious anarchists dismissed Bradford as a cartoon character and called SAG his fan club. Bradford dismissed serious anarchists as a bunch of no-hopers who sat around drinking Fairtrade coffee and talking about things rather than doing them.

James had to study anarchist theory while preparing for his mission and quickly reached the conclusion that it was completely dumb: nobody likes being told what to do, but it doesn't take a genius to work out that there'd be chaos if everyone could do whatever the hell they liked.

He'd taken six weeks to win Bradford's trust and now agreed with the serious anarchists on one point: SAG's existence had little to do with politics and a lot to do with Chris Bradford deciding it would be more interesting to spend his life starting riots and blowing stuff up than to finish his Business and Economics degree and get a job with his dad's accounting firm.

They took fifteen minutes driving from central London to a posh hotel called The Retreat. It was the kind of place where wealthy couples spent the weekend, with the wives on beauty treatments and the husbands on the golf course.

'Soft tarts,' Bradford snarled, as they drove past rows of parked Jaguars and Mercedes. 'I'd love to send some of the SAG boys in here with cans of paint stripper.'

'I could go for that,' James smiled, but the juvenile remark reminded him that Bradford was getting out of his depth.

They drew stares from women whose earrings were worth more than the antique VW, and the doorman wouldn't have looked at their combats and scruffy boots any more suspiciously if they'd stepped off a flying saucer.

'Are you going inside, sir?' the doorman asked.

'I assume there's no dress code for the lobby,' Bradford replied, practically snatching the handle out of the doorman's hand.

Reception had a black and white marble floor, dried flowers and a water feature. James' green hair was attracting eyeballs and he pulled his hood up over his head as they headed for the lift.

'Could you two be any more bloody conspicuous if you'd tried?' a man with an Irish accent asked as he rested a hand on Bradford's back. James clocked the muscular man and saw that he was too young to be Rich Davis.

'Where are your phones?' he asked.

'Ditched them,' Bradford said. 'Just like you asked.'

'And nobody tailed you here?'

Bradford shook his head. 'Buses and taxis. The VW's registered to a dealer.'

'OK,' the man said.

'I didn't catch your name,' Bradford said uneasily, as the lift doors opened gently.

'I didn't tell you my feckin' name, Mr Bradford, because you don't need to know it. The only name you need to know is Rich Kline. And I warn you now that he's pissed off with you.'

The Irishman pressed the button for the fifth floor.

'He told me room 603,' Bradford said.

'He's a cautious man,' the Irishman replied.

James studied him as the lift rose. He was clearly a bodyguard. His accent came from the wrong side of Belfast and he had gnarled skin; but his suit was nicely cut and the Omega watch looked real.

When they stepped out on the fifth the bodyguard walked four paces before taking out a flip phone and dialling. 'Did you see anyone else come in with them?'

James couldn't hear the other half of the conversation, but it seemed Rich had at least one additional set of eyes down in reception. When the first call ended, the bodyguard immediately dialled another number.

'Rich,' the bodyguard said. 'I've got Bradford here . . . Right . . . Right. I'll tell them.' After a moment he flipped the phone shut, pulled a plastic key card from his trouser pocket and turned towards Bradford. 'The boss is eating dinner. He'll see you up in his room in about forty-five minutes.'

Bradford bristled. 'Are you kidding me?'

The bodyguard raised one sinister eyebrow and aimed his hand towards the lift. 'Go to the room and wait, or leave. Rich is a serious man and after today's fiasco you're lucky he's willing to see you at all.'

James understood, but Bradford was irked. 'What's that supposed to mean? The meeting was all set for seven.'

The bodyguard took a step closer to Bradford, cracked his knuckles and eyeballed him. 'Mr Bradford, you're public enemy number one after today's shenanigans. You've turned up here in a car that sticks out a mile and a schoolboy with a bright green bog-brush for a hairstyle. So Mr Kline wants you to sit in a room and wait it out in case some geriatric busybody saw you on the six o'clock news and decides to give the fuzz a tinkle. Got it?'

Bradford had a temper and James knew he had to calm him down.

'There's no law against sitting in a hotel room, boss,' James said calmly, as he took the entry card from the Irishman. 'We'll wait, no worries.'

'OK,' the bodyguard said. 'Order up some room service on us if you like. I'll give you a call when Rich's ready.'

James led the way down the corridor towards the room while the Irishman took the fire stairs up to the next floor.

'This is bull,' Bradford said quietly. 'It's either a set-up or a pissing contest so that this Rich can show us who's boss. Either way, I don't bloody like it.'

*

Dennis King dropped the five boys and two girls near a housing estate on the outskirts of a Midlands town, leaving them a three-kilometre walk to the air traffic control centre. When they got close the boys vaulted a gate and squelched across farmland, while Bethany and Lauren kept to the roadside, heading for the main gate.

The ATCC was a typically bland government building, three storeys high, made of concrete with plastic framed windows. It could have been a newly built school or hospital but for the satellite dishes on the flat roof and a hundred-metre-tall pylon with three rotating radar sensors and a dome at the top, like a golf ball atop a giant tee.

Headlights streaked by as the girls walked along a strip of gravel sandwiched between a heavy-duty perimeter fence and a gloomy A-road. The drizzle was cold and they had no way to shield the spray blown up by the back wheels of larger vehicles. When they reached a low tree, Lauren ducked behind it and crouched down.

'So does James suspect?' Bethany asked, branches rustling as she unzipped a backpack.

Lauren shrugged. 'I don't think he knows Dana's cheating, but the last time I phoned him he said she was acting weird.'

'If you ask me, they've been on a downward slope for a while,' Bethany nodded. 'Remember that resuscitation course we all did? They were partners, but they barely spoke to each other all day.'

'I'm not gonna tell him,' Lauren said, shaking her head. 'Not four days before Christmas.'

Bethany gasped. 'But if he finds out that you knew he'll be really angry.'

'I know,' Lauren said. 'It's a risk. But James is in the middle of a mission and he's only coming back for a few days. If Dana wants to confess and ruin James' Christmas there's nothing I can do, but I'm not gonna be the one to do it.'

'But all the boys who were on the bus know. You can *ask* them to keep quiet, but it's bound to spread around.'

'I know,' Lauren sighed. 'It's only gonna be speculation though 'cos I made Kevin delete the photograph.'

As Lauren said this her phone rang. 'Yo, Rat.'

'Just telling you that we're in position, slingshots ready and waiting for your signal,' Rat said.

'Are the three little pigs behaving themselves?'

'They will if they know what's good for 'em,' he answered. 'Ronan's sulking, Kevin's a bit upset.'

'And Jake?'

Rat laughed. 'Jake's lippy and obnoxious, same as always.'

Lauren overheard Jake saying, '*I heard that*' in the background. 'We'll be at the front gate in two or three minutes,' she said. 'I'll call you when we get inside.'

'You know what?' Bethany smiled. 'I don't mean to be nasty, but the way James takes girls for granted, getting dumped might actually do him some good.'

'Can we drop this?' Lauren asked irritably, as she pushed her phone back into the pocket of her jeans. She hated the friction between her brother and best friend. 'Right now

James' love life is a long way down my list of priorities. Have you got the fake blood?'

'Check,' Bethany said, as she unscrewed the cap on a metal tub.

Lauren grabbed a handful of gravel and started rubbing it into her jeans, but she realised this method would take ages so she laid out on the damp roadside and rolled in the dirt. Once her clothes were filthy she peeled off her hair band and mussed her hair.

'Looks good.' Bethany pulled out a chunky penknife and used it to make holes in Lauren's top. 'Hold still or I'll stab you.'

'I can claim expenses and buy new jeans and a couple of tops in the sales.' Lauren smiled as she dug her fingers into the nicks made by the knife and turned them into a series of holes.

'You got that sweatshirt in Matalan for *three* quid,' Bethany sneered. 'What are you gonna buy with that?'

'Don't be a mushroom,' Lauren grinned. 'I'm not gonna say it was the three-quid one, am I? I'm gonna claim at least twenty.'

'Nice,' Bethany smiled, as she looked down at her bum. 'That's not a bad idea. I might say I ripped my jeans on something. Remember those Diesels we looked at last time we went shopping in London?'

8. BLOOD

Joe Prince was at the start of a twelve-hour shift in the security booth behind the main gate of Britain's newest air traffic control centre. He was twenty-eight with three young kids and delighted to be back in a job after he'd been laid off when a nearby dairy farm went bust two years earlier.

It got boring watching the rows of LCD screens, and the high point of the night shift was half a dozen tech staff heading for home in identical company BMWs between 7 and 8 p.m. They were ironing out the glitches before the centre opened in the new year and Joe was jealous because he got minimum wage while they were all on sixty-grand bonuses if it opened under budget and on schedule.

'You've got to help me,' a voice squealed from a loudspeaker up near the ceiling.

Joe knew it was the intercom on the pedestrian gate, but nobody ever arrived on foot in these parts and it was the first time he'd heard it used. Joe's *Carp Fishing* magazine plummeted off his lap as he rolled his chair forward towards the control console.

The CCTV at the brand new facility recorded clear colour

images and he was appalled by the sight on his main screen. The young teenager who'd pressed the entry buzzer had ripped clothes, blood smeared over her face and she seemed to be crying.

'Hello,' the girl sobbed again. 'Is anybody in there? *Please* help me.'

The security system gave Joe a range of options, from opening the gate to let someone in, all the way up to a button that would trigger a centre-wide lockdown and security alert. But the girl's desperation brought out Joe's more basic instincts and he scrambled out of the booth and ran down towards the main gate.

'Sweetheart,' Joe said sympathetically, as he saw Lauren sobbing through the bars. 'What on earth happened?'

'I was in town,' Lauren sniffed, as Joe put a magnetic card up to a control pad to open the gate. 'These men pulled me into their car and . . . Oh god!'

CHERUB agents are taught to make themselves cry by thinking about sad things, and how to lie without feeling embarrassed. Lauren was a star pupil and Joe was welling up just looking at her.

'You're safe here, sweetheart,' Joe gasped. 'I'll take you inside. We'll call the police and your parents and I'll make a hot drink to warm you up.'

Lauren limped through the gate as soon as it was open and wrapped her hands around Joe's chubby waist before he could pull the handle to close it.

'Thank you,' Lauren sobbed. 'They threw me out in the dirt and . . .'

'It's OK, sweetheart,' Joe said, rubbing her back.

'You're safe now, that's all that matters.'

Lauren felt guilty as she felt her way around Joe's belt until her fingertips touched a canister of pepper spray. The guard seemed like a really nice guy and there was every chance he'd lose his job for letting her inside.

'My shoulder really hurts,' Lauren moaned, as she carefully slid out the pepper spray before taking a quick step backwards and squeezing the trigger.

Joe screamed then stumbled backwards, clutching his eyes as Bethany rushed through the open gate. Lauren kicked Joe hard in the kidneys, doubling him over as Bethany ran behind and pulled the penknife out of her pocket.

'Move one muscle without my say-so and I'll jam this in your back,' Bethany said ferociously. 'Walk back to your booth, *quickly*.'

There were other guards on the base, so the girls were anxious to get inside before anyone else saw what was going on. Lauren swiped Joe's pass to close the electronic gate as Bethany marched him back to the booth.

'There's nothing here worth stealing,' Joe said nervously. 'You should leave now before you get in serious trouble.'

'Shut *up*,' Bethany ordered. 'Speak when you're spoken to.'

Despite Bethany's knife, Joe fancied his chances against two thirteen-year-old girls and lunged for his control panel as they entered the cramped booth. He kicked the wheeled chair backwards, trying to knock Bethany down before hitting the alarm. But Bethany sidestepped the chair and used a Karate technique, jabbing two fingers hard under Joe's ribcage.

He missed the console as his whole body jolted into spasm.

Unable to save himself, Joe's face hit the vinyl floor with a painful thud.

'What did I tell you?' Bethany shouted, as she pressed the blade against the back of Joe's neck. 'You think we're not serious?'

'I don't know what this is, but there's nothing in here for you,' Joe gasped. 'Take my wallet. There's about thirty quid in there.'

'One more word,' Bethany warned, feeling a twinge of conscience as she saw the family picture resting on the desktop. Joe had three daughters spread over his lap. The youngest was a baby and the oldest a gap-toothed six-year-old.

While Bethany kept Joe in check, Lauren sat astride his thighs and wound thick insulating tape around his ankles. When this was done she told Joe to put his wrists together so that she could bind them.

Once Lauren was finished, Bethany stood the photo of Joe's daughters on the floor, right in front of his eyes, which still streamed from the blast of pepper spray.

'Three pretty daughters,' Bethany said, as she grabbed the walkie-talkie from Joe's belt. 'Do you want to see them again?'

'Yes,' Joe said. 'Of course I do.'

'Great,' Bethany smiled grimly. 'I want you to speak into your radio. Tell the security team that you've spotted something on the cameras out back near the grain silo.'

'Make it sound good or I'll cut off your ding-dong,' Lauren added.

'Whatever happened to sugar and spice and all things nice?' Joe groaned.

Bethany placed her trainer between Joe's shoulder blades and shifted her whole weight on to the heel.

'God,' Joe said, moaning in agony.

'Plenty more where that came from for a man who says the wrong thing,' Bethany warned, as she leaned forward and held the walkie-talkie in front of Joe's mouth. 'Speak.'

'Joe at the entry point here, guys. Sorry to disturb you but I just saw something out back by the grain silo.'

'Probably a sheep,' came the reply, as laughter rattled in the background. 'We're watching a DVD, Joe. And it's bloody *freezing* out there.'

Lauren was shocked by the casual reply. All radio traffic during the security test was being recorded and that line would probably be enough to cost the private security company its contract.

'Lazy buggers,' Bethany hissed, glowering at Joe as she held the handset in front of his mouth. 'Tell them it's a definite intruder.'

'Guys, I'm not messing here,' Joe said. 'Someone's moving around out there. If you don't check it out I'm gonna have to report you.'

'Whoooo, *Joseph*, laying down the law,' the dude on the other end of the radio laughed. 'OK, big man, if you want to be a hard arse. We'll go check it out, but you can keep your mitts away from the Cup-A-Soups and Lemsips in my locker from now on.'

'Well done,' Bethany said, as she took her trainer off Joe's back and pocketed the radio. 'Now open wide.'

Joe reluctantly allowed Bethany to stuff his mouth with a ball of screwed-up tape before winding the roll several times around his head, covering his eyes and mouth but leaving his nostrils free to breathe.

Lauren pulled out her phone. 'Rat,' she said. 'Security team should be coming your way. And based on what we've just heard, you shouldn't have too much to worry about.'

'Lauren says the security team are a bunch of pussies,' Rat said happily, as he pocketed his phone.

*

When the team had studied the plans for the new control centre, they'd noticed that while the front was protected with heavy railings, the large expanse of land behind was secured by the kind of wire-mesh fencing you'd expect to see around your local swing park rather than a high-security installation.

The original design had called for the heavy railings all around, but the local council had objected because it would spoil the landscape, and nobody had made a fuss because the lighter fence saved half a million in building costs. It was exactly the kind of design weakness that security-test programmes run by CHERUB and MI5 were designed to unearth.

While Lauren and Bethany entered from the front, Rat and the other four boys had squelched across the surrounding farmland. Once they got within twenty metres of the perimeter, Rat, Andy and Jake kept watch while the two youngest boys had crawled up to the fence on their bellies and each made a hole with their wire cutters.

Ronan's hole was large and obvious. He'd folded back the wire and left a bright orange skiing glove snagged on it. Kevin's hole was twenty metres away. It was smaller and he'd pulled the wire back tight, making it near impossible to spot in the dark.

Andy was first to spot several torches flickering between newly planted saplings in the grounds.

'I see five, I think,' Jake said, as he peered through a tiny set of binoculars.

'Shit,' Rat said. 'Means there's probably still one guy wandering around inside. Jake, Andy, Ronan, you move up and get ready to go inside.'

'Aye aye, Captain Rathbone,' Andy said, before saluting his friend and scuttling off over the soft ground with Jake and Ronan in tow.

There were three hundred metres between the back of the control centre and the fence. The five uniformed guards were walking together, chatting casually, mucking around with their torches and one was even lighting up a cigarette.

'They're not taking it seriously,' Rat said, as he turned towards Kevin. 'How much security training do you reckon they've had?'

Kevin smiled uneasily. 'Half a day, at most.'

'You feeling OK now?'

'Bit nervous,' Kevin admitted. 'I know this isn't a big deal compared to some missions, but it's my first time doing CHERUB stuff out in the real world.'

Rat put a reassuring hand on Kevin's shoulder as he pulled out his mobile. 'It's definitely only five guys,' he said. 'I'd better call Lauren and tell her to go find the sixth.'

'Someone could be off sick or something,' Kevin said.

Andy, Jake and Ronan had reached the fence. The area inside was alarmed and they couldn't enter the compound until they were sure the motion sensors were switched off.

'Faces down, boys,' Andy whispered, as a powerful torchlight swept across the ground.

As expected, the guards spotted Ronan's hole and the bright orange glove.

'Hey, Karen,' one of the guards shouted into his radio. 'Looks like Joe was right. Someone's cut the fence, but they can't have got in because they'd have set off the alarm. I'm gonna go take a look, so I need the sensors off.'

Andy didn't hear the reply, but he knew that the sensors were off when two of the guards started walking towards the hole. Their three companions seemed content that they'd found the source of the problem and stopped searching with their torches.

'Like a charm,' Andy whispered, grinning to Jake and Ronan as he led the way through the other hole. 'Keep the noise down and don't look up unless you have to 'cos your faces will catch the light.'

Jake tutted as he followed Andy through. 'Do I look like an idiot?'

'Pretty much,' Ronan smirked.

Kevin breathed deeply as the two guards approached the other hole. Rat took his slingshot and a cloth bag filled with ball bearings out of his jacket. The fence was ten metres away, it was dark and there was drizzle in the air but he was still confident about making the shot.

'Kids,' the guard said dismissively as he picked up the child-sized glove hooked to the gap in the fence. 'Little fellow left his glove behind.'

Ronan had deliberately left hand and trainer prints in the

mud and the guard shone his torch at the ground, inspecting them. 'Ten or eleven years old, I'd guess,' he said finally.

His bald-headed colleague nodded. 'We'd better go under and see if they're still out there,' he said. 'Joe only saw them a minute ago.'

'Sod that,' came the reply. 'You fancy crawling through all that mud? And if we catch the little buggers we're just as likely to get done for assault.'

'I'm just saying, Ken,' the baldy said, as he straightened up and put his cap on his head, 'the high-ups are bound to launch an investigation, so we'd better make ourselves look good.'

Ken realised his colleague was right, but he paused, looking for any excuse not to get muddy. 'Handprints,' he said happily. 'That's forensic evidence, and there's no way I can get through without disturbing it.'

'Dammit,' Rat muttered. He'd hoped to ambush the guard as he crawled through the fence.

The trouble with shooting while the guards were inside was that the ball bearing could hit the wire mesh and ricochet. The two guards were about to walk away and Rat realised it was his best chance.

He bobbed out of the damp grass, stretched the slingshot to its fullest extent and aimed for Ken's body. A head shot would have been more effective, but the midriff was a larger target and they weren't trying to kill him. The steel ball hit the fencing and ricocheted upwards, knocking off the guard's hat.

'What the heck?' Ken said, mystified by the sudden loss of his hat but not realising that he was under fire.

Rat moved closer and his second shot passed clean through the mesh, slamming Ken in the gut and knocking the wind right out of him. Kevin was a metre behind and fired at the bald guard. They didn't want to seriously hurt anyone, but Kevin had only had one short slingshot practice and the metal ball went high. It hit in the neck, making the guard yelp with pain.

Five seconds had elapsed since Rat's first shot and the other three guards now realised their colleagues were under attack. Their first thoughts were terrorists with silenced hand guns, rather than boys with slingshots.

'Get out of here,' one of them shouted.

But the trio of guards had been outflanked by Andy, Jake and Ronan. As they turned to run back to the building the three cherubs broke cover and fired a volley of ball bearings from less than ten metres. The first round of shots knocked down two guards with blows to the gut and chest, but Ronan missed the one farthest away and gasped in horror as the man went for his radio.

One message to the remaining guard in the control room and they'd have a dozen expertly trained military police officers plus the local on their backs. Luckily, Rat had pushed through the hole in the fence and knocked the guy who'd been hit in the head cold with a well aimed kick. As he stood up, he grabbed one of the metal balls from inside his coat and fired a superb long-range shot at the last guard. As he fell, a second shot from Jake slammed him in the back.

The five guards were all down, but only one was unconscious. Kevin launched an assault on the first guard by the fence, thrusting his palm against the man's temple and then snatching the pepper spray off his belt while he was in a daze. After subduing the guard by the fence with two squirts from the canister and a threat of more, he worked with Rat to bind his wrists and ankles with tape while the other lads moved to quickly incapacitate the others.

Andy had the toughest looking guard to deal with, but the steel ball to the gut had knocked the wind out of him and he meekly offered his wrists up to be bound after a hard kick in the stomach.

Ronan and Jake had a fight on their hands, but they pinned the guard down between them and subdued him with half a can of his own pepper spray. Rat simply reloaded his slingshot and closed the last guard down, aiming at his head from point-blank range.

'Toss your radio,' Rat ordered. 'Put your hands where I can see 'em and wait for my little friend with the gaffer tape.'

Kevin took less than a minute to bind up the unconscious guard by the gate, then he rushed over to deal with Rat's prisoner. Once everyone's hands and feet were secure, Rat looked around.

'Nice work boys,' he said, as he grabbed his phone out of his pocket to call Lauren.

'How's it going?' she asked.

'We've got the security team all bound up out here. You'd better head inside and grab that last man before he starts wondering why all his buddies have gone so quiet.'

9. RICH

He might have called himself Rich Kline, but as soon as the door of his hotel suite opened James recognised Rich Davis. He was fatter, balder and the seventies-style sideburns were gone, but this was definitely the man who'd once topped the Ulster Constabulary's most wanted list.

'Mr Bradford,' Rich said, as he grudgingly reached out to shake hands.

James was pleased to see clean laundry hanging on the wardrobe door and half eaten room-service sandwiches. These personal effects would make planting the tracking device much easier.

'Everyone calls me Bradford,' he smiled, as his big hands met with Rich's. 'Good to finally meet you.'

'Wish I could say the same,' Rich said, before breaking into a rattly cough. 'I never thought I'd be out on the streets again, Bradford. Cops gave me thirty years on fit-up charges. If it wasn't for the peace accord I'd still be in maximum security lockup. The British government did everything they could to get me and now you're public enemy number one, they'll do everything they can to get you.

'If they can't get you the honest way, they'll fit you up and you'll be doing twenty-five years before you know it. That's why you can't take *stupid* risks, like turning up here in that shit-box car with a kid with bright green hair.'

'He's sixteen,' Bradford said defiantly. 'Knows how to fight. Too young to be a cop or a journo.'

James knew Rich Davis was trying to establish dominance: making them wait, the overbearing tone and the slab of a bodyguard standing in the doorway behind them cracking his knuckles. Davis didn't want to negotiate with Bradford, he wanted to show him who was the boss.

Davis addressed his bodyguard. 'Check both of them for bugs, then take the boy downstairs and buy him a lollipop.'

'James stays here with *me*,' Bradford said, trying to sound tough, but a tremor in his voice gave him away.

The bodyguard grabbed a bug detector and closed up behind Bradford, sweeping it over his clothes. James had a listening device and two trackers but wasn't worried: CHERUB used technology way too advanced for such a crude device to pick up.

'No phones, no bugs, guv,' the guard said to Davis. He turned to James. 'Come on son, let the grown-ups talk.'

James gave the bodyguard evil eyes. He had to gather intelligence and plant the tracking device and he couldn't do either if he wasn't in the room. On the other hand, forcing the issue would risk destroying the relationship between Bradford and Davis before they learned anything about the Irishman's weapons smuggling operation.

'I want him to stay,' Bradford said. 'You can't order me around like this.'

'You need to learn some manners, son,' Davis snarled.

'Who do you think you are?' Bradford shouted, as the bodyguard put a meaty hand on James' shoulder.

The guard had been behind the door when they entered which meant James hadn't been able to size him up, but the casual way he was manhandling James showed that he didn't rate him as a serious threat.

'OK, fine,' James said, acting the stroppy teenager as he raised his hands and turned to face the bodyguard.

'Green-headed ponce,' the bodyguard laughed, before shoving James in the back.

Bradford had made it clear that he didn't want James to leave and the insult gave James an excuse to lash out. As soon as there was a metre of space between himself and the bodyguard, James launched an explosive roundhouse kick.

The bodyguard clattered backwards into a chest of drawers and James felt a jolt of panic as he reached inside his jacket for a gun. James closed in, grabbing the bodyguard's thumb and twisting it back until the bone snapped. A knee in the stomach sent the guard crashing to the ground.

'You want to take the piss out of my hair?' James shouted, booting his opponent in the guts before leaning forward and ripping the gun from the holster under his jacket.

'Still want to shoot me?' James asked.

The bodyguard was coughing blood and wouldn't be getting up any time soon, so James pointed the gun at Davis.

'Whoah! Careful son,' Davis said, waving his hands warily. 'We can talk about this.'

'Don't patronise me,' James shouted. 'If you offer to buy

me a lollipop again, I swear to god I'll take this gun and shove it right up your arse.'

After this, James expertly removed the clip from the gun – perhaps a little too expertly for someone who was supposed to be an ordinary teenager. He pocketed the bullets and checked the chamber was clear before handing the empty weapon to Davis.

The room went into an uneasy quiet. Bradford and Davis glowered at each other, James scowled at the bodyguard, defying him to stand back up and take another swing at him.

Finally, Davis looked down at the empty gun in his hand and burst out laughing. 'I've seen some things in my time, but that's a right nasty little green-haired thug you've got yourself there, Mr Bradford.'

James taking out the bouncer had given Bradford confidence and he allowed himself to smile slightly. 'James is a good man,' Bradford nodded. 'I've got a lot of good men. Now do you think we can forget all this macho shit and talk some business?'

*

When it opened in a month's time the air traffic control centre would be the workplace of a hundred and fifty civilian and eighty military air traffic controllers, along with more than two hundred support workers ranging from canteen staff to software engineers and senior management.

Right now it was ghostly. Many of the main lights were switched off to save energy and Lauren and Bethany crept down a corridor lit only by green emergency exit signs.

'The arrow said that the security office is along here somewhere,' Lauren whispered, as Bethany clattered into a bucket half filled with water.

'Oww,' Bethany moaned, as she flipped on her torch to see what she'd hit.

'Keep the noise down,' Lauren warned. 'If that last guard radios out we're totally screwed.'

'Looks like the builders did a good job on the roof,' Bethany said, as she shone her torch up at a mouldy glass skylight that was feeding the water into the bucket.

Lauren had carried on walking and saw light shining around the rim of a door. She flicked her torch on and was delighted by the sign on the door: ROOM G117 - SECURITY STAFF LOUNGE & TRAINING AREA.

Lauren put her ear up to the door and could hear a woman speaking into her radio. 'Guys, what's going on out there? Respond please. You tossers better not be jerking me around.'

'One woman, and she's close to losing her cool,' Lauren said, as Bethany got close. 'Get the bucket.'

'Bucket?' Bethany said, sounding like she'd misheard.

Lauren didn't know the layout of the security lounge, but there was almost certainly an emergency alarm trigger somewhere in the room. If they burst in, the female guard might reach it before Lauren and Bethany could grab her.

'Cheers,' Lauren said, as Bethany heaved over the plastic bucket. It was so full that the weight of grubby water inside buckled it out of shape.

Lauren began pouring the water under the door of the security lounge. Some ran back into the corridor and swirled around her trainers, but the majority of the brownish liquid ran under the door and the guard inside heard it splashing on the vinyl floor.

'Goddammit,' the woman yelled to herself. 'Poxy roof. Now let's just add mopping up to my job description.'

The guard was startled to open the door and see Lauren standing in front of her. In a move not out of any combat training manual, Lauren swung the empty bucket at the guard's head. It hit with a hollow thunk but the plastic was too light to do serious damage and the guard screamed and tried slamming the door in Lauren's face.

Lauren barged in as the guard ran towards the control panel. She locked arms around the guard's chunky thighs and brought her down on to the damp floor with a rugby tackle. Bethany had picked up the bucket as she entered and couldn't resist wedging it over the guard's head.

The sight of the guard thrashing about with the bucket on her head and her muffled shouts of '*Oh my god!*' touched the girls' warped sense of humour and they both started to laugh.

'Give us the tape, Bethany,' Lauren snorted.

While Lauren pinned the guard to the floor and bound her wrists and ankles, Bethany spotted a marker pen beneath a whiteboard used for the security team's shift rotas and used it to draw a smiley face on the bucket.

When Lauren saw it she started laughing so hard that she could hardly breathe. 'Oh god,' she snorted. 'I'm gonna die.'

Bethany wasn't laughing quite so hard, but still had trouble standing up straight as she wrapped a giant length of tape over the top of the bucket and looped it under the woman's armpits so that it wouldn't come off.

'I'm *such* a bitch,' Bethany shouted triumphantly. 'Don't you just love being evil?'

'You can't leave that on,' Lauren said, trying to be serious between the howls of laughter. 'She could be pregnant, or have asthma or something.'

'Spoilsport,' Bethany moaned, snapping a picture on her mobile before pulling off the bucket.

The woman let out a piercing scream before Bethany made a proper gag the way she'd been trained: a loosely wrapped ball of tape that would depress the tongue but not induce choking and a single strip of tape over the mouth, being careful not to block the nose.

'We shouldn't laugh,' Lauren said, as she pulled out her phone and tried to calm down slightly before calling Rat. 'But that bucket looked so damned funny.'

The guard was spluttering words into her gag and Lauren was pretty sure that they weren't nice ones.

'What's so funny?' Rat asked, when he answered his phone.

'Don't worry about it,' Lauren sniffed, rubbing a tear from her eye. 'How you doing?'

'It's below freezing out here, so we've dragged all the guards into the shed under the radar tower. Now we're waiting on you.'

'I'm sitting on the last guard,' Lauren said. 'So get your worthless male butts inside, it's time to trash this joint!'

10. DIALOGUE

'The question is, can we do business?' Rich said, as he pulled a set of long velvet curtains and invited Bradford to sit at a circular table set in the hotel suite's bay window. James took a bottle of mineral water from the mini-bar and handed it to the bodyguard who was still down on the floor. He accepted it grudgingly, before swishing it around his mouth and spitting bloody water out on the carpet.

'Where'd you learn your tricks?' he asked, as James gave him an arm up.

'My dad was a Thai kickboxing champion,' James lied. 'Taught me moves almost from the day I could walk.'

'I could have had you, kid,' he said, half smiling as he stared down at his dislocated thumb. 'Just never expected it.'

James didn't want another ruck, but wasn't impressed by the attempt at camaraderie from a man who'd patronised and pulled a gun on him five minutes earlier.

'All these phone calls, all this mystery,' Bradford said, as he stared at Rich across the table. 'You said something about a cache of Russian weapons.'

Rich grabbed a pair of ice cubes and dropped them into

his whisky tumbler before nodding. 'There's still plenty of IRA kit floating around, but I can also get better things: plastic explosive from eastern Europe, Italian grenades, Israeli machine guns . . . The problem is it all costs and judging by that car you came in, you and your little bunch of anarchist friends aren't exactly swimming in money.'

The conversation was just getting interesting, but James' priority was to plant the tracking device inside something belonging to Rich. Busting Rich before anything was known about his organisation would be like cutting off a weed at the stem: if you don't destroy the roots, it just grows back in a different shape.

'Mind if I take a leak?' James asked.

Rich turned and smiled. He clearly found the green-haired thug amusing. 'Go for it,' he nodded.

'*Don't* lock the door,' the bodyguard warned.

That wasn't ideal, but James pushed the bathroom door closed and kicked one of the damp towels on the floor against it so it would be difficult to open quickly. The shower cubicle was a mess and he was delighted to see Rich's toiletries spread out over the cabinets.

He lifted the toilet seat and studied Davis' stuff as he started to pee. After zipping up he turned on the tap, but rather than washing his hands he glanced back over his shoulder to make sure Rich's bodyguard wasn't peeking before taking a tiny tracking device out of his jeans.

The three-centimetre disc was roughly the thickness of a CD. Although it wasn't particularly large, the tracking device didn't look like anything else and needed to be hidden somewhere out of sight, like the lining of a suitcase or the battery compartment of an electrical device.

Rich had a roll-open toiletry bag hooked on to the shaving mirror, but James was disappointed to discover that all the compartments were made from loose nylon mesh which made it impossible to hide anything.

The longer James took the greater the chance of the bodyguard getting suspicious and sticking his head around the door. He had half a mind to cut his losses when he eyed Rich's shaving kit.

Rich used a Mach-3 razor, with a traditional bristle shaving brush and an upmarket brand of hard shaving soap in its own plastic tub. James grabbed the tub and twisted off the lid as he backed up to the door. The bodyguard couldn't see James in this position and if he did push the door, it would hit James in the back giving him two or three seconds to disguise what he was up to.

With the tap running it was hard to follow the conversation at the table, but James' nerves worsened as he caught a half a sentence from Bradford and realised that his voice was high and tense.

James moved fretfully, squeezing the circular tub so that the almost new bar of white shaving soap popped out. He took the sticky backing off both sides of the tracking device and pressed it against the bottom of the plastic tub, before squeezing the lump of soap down on top of it.

This was close to ideal from a disguise standpoint: Rich probably wouldn't use the soap down to the last dregs where the tracking device would be revealed, and even if he did he'd hopefully assume that the disc was a part of the packaging designed to hold the soap in place.

James stepped back into the main room but nobody paid attention. The bodyguard sat on the end of the bed clutching his thumb while Rich Davis and Chris Bradford scowled at each other across the table.

'*Listen* to me,' Rich said angrily. 'You're living in cloud-cuckoo land. If you want expensive toys you need money. I want to work with you, Bradford, but every successful terrorist organisation has to have two arms: one to raise money and one to spend it.'

'I'm not a bank robber,' Bradford said incredulously. 'Or a con-artist. And I certainly don't go around extorting money from stallholders and shopkeepers.'

'Then how *do* you make it work?' Rich bawled. 'I hate the British establishment as much as I ever did. I can bankroll enough weapons to get you started, but I'm no billionaire. We can't turn SAG into a serious threat unless there's money coming into the kitty.

'You've got enthusiastic young supporters like James over there. I've got *thirty* years' expertise in raising money for terrorist groups, plus contacts in the defence industry that can bring in everything you need to get the job done.'

'I didn't come here looking for a partner,' Bradford said firmly.

'Well what did you come here for?' Rich said angrily. 'A handout?'

Bradford shrugged. 'I guess I hoped you supported our cause.'

'You expected me to hand you a bunch of weapons and tell you to go off and do whatever you liked with them?'

Bradford lowered his head and ground his palms against

his temples. 'I don't know what I was expecting from you, Rich,' he said. 'But I'm not looking to rob banks and I'm certainly not looking for a partner.'

'Fine,' Rich said, in a tone that made it perfectly clear that it wasn't. 'Ain't no point talking in circles. There's no basis for us to work together.'

Rich glanced at his watch and looked over at the bodyguard slumped on the end of his bed.

'Pack my things,' he said contemptuously. 'No reason to stay here.'

Bradford was a confident man who was used to running the show, but he now sat with his elbows on the table and his face gaunt. He'd put all of his hopes into the idea of turning SAG into a terrorist organisation and Rich represented his only realistic chance of doing so.

'You can leave now, Mr Bradford,' Rich said firmly. 'I have to make a private call.'

James kept up a sombre appearance as he opened the door of Rich's suite, but he was smiling on the inside: he'd planted the tracker, which would enable MI5 to track Rich's movements until its tiny internal battery ran out of juice. He'd more than proved his loyalty to Bradford when he flattened the bouncer and the fact that negotiations broke down so quickly meant that SAG had no chance of building a terrorist arsenal any time soon.

As James' boot hit the thick green carpet in the corridor, he glanced down the hallway and saw a policewoman in full protective gear lean out of a stairwell. She hid so quickly that James thought he might have imagined it, but he was on edge as he started down the corridor with Bradford alongside.

'What went wrong?' James asked edgily, as he cast an anxious glance over his shoulder.

'I'm not a fool,' Bradford stuttered. 'I knew we'd need money, but I don't think Rich was looking for a partner. I think he'd end up being the one that called all the shots.'

'Reckon you're right,' James nodded, as the doors of two rooms on opposite sides of the corridor in front burst open.

'Police, freeze!'

More cops started pouring off the fire stairs at the end of the corridor behind them.

'Bollocks,' Bradford shouted.

James couldn't understand. This wasn't part of any plan he'd seen and what could have changed in the two and a half hours since he'd last spoken to his mission controller?

11. RAMPAGE

The five boys were in high spirits as they raced towards the front entrance of the air traffic control centre. Rat led the way around the final corner and grabbed his slingshot as soon as he saw the fancy BMW parked in front of the main doors.

Slowing to walking pace, his first shot punched through the front windscreen, while the other lads followed up with shots that demolished all four side windows. A few that missed glass left huge dents in the metalwork and smashed one of the headlamps.

'Yeeeeeah baby!' Jake shouted, as he jumped on to the bonnet and ripped off the windscreen wiper.

Ronan and Kevin tore off door mirrors as Jake scratched up the paintwork along the side of the car with the wiper and Rat clambered up and stamped through the glass sunroof. The girls were waiting in the doorway as Rat jumped down.

'Having fun?' Bethany asked.

'Hell yeah!' Andy shouted, as he tried levering off the petrol filler cap. 'If I can get in here, we'll blow this baby sky high!'

'Don't be an idiot,' Lauren yelled. 'They'll hear the explosion for miles and we'll have the cops on our arses. Gather round, listen up.'

They formed a little huddle near the doorway, but Ronan, Jake and Kevin had enjoyed trashing the car and couldn't stop giggling.

'Remember,' Lauren said firmly. 'This has *got* to look like a bunch of kids went crazy, attacked the security guards and trashed the joint. You've got fifteen minutes. This is a state-of-the-art facility so make the vandalism look good, but *don't* go burning the place down or start having a go at the government's brand new thirty-million-pound computer system. Understood?'

'We'll try our best,' Ronan laughed.

Lauren gave the eleven-year-old a shock, grabbing him by his muddy jacket and shoving him against a plate glass window. 'I've had enough of you tonight,' she growled. 'So unless you fancy going head first down a flight of stairs, I suggest you shut your mouth and start doing *exactly* what I tell you.'

Bethany led the way inside. Jake and Kevin charged into a gents toilet off the reception area and stuffed the sink's holes and overflows with toilet tissue before turning all the taps on full blast. While the basins flooded, they launched powerful Karate kicks at wall-mounted soap dispensers. They splintered open, spraying pink goo in all directions, including on to the boys' already muddy clothes.

'WHOOOOOOOOOOOOOO!' Kevin chanted, skidding precariously on the soapy floor tiles as he chased Jake back into the reception.

Bethany was trashing the reception desk while Lauren was wading through indoor greenery, ripping up some plants and blasting others with white carbon dioxide powder from a fire extinguisher while singing *Let It Snow*, badly.

'Where did Rat and them go?' Jake asked.

Lauren pointed to the back of reception and hooked her hand to the right. 'Main control room, I think.'

Kevin and Jake bolted down a thirty-metre corridor, passing a glass-sided room containing the enormous mainframe computer which controlled the entire centre. The pair gasped as they found themselves in a vast space with a wooden ceiling high above, a sloped floor leading down to a bank of massive display screens and rows of identical monitoring stations which would eventually be used by the controllers.

Some screens were already attached and had been left switched on overnight to bed in the new software. In other areas, the terminals were still being wired into the main computer and the floors were tangled with a mass of unfinished computer and electrical cabling.

'Man, I wish we were allowed to trash this bit!' Jake said, as he read a number off an active screen, grabbed one of the controller's headsets and pressed the speak button. 'Flight AQ71, descend to two hundred metres and do a barrel roll, over.'

Kevin burst out laughing, but they were both stunned by the reply coming out of the speaker alongside the screen. 'AQ71 pilot to control. Please repeat instruction, has control switched to new frequency, over?'

'Ooops!' Jake said, as he threw down the headset and

jolted backwards as if he'd been electrocuted. 'I never knew the system was live.'

Kevin laughed. 'You'll never get your navy shirt if you bring down an airliner.'

'Shut up,' Jake said. 'And don't tell *anyone* about this.'

As he hurried away, there was a huge crash of glass in the conference room off to one side and they heard Rat screaming and yelling, 'What a shot!'

'What happened?' Kevin shouted, as he raced into the room behind Jake.

But he didn't need to ask, because he could see a long conference table showered with chunks of glass where an elaborate light fitting had crashed down on top of it.

'You should have seen it,' Andy gasped.

'One shot at the base and the whole thing came down,' Rat said proudly. 'I'm the master of the slingshot!'

Jake saw a line of wheeled metal trolleys filled with tools which belonged to the engineers fitting out the control room. He pulled open one of the drawers and flung out a bunch of Allen keys and screwdrivers.

'We could race these,' Kevin noted. 'You know the slope in the main control room?'

'Yeah,' Rat said excitedly. 'We might kill ourselves, but what the hell.'

Kevin, Jake, Rat and Andy pulled the trolleys out of the conference room and lined them up at the top of the sloping pathway down the middle of the control room. It was covered with carpet tiles and led all the way to the front of the room, with rows of controllers' screens branching off on either side.

'Go!' Rat shouted, as he leaned over his trolley and kicked against the back wall.

'Cheat!' Jake shouted. 'I wasn't ready, you Aussie butt licker.'

The trolleys were around waist height and packed with tools and equipment which rattled like crazy. The slope was steep and large rubber wheels enabled them to gather considerable speed as the four boys clattered towards the front wall.

Rat led the way, but his trolley snagged on the stuck-up corner of a carpet tile. It spun three hundred and sixty degrees before crashing into the side of a console. Andy rammed him from behind and crashed to the floor as his trolley tumbled over on top of him, but not before Jake and Kevin squeezed through the remaining gap at speed.

The two lads were determined to make it to the bottom first and the ride turned into a game of chicken as they picked up speed while getting ever closer to the bottom of the slope. Both lads dived clear, barely a second before the pair of trolleys smacked into the wall.

Lauren and Bethany had arrived at the back of the control room, both covered in powder from fire extinguishers.

'What the hell,' Lauren laughed, as she saw the metal trolleys with their drawers hanging open and bits of rogue computer equipment scattered all along the slope.

The four boys were quiet for a few seconds as they stood up and inspected their injuries, but they were all OK.

'Good job we jumped off,' Kevin said, as he inspected a huge dent in the wooden panelling where his trolley had hit the front wall. 'That could have been my head.'

'Wouldn't have made much difference,' Jake snorted.

As Kevin flicked Jake off, Rat looked along the aisle between two rows of consoles and noticed an engineer's open tool case and one of the display screens with the access panel underneath left open. This wouldn't have grabbed his attention, but for the steam rising off the cup of coffee standing on the desktop above it.

'Lauren,' Rat shouted. 'I think we've got a problem.'

'What?' Lauren asked curiously as she strode briskly down the slope towards the scene.

Rat dabbed his fingertip in the cardboard cup. 'Black coffee still almost boiling. One of the engineers must have been working late.'

'I *thought* that BMW you boys trashed was a bit flash for a security guard,' Bethany noted.

Jake groaned. 'Well why didn't you say so at the time?'

'We'd better hunt him down,' Andy said.

'What's the point?' Lauren said, shaking her head. 'There's got to be two hundred rooms in this building and he'll have called the cops already.'

'Great,' Kevin moaned. 'We've got no transport and we're five kilometres from where Dennis is picking us up.'

'Ronan,' Rat shouted into his phone. 'Where are you, mate? You what? Right . . . Right, I understand. You'd better get your butt down here sharpish.'

'What's up with him?' Lauren asked anxiously, as Rat snapped his phone shut.

'Ronan went up to the first floor and started trashing a refreshment area, but he saw a woman running along a hallway.'

'A woman as well,' Jake gasped. 'What was she, a cleaning lady or something?'

'The engineer was a woman,' Rat said, shaking his head.

Bethany glowered at her brother. 'You're *such* a sexist pig.'

Lauren gave Bethany a little shove, as if to say *don't you two start arguing now*, then she looked at Rat. 'So why didn't Ronan tell us?'

'It's just happened,' Rat explained. 'He tackled the woman, but she got away and now she's barricaded herself into an office. But she dropped her handbag, so Ronan checked the call log on her phone. She called an emergency number, eleven minutes ago.'

'Must have heard us smashing up the car,' Lauren sighed. 'They could be here any second. We've got to get out of here.'

As Lauren said this, all the lights and screens in the giant room flickered before going out. The control room was below ground level with no windows and the dark space turned eerily silent as the air conditioning system and the whirring fans inside hundreds of computers came to a stop.

'Someone pulled the electricity *and* the backup generator,' Rat said, his voice echoing around the room.

'OK,' Lauren said, trying to sound calmer than she was. 'They're probably going to be military police, which means they're tough and they're gonna know what they're doing. I'd say our best chance is if we split up.'

'Agreed,' Rat said, and the others all murmured as they heard Ronan running down the hallway and bursting through the doors.

'I just ran through reception and saw them,' Ronan gasped, in a state of complete panic. 'There's two vanloads of soldiers, plus coppers, and they're unloading dogs from the back of their vans. We have got to get the *hell* out of here.'

*

James had been arrested a few times. It was never pleasant: the cops shoved you around, then you'd spend for ever stuck in an evil-smelling cell with nothing to eat or drink and a toilet that was invariably busted.

So he didn't fancy getting pulled and the cops bursting out of the hotel rooms in front of him would take a few seconds to get into position, so he sprinted forwards with no idea whether Bradford would have the presence of mind to go with him.

An officer went flying as James clattered into him and he almost hit the carpet himself as a hand grabbed his ankle, but James kept going. He looked back and saw Bradford bundled to the ground by three officers as more piled in from the opposite end of the hallway and used a battering ram to shatter the door of Rich's hotel room.

There were armed officers on the scene, but James wasn't too worried. Police marksmen have strict rules of engagement and he knew they wouldn't shoot unless he posed an immediate threat to someone.

As he reached the main staircase, the female lookout officer he'd glimpsed moments earlier stepped in front of him and swung her baton, trying to hit him in the stomach. But she was small and she moved too early. The blow swept harmlessly across James' jacket and he was moving so fast that he knocked hard into her.

She bounced off the wallpaper and her cap flew down the staircase as the back of her head hit the wall with a nasty thunk. As the officer grappled the banister trying not to fall down the stairs, James charged down taking three steps at a time with no clue what he was going to encounter when he reached the next landing.

'What's going on . . .' he mumbled to himself as he reached the first floor and looked over a long balcony into the hotel's main lobby. To his left and right were grand staircases leading down to ground level, but half a dozen yellow-jacketed cops stood around in the lobby.

James' boots and bright green hair didn't exactly blend into his surroundings, so he slowed to walking pace and tried a set of double doors behind where he was standing. These led into an empty function room and he managed to slip inside before any of the cops downstairs spotted him.

The room had dining chairs stacked up against the wall, and large chipboard-topped tables designed to be disguised with fancy table linen. At the back of the room were a fire exit and a small bar. James vaulted over the polished bartop and crouched down low between the beer taps and the glass-doored fridges filled with soft drinks.

He needed to know what was going on, but he didn't have his mobile so he grabbed the telephone on the wall next to the packets of peanuts and was pleasantly surprised to find that he remembered his mission controller's mobile number.

'John, what's going on? Why's the joint swarming with cops?'

'Eh?' John exclaimed. 'Who says it is?'

'*I* say it is,' James said angrily. 'They just busted Rich and Bradford and I don't know what to do . . . You mean you know nothing about this?'

'No,' John said, flabbergasted. 'I . . . There must be another team working the case, or something.'

'Arse and balls,' James spluttered bitterly. One of the greatest problems with highly secretive operations is that occasionally two different teams end up working independently on the same case. 'What do you want me to do?'

'Get out if you can, but don't take any stupid risks. If you get nicked, I'll find out where you're going and pull you out ASAP.'

'Right,' James whispered. 'Where are you . . . ?'

'Parked up near a country pub about half a–'

James didn't hear the rest because a bunch of cops were running into the room.

'Green-haired bastard must have gone through here,' one cop said, as he raced across the carpet towards the fire exit.

'Gotta go,' James whispered, but he couldn't reach up to replace the receiver without his arm being seen.

The officer shoved the fire door and an alarm rang out. 'Can't have got through here without setting it off,' he noted. He turned towards the bar as one of his colleagues searched behind an elaborate Christmas tree and the other leaned forward looking under the tables and behind the stacks of chairs.

James half smiled as the burly cop leaned across the bar and looked down at him.

'What can I get you, officer?' James asked. 'Beer, wine, peanuts?'

He thought about springing up and having a go but the officer went for his stun gun and James had no appetite for 50,000 volts.

'On your feet, hands on head,' the officer barked.

As James stood up, the other two officers grabbed him by the arms, yanked him across the top of the bar then slammed him hard against the floor before tying a set of plasticuffs tightly around his wrists.

'Suspect in custody,' one cop said into his radio, as another sarcastically read James his rights.

James had his face down on the floor and couldn't see much except the officer's boots, but he noticed a smaller set of boots coming across the carpet. The shiny black toes stopped just in front of his nose.

'All right,' the officer said, ripping her baton out of her belt before crouching down in front of James.

He looked up and knew what was coming as soon as he saw the bloody-nosed officer he'd bundled down the stairs.

'Wanna mess with me now you little punk?' the officer shouted, as she stood up and smashed James in the back with her baton, before taking a short run-up and booting him in the kidneys.

'Jesus,' James groaned, as the female officer joined her colleague in pulling him to his feet.

'You don't like that, tough guy?' she grinned. 'Well you wait and see what happens when we get you in the back of our van.'

12. CUPBOARD

Jake, Ronan and Kevin sprinted out of a set of fire doors at the rear of the air traffic control centre. The military police were taking their time getting organised at the front of the building, but it was pitch black and the three boys pulled their hoodies up to stop their faces catching any stray light.

'What's the plan?' Kevin asked warily.

Jake shrugged. 'Run like hell and try climbing over the fence.'

'Does that actually count as a plan?' Ronan asked.

Jake huffed. 'Ronan, I'm all ears if you've got a better one.'

Kevin thought aloud as they crept along close to the concrete wall: 'That fence is four metres high with razor wire on top. We can't climb over but I've still got the cutters I used to make the hole.'

Ronan smiled. 'I've got a pair too.'

'So we've got both pairs of wire cutters?' Jake said. 'What about Rat and the others?'

'Who gives a toss?' Ronan said. 'Lauren's been bossing us around all day. She's so smart, let her sort it out.'

'Ronan's right,' Jake said. 'It's every man for himself and we're never gonna find them in the dark anyway.'

*

Rat and Lauren took a riskier strategy, racing through reception seconds before the RAF police officers entered and heading along the corridor to the room where the female security guard was tied up.

'Hey sister,' Lauren said, as she shone her torch at the guard. Her limbs were bound tight, but she'd freed the tape over her mouth and spat out her gag.

'Kiss my arse, brat,' the guard shouted.

While the two females scowled at each other, Rat found the security guards' outdoor jackets on a row of coat hooks along the back wall and he searched pockets until he'd found two sets of car keys.

'Fiat or Volvo?' Rat asked.

'Volvo's bound to be heavier for smashing through the fence,' Lauren said. 'But take both sets. The Fiat might be parked further away from the cops.'

*

Andy and Bethany sprinted across the muddy field at the rear of the compound as the police Alsatians barked in the distance.

'Don't like that sound one bit,' Bethany gasped. 'You'd better put that torch out; the cops will spot us a mile off.'

'I definitely saw it round here somewhere on the way in,' Andy said irritably, as he swept the ground with the beam of his torch. 'A dirty great builder's tarp stretched over a hole.'

'Maybe we should just try climbing over the fence,' Bethany suggested.

'Go try if you want,' Andy said. 'But it's eight strands of razor wire in a V shape, with coils of barbed wire running through the middle. Snag your leg in that lot and it'll come out in ribbons.'

'There, beside the shed,' Bethany said, as she saw an orange glow in the beam of Andy's torch.

They raced forward, finding the heavy orange tarpaulin stretched over a circular hole which would eventually house the rotating base of a large satellite dish. It was only held in place with breeze blocks and the pair moved around the edge of the hole kicking the blocks away.

When there were only a couple left along the far side, Andy gave the heavy sheet an almighty tug. This shifted the tarp, but at the same time drenched Bethany with the rainwater that had been lying on top of it.

'AAARGH,' Bethany shuddered, as freezing cold water dripped out of her hair and ran down inside her clothes. 'You *bloody* idiot!'

But the pair didn't have time to argue. The police were finally getting organised and a dozen RAF police had spread out to form a search line. Torch beams swung methodically over the ground as they marched briskly away from the control centre. Behind the search teams were dog handlers with Alsatians. Luckily, Bethany and Andy were less than sixty metres from the fence.

*

When the cherubs split up Jake had taken a more cautious approach than Andy and Bethany. He was still creeping around the outside of the air traffic control building, behind the search team that had set off across the grounds.

He peeked around a far end of the building, then stepped back and looked at Ronan and Kevin.

'Three guards and two dogs,' Jake whispered. 'They're just milling around, less than fifteen metres away.'

Kevin was scared. 'We'll never make it,' he said, looking at the twenty metres of open ground between the end of the main control centre building and an ancillary building designed for admin staff.

'We haven't got a choice,' Jake said, struggling to keep up the spirits of his slightly younger companions. 'Just move quietly. Go!'

As Jake ran out, he tripped on a metal doorstop sticking up from the ground and grazed his hands as he sprawled over the damp concrete. Ronan grabbed Jake's collar to help him up, but Jake couldn't help moaning and the Alsatians reared up on their leads, barking, the instant they heard.

'Visual,' one of the RAF officers shouted, as he blasted his torch beam in Ronan's face.

Ronan was taller and stockier than Jake and he yanked the older boy to his feet.

'Come on,' Kevin shouted, as he ran across the gap between buildings before looking back at the others.

Jake's knee buckled as he took his first step. Realising that he wasn't going anywhere fast, he shoved Ronan away. 'Get out of here.'

Ronan started running, but after less than three steps he looked over his shoulder and saw the huge Alsatian charging across the concrete. It pounced and knocked Ronan forward, but before the dog could bring its whole weight on top of him it crumpled to the ground with a pitiful yelp.

Ronan was mystified until he'd made it a couple of steps and glimpsed Kevin aiming his slingshot at the second dog.

But Kevin only had shadows to aim at and his second shot vanished harmlessly into the darkness.

Jake screamed in terror and tried to crawl as the Alsatian's narrow snout closed in on his arm. He managed to wriggle clear, but only for the dog's sharp teeth to pierce Jake's tracksuit bottoms and sink deep into his buttock as a pair of dog handlers charged forward to save him.

'Oh god,' Kevin trembled, as he looked at Ronan. 'Maybe we should surrender.'

Ronan shook his head. 'Surrender is weak. With two sets of cutters we'll be through that fence in no time.'

The pair ran off desperately, knowing the military police and their dogs wouldn't be far behind. Jake sobbed with pain as dog handlers ordered their Alsatians to heel, while a burly military policeman hauled him up with one hand and shoved him up against the wall.

'You're in a *lot* of trouble, young man,' he barked, before laughing as he shone his torch beam at Jake's torn and bloody tracksuit bottoms. 'And I bet you won't forget Fluff the Alsatian in a hurry either.'

*

There were footsteps and torch beams in the vandalised lobby by the time Lauren and Rat emerged from the security office, cutting off their route to the car park.

'Dammit,' Lauren said.

As she tried remembering the building plans she'd seen back in her room on campus, Rat moved confidently in the opposite direction. Lauren followed, sticking close to the wall to minimise the chance of being spotted by a torch beam.

'There's stairs at the end,' Rat explained. 'We can go up to the first floor, double back, run the entire length of the building, then go down the fire stairs into the car park.'

Rat was intelligent even by the high standards of CHERUB agents. He had one of the highest IQs on campus and a superb memory, but he also had a planet-sized ego so Lauren made a point of not offering a compliment.

As they neared the top of the stairs, they stepped through water trickling down the steps. It ran from a bathroom flooded by Ronan The first-floor hallway had also been completely trashed. Two vending machines were toppled, dozens of polystyrene ceiling tiles were poked through with the end of a broom and light fittings and glass panes inside several doors were shattered.

'Ronan's a destructive little bugger,' Lauren smiled, as she shone her torch around.

Rat climbed over the first vending machine blocking the hallway, before peeking out of a window. There was enough light coming from car headlights, flashing blue lamps and torch beams for him to get a good idea of what was occurring. More police were arriving, along with backup teams from the RAF base and even a local TV news van with a satellite dish on top.

'Crap,' Lauren said. 'That's something we could do without.'

'Somebody must have tipped the press off,' Rat nodded. 'And we can say goodbye to missions for a couple of years if we land a starring role on the evening news . . .'

They moved down the corridor as fast as darkness and the need to keep quiet would allow. After passing above the reception area they opened a set of doors and found themselves on a gallery overlooking the huge control room where they'd crashed the engineers' carts a few minutes earlier.

The emergency lights had been turned back on and a mixture of regular and military police officers swarmed around between the consoles on the floor below them.

'Kids,' a peak-capped RAF officer said, as her civilian counterpart took flash photographs of the destruction. 'Planned it all out, tied up the guards . . . Unbelievable.'

The gallery was exposed, but luckily the flooring was still being laid. Lauren crawled along behind a giant roll of carpet with Rat directly behind her. She had to go up on her knees to open the door at the end of the gallery. The hinge had a squeak, but nobody down below seemed to notice and the pair passed into a bare office.

The narrow room had large square windows along one side and an emergency door leading on to metal fire-escape stairs at one end. The engineers were in the early stages of installing the wiring and reels of cable littered the floor.

'Mind you don't trip,' Rat said, hopping over the cables.

When Lauren reached the fire exit, she stared out of the large window alongside it and cursed their luck. 'Cops everywhere.'

'It's not our night tonight,' Rat sighed.

They were in a bare room with no hiding places and it could only be a matter of minutes until the police teams sweeping through the building caught up with them. Rat ran to the opposite end of the room, looking out of the windows as he went.

'I see the Fiat,' he said. 'I can't see anyone down this end. Do you reckon we could jump down?'

Rat grabbed the handle on the side of the plastic window frame and pushed it open. Cold air blasted Lauren's face as she peered down into the darkness.

'I've dropped from twice that height in training,' she nodded. 'Bit of a squeeze-through though.'

Rat quickly closed the window and grabbed another handle on the side of the frame. This made the entire square of glass swivel on a central pivot designed to allow the outside of the glass to be cleaned from indoors.

'Even *your* big butt should fit through there now,' Rat said.

'Smartarse,' Lauren replied, as she swung her leg up on to the window ledge. Rat quickly flicked on his torch to make sure she wasn't going to land on anything apart from an empty parking bay. It was a four-metre drop and Lauren couldn't help groaning as she landed heavily on her ankle.

Rat came down a few seconds later and quickly found his feet. 'You OK?' he asked edgily.

'Twisted,' Lauren said as Rat helped her up.

Fortunately the little Fiat Punto belonging to one of the guards was parked in front of a hedge less than ten metres away.

'I've got you,' Rat said, taking the car keys from inside his jacket before grabbing Lauren under the arm and making a dash towards the car. As they got close Rat pressed the plipper to unlock the doors. The car emitted a double blip and all four indicator lights blinked in the darkness.

'Visual,' a policeman shouted. 'The Fiat!'

Lauren moaned in pain, clambering in the back door as Rat fumbled with the ignition key up front. He fought to get the little car into reverse gear as three RAF police officers charged towards them. The swiftest officer grabbed the door handle as Rat lifted the clutch. The door flew open, but the car shot backwards, tearing the officer's fingers away before the flapping door knocked him down.

Every car has a slightly different feel that takes time to get used to. Rat stalled the engine as he juddered off in the wrong gear.

'Shite!' he yelled, as he jangled the key to restart the engine.

'I thought you knew how to drive,' Lauren shouted frantically.

'Your sarcasm *really* helps my concentration,' Rat shouted back as he found the right gear and made a successful second attempt at driving away.

The front bumper shattered as the car hit the kerb at speed and reared up into the mud. Rat straightened up the steering wheel, floored the accelerator and aimed straight for the fence.

13. COPS

James lay face down on the floor of a speeding police van, plasticuffs tearing into his wrists and four officers sitting on the wooden benches alongside him. The female officer he'd knocked against the wall kept a boot on the back of his head, pressing his face against the floor and forcing him to breathe the smells of urine, dog and whatever else ends up stuck to the bottom of a police van.

'Here driver,' one of the cops said loutishly, as he leaned towards a grilled porthole and looked into the cab. 'Can't you find some nice bumpy roads for our boy on the floor here?'

The cops were breaking all sorts of rules on the handling of prisoners, but if you assault a police officer you can be sure they won't treat you nice when they arrest you. Not that James needed any extra bumps: police vans have firm suspension designed for speed not comfort and every pothole or dink in the road sent a jarring pain through the spot on his back where he'd been whacked by the baton.

'Conspiracy to commit acts of terrorism,' one of the three male officers said cheerfully. 'Possession of a deadly weapon, assaulting a police officer and resisting arrest. You'd better get yourself a good lawyer.'

'Not to mention a criminal hairstyle,' the woman added.

As a CHERUB agent James knew he'd never face any of those charges but the ribbing still riled him as laughter filled the steel box. More came when his body flew up and slammed the floor as they rode up over a speed bump at more than thirty miles an hour.

'Ooopsie daisy!' someone laughed.

The driver shouted through the grille between the cab and the rear compartment. 'Was that too fast?'

'I dunno,' the female officer said, as she pressed the heel of her boot down a bit harder. 'We'll find out if you drive round the block and go over it again.'

'Quite a pretty boy too,' one of the men joked. 'The gays in prison will *love* you.'

James was close to blowing up, but sensible enough to realise that it would be all the excuse they'd need to lash out with their batons and maybe throw in a few volts from their stun guns for good measure.

After a slam from another speed bump the van slowed right down, and while James couldn't see where they were going it was obvious they were pulling into some kind of parking compound.

'On your feet, toss-pot,' the biggest officer ordered, before opening the back doors and jumping out.

James rolled on to his back, but with his hands cuffed behind him it was tricky getting off the floor and jumping out. He looked around and saw that he was in the well lit parking lot at the rear of a police station.

'Getcha butt inside,' an officer barked nastily. He poked James in the back, but his body language changed when he saw a superintendent accompanied by another man walking across the tarmac towards them. James was relieved by the sight of Mission Controller, John Jones.

'Is this your boy?' the superintendent asked John.

John nodded and looked at the giant officer. 'Slice his cuffs and return his belongings.'

The female officer looked pissed. 'What's going on, boss? The little shit was in the meeting with Bradford. Then he body-checked me and damned nigh threw me down a flight of stairs.'

'Ours is not to reason why, Catherine,' the superintendent said firmly. 'The green-haired boy got away. Anyone who says otherwise can expect the remainder of their police career to be brief and unpleasant. Is that *clear*?'

'Crystal, boss,' the woman sighed, shaking her head as another officer sliced the plasticuffs off James' wrists.

'Have a nice life, officers,' James chirped.

'I don't care who you are, boy,' the woman growled. 'I wouldn't recommend showing your face around these parts ever again.'

James waved his hand contemptuously. 'Why don't you go home and shove a broom handle up your–'

'Hey, hey, *hey*,' the superintendent interrupted.

'Don't make a bloody scene,' John growled, as he grabbed James by his arm and shoved him towards a Jaguar parked on the opposite side of the car park.

'My back's *killing* me,' James moaned, as he lowered himself into the front passenger seat. 'Bitch slammed me in the back with her baton.'

'Sounds fair enough,' John said sarcastically as he started the engine. 'Pushing that *nice* lady officer down the stairs.'

James shook his head. 'She might be small but she certainly paid attention the day they did baton training at the academy.'

'Oh yeah,' John smiled. 'I knew some seriously vicious WPCs when I was on the force and the titchy ones always compensate for their size by acting like hard arses.'

'What the hell happened back there anyway? Who was running that surveillance? Who made the arrests?'

John waited until he'd negotiated the tightly packed police parking lot and pulled into the street before starting his explanation.

'I haven't heard all the details yet, but it comes down to a freak coincidence. Apparently Rich lost a bank card under his Richard Kline alias. He went into the branch to order a replacement, kicked up a bit of a fuss for some reason and it turned out that one of the tellers was a Belfast boy who recognised him as Rich Davis, ex-IRA. He called Special Branch anti-terrorist unit and they put him under surveillance at the address where they sent the replacement card.'

'When did that happen?' James asked.

'Over the last two or three weeks,' John said, as they stopped at a red light. 'Pure coincidence: MI5 and the anti-terrorist squad working the same case from different ends.'

'Have they got enough evidence to nail Davis and Bradford?'

John nodded. 'They wouldn't have moved in if they hadn't. We couldn't bug the meeting because we had no idea where it was going to be. They obviously did, and as soon as they got the pair of them talking about a terrorist conspiracy they swooped.'

'Oh well,' James sighed. 'Can't win 'em all.'

'And it's still a result,' John said. 'The bad guys will be going down for a long time.'

'Yeah . . .' James huffed. 'But that would have happened whether I'd been there or not, and I just spent six weeks walking around with this stupid *bloody* hairstyle.'

*

Bethany and Andy stretched the tarpaulin out between them and wrapped it over their shoulders before starting to climb the fence. It was hard to get hold of anything with cold fingers and trainers slippery with mud, but fear drove them upwards.

'Don't seem to have seen us,' Andy said, as he looked back over his shoulder at the guards and torch beams.

'Won't take long once they see the giant orange tarp,' Bethany said.

Smaller feet gave Bethany better purchase on the fence and she reached the point below the razor wire first.

'OK, ready to drop,' Andy said.

This was the trickiest part of Andy's escape plan: holding on to the fence with one hand, while unfurling the tarp and then somehow throwing it over the strands and coils of wire.

'Ready?' Andy said. 'Go.'

They both swung the thick tarp, trying to get it to flick upwards and cover the barbs, but the wind was blowing the wrong way and the tarp tangled hopelessly before a gust blew it on to Bethany. She couldn't hold the tarp's weight with her free hand and it knocked her feet out of the rungs, leaving her suspended by two fingers.

Andy tried moving across to grab her, but Bethany was in agony and let go, falling from four metres and grateful for the muddy ground. Andy jumped down and helped pull the crumpled tarpaulin off her head.

'It's never gonna work,' Bethany said, as Andy hauled her up. 'We'll never get the tarp over the wires and hold on at the same time.'

'We could tie the corners to the fence, then go under the tarp and push it up as we climb.'

'Might work,' Bethany nodded. 'There's holes in the corners. Have you got string?'

'I hoped you might have some,' Andy said uneasily.

'We're screwed,' Bethany said, stamping furiously. 'My clothes are wrecked, I'm completely knackered and my knickers are *soaked* in freezing cold water.'

'Unless we try and find one of the original holes in the wire,' Andy suggested. 'I know roughly where they are.'

'In pitch darkness?' Bethany huffed. 'And the cops will find out where they are as soon as they untie the guards.'

'You're probably right,' Andy sighed. 'But we'll never get that tarp over the wire, so why not give it a go?'

As Andy turned around he saw two small figures racing across the grass, with half a dozen RAF police and a pair of dogs on leads chasing after them.

'Over here,' Andy shouted, waving.

'What are you doing?' Bethany gasped, batting Andy's arms down and trying to cover his mouth. But Kevin and Ronan had already turned towards them.

'Straighten out the tarp,' Andy ordered. 'Let's get back up there.'

'Why?' Bethany shouted. 'And who put you in charge?'

'Trust me,' Andy said firmly.

He seemed confident, so despite complaining Bethany helped him flatten the tarp, draped it over her shoulder and they started climbing again. As they neared the razor wire, Ronan and Kevin arrived, with cops and dogs a couple of hundred metres behind and gaining.

'You two climb up under this tarp, then push it over the wires,' Andy ordered.

Ronan didn't get it straight away, but Kevin had done a training exercise where his team used a similar technique to get through coils of barbed wire by trampling it down under tent fabric and planks of wood.

The small footholds meant the eleven-year-olds had an easier time climbing up the four metres of wire than their older team-mates. As Bethany and Andy stretched the hanging tarp between them, Kevin led the way climbing the fence beneath it.

When he got near the top he pushed the tarp outwards, so that the top bulged out around his head, then gripped the fence with one hand while using the other to start feeding it over the razor wire. Ronan had now worked out what they were trying to do and joined in, while with the tarp's weight now shared by four instead of two, Andy and Bethany could reach up and fling the corners.

'Are we there?' Kevin asked, as the barking dogs closed to within ten metres of the fence.

Andy nodded as he saw the thick tarp spread over the

wires, but it was too dark to see whether any of the barbs were poking through, or know for sure that the razor wire wouldn't slice through both the tarp and his fingers when he grabbed hold of it.

'Feels OK,' Andy said, relieved, as he swung his leg over and bounced gently on the coils of barbed wire.

'Get down from there!' an RAF officer shouted. Two dogs snarled and jumped at the fence, but didn't get within a metre of the quartet's legs.

Andy swung his legs over on to the far side of the fence before jumping clear and rolling as he landed on the soft ground.

Kevin and Bethany followed within seconds.

'AARGHHH,' Bethany screamed. 'I landed in a cow pat. It's all over me!'

There was nothing to stop the RAF officers from scaling over the tarp behind them, so before jumping down, Ronan squirted it with the pepper spray he'd taken from a guard and lit it with a lighter.

As Ronan landed, the pepper spray ignited and the plastic covering over the tarp began to smoulder. But one RAF officer seemed determined to hoist himself over the flaming sheet and the razor wire, so Andy grabbed the last bearing out of his coat pocket and shot him in the chest from less than five metres.

'Does anybody have wire cutters?' a policeman shouted.

'Flank them,' a military policeman yelled. 'Get men out the front gate into the fields to hunt them down.'

Andy was impressed at Ronan's quick thinking. 'Where'd you get the lighter from?'

'Had it in my jeans,' Ronan said, ankles slipping as he ran through heavy mud. 'I've always enjoyed setting light to stuff.'

'Nice one,' Andy said, grabbing his phone to call his mission controller as the four cherubs set off across the dark field. 'Dennis it's Andy, we need a fast pick-up . . . That far? I know there's cops everywhere boss, but–'

'What's the matter?' Ronan asked, as Andy snapped his phone shut angrily.

'Dennis won't drive in to pick us up. He says too many questions will be asked if he's spotted picking us up on a main road. He's set a new rendezvous point five kilometres across country.'

The four cherubs groaned. After all they'd been through, none of them fancied a five-kilometre run across muddy farmland.

They jogged at a steady pace, occasionally bumping into each other in the dark.

Kevin looked at Bethany. 'Did you really land in cow shit?' he asked.

'Yes I did,' Bethany snapped. 'I'm covered in it and if any of you so much as smirks, I swear I'll kick you *so* hard . . .'

'So the dogs got Jake,' Kevin said, trying to change the subject because he didn't want to start laughing. 'What's happened to Rat and Lauren?'

*

Rat had seen this moment in movies a hundred times. The car hits the fence, the posts holding it up shatter and it blasts on to the road with a shower of sparks dragging behind it.

'Brace yourself,' Rat shouted to Lauren, as he realised

to his horror that he hadn't buckled his seatbelt in the rush to escape.

He glanced at the speedo as the small Fiat ploughed towards the fence. But the front wheels couldn't grip in the mud and they ploughed into the fence at less than twenty miles an hour. There was a great metallic crash and a loud bang as the front airbag exploded in Rat's face. One of the concrete posts snapped and the nose of the car reared up high into the air until they were almost vertical.

Lauren thought the car was going to topple backwards on to its roof, but the other fence post finally snapped. The car tipped forwards and began sliding down a muddy embankment.

'Hit the gas,' Lauren screamed. 'Have you stalled it again?'

Rat's ears rang from the airbag explosion and he could only just hear Lauren's orders.

'Engine's dead,' he yelled back, as a haze of white powder from the airbag filled the air. 'Must be a safety cut-out when the car tips up that much.'

It was pitch dark and Rat couldn't see over the semi-inflated remains of the airbag, but he could feel the car sliding gently down an embankment. He squeezed the brakes full on, but it had no effect because the wheels were aquaplaning.

After a ten-second slide, the front of the car hit a tree, turned sideways and came to a halt in a twenty-five centimetre deep puddle. Lauren pushed her door, but it only opened far enough to embed itself in the mud and flood the car with brown water.

As they crawled over to the passenger side, which pointed

into the air, a mixture of regular cops and military police scrambled down the muddy slope and surrounded the car. Lauren heard the unmistakeable click of a rifle being loaded, and while she doubted the RAF police would shoot a couple of unarmed kids, the sound still sent a shudder down her back.

'Get out of the car, keep your hands where I can see 'em,' a man shouted as he grabbed a door and wrenched Rat from the front passenger seat. Lauren found her own way out, but in the chaos she'd forgotten her twisted ankle and collapsed into the deep puddle.

A huge RAF policeman yanked Lauren up and pushed her against the car. As she struggled to blink muddy water out of her eyes she looked up and saw a series of photographic flashes fired off from the edge of the puddle.

Lauren buried her face in her hands as the military policeman dragged her backwards out of the water.

'Get that camera out of my face,' she screamed. 'Go on, piss right off!'

14. SCOOP

'So it's all over?' Dana said.

It was Saturday morning. James sat on a swivel chair in the middle of his room. There was a bath-towel stretched underneath it to catch falling hair.

'Yep,' James nodded. 'Bradford was my target, but he's been busted and I can't go back undercover because officially I'm on the run.'

'The riot looked like a laugh,' Dana smiled, as she clipped a plastic comb to a set of hair clippers. 'Are you sure you want a number one? 'Cos once I start there's no going back.'

James nodded. 'I only re-dyed it two weeks ago. If you leave it any longer I'll still have green bits at the tips. Besides, the last time I cut it really short you said it was sexy.'

'If you say so,' Dana said half-heartedly, as she turned on the battery-powered clippers.

She started with the tallest part of the Mohican and clumps of green-tinted hair rolled down James' back and landed on the towel.

'Is everything OK with you?' James asked.

'Pardon?' Dana said, switching off the buzzing clippers.

James tilted his head up to look at Dana standing behind him. 'While I was away, you acted kind of distant . . . I mean, I sent you messages and you never answered me half the time, or called back.'

Dana turned the clippers back on. 'Keep your head still or we'll be here all day.'

'That's *exactly* the kind of thing I'm talking about,' James said bitterly.

'What *are* you on about?'

'Changing the subject.'

Dana leaned forward and kissed James' cheek. 'I've been busy,' she said. 'I had that rotten cold and the coursework for my art A-level is doing my head in.'

'But everything's OK, isn't it?' James said. 'I've seen your paintings. Even the ones you say are rubbish are a million times better than anything I could do.'

Dana tilted James' head forward and started clipping the back of his neck. As she worked, James reached backwards and pushed his hand up Dana's baggy shorts.

'Stop buggering about you randy git,' she snapped. 'If you don't keep still, your hair's gonna end up a right state.'

But James ignored Dana and yanked her shorts down to her knees.

'Get off,' she said, turning off the clippers before rapping James on the head with them.

James tutted. 'We were all over each other before I went off on the mission.'

'I'm not in the mood,' Dana said firmly. 'Keep your head *still*.'

'Come *oooooon*,' James begged, before jumping off the chair and making a grab for Dana's bum. 'I haven't seen you for three weeks. My nuts are swollen up like mangos.'

'Quit pestering me,' Dana yelled, giving James a shove and throwing the clippers at his bed. 'You can cut your own bloody hair.'

'What!' James gasped, as he chased Dana out into the corridor. 'I'm sorry. I was only messing about.'

'Learn some respect, arsehole,' Dana shouted, before heading up the stairs to her room. 'If I say I'm not in the mood, it means I'm not in the mood.'

As he headed back towards his room, James saw Kevin leaning sleepily out of his room across the hallway, dressed in the grey CHERUB T-shirt and underpants he'd slept in.

'Sorry mate,' James sighed. 'I know you had a late night. I didn't wake you up did I?'

Kevin was a recently qualified agent and he hadn't settled into life in the new building. He wanted James to be his friend and wouldn't have complained even if he had been woken up.

'Nah,' Kevin yawned. 'I need to get down to the dining-room before they stop serving breakfast, anyway.'

James saw his hair in a mirror as he stepped back into his room. In some spots he was virtually bald, while other areas still had long tufts of spiky green hair.

'What a state,' James said.

'Do you want me to help tidy up your hair?' Kevin asked. 'We used to do each other's over in the junior block, rather than queuing up for hours when the barber comes around.'

'I wouldn't mind,' James said eagerly. 'I could probably

reach around and finish it off myself, but it's a lot easier when someone else does it.'

'I'll just get dressed,' Kevin said.

James sat back on the chair as Kevin came into the room, tying the waistband of his tracksuit bottoms before picking up the clippers.

'Women,' James sighed. 'If you want my advice Kevin, keep them out of your life as long as you possibly can.'

'I'll try,' Kevin smiled, as he turned on the clippers and started working on the tufts of green hair. 'Keep your head still.'

'I don't know what's up with Dana. Before I went away we were in the zone, you know? Now it's like, *poof*. She doesn't answer my calls; she doesn't like me touching her. I mean, what the hell is with that?'

Kevin wondered if he should tell James that he'd seen Dana cheating. But Lauren had warned him not to get involved and James had a reputation for lashing out at the wrong people when he got angry.

'Sorry, mate,' James said, as the mirror on the front of his wardrobe caught the look of discomfort on Kevin's face. 'I didn't mean to embarrass you by talking about my love life.'

'Guess I'll be going through the same in a few years,' Kevin said awkwardly.

'You're better at haircutting than Dana, anyway,' James smiled, as Kevin skilfully moved the clippers over James' head.

Kevin smirked. 'I'll be expecting a decent tip then.'

After Dana's moodiness, James appreciated the company of a cheerful eleven-year-old who he knew looked up to him.

'So how was your little mission with my sister last night?' James asked. 'I hear there was some trouble.'

'It was good,' Kevin smiled. 'At least I got away OK. Lauren and Rat got busted, but Dennis King got them released after a couple of hours in a police cell. Jake came off worst of all. He ended up with twelve stitches in his butt from a dog bite.'

James burst out laughing. 'Sounds nasty. Remind me to wind him up about it when I see him.'

'Oh, I forgot the bit you'd have liked most,' Kevin added. 'Bethany jumped off a fence and rolled through some *vast* cow pat. It stank *so* bad and when we got back to the car it was all mashed into her hair. I think she wants to kill me and Ronan now 'cos we were pissing ourselves laughing.'

'Excellent,' James smiled. 'I wish I'd seen that.'

'I reckon that's about done,' Kevin said, as he gave James a final trim behind his ear before switching off the clippers.

James was pleased with the result, although his scalp looked pale and the clippers had beheaded a couple of zits on his neck, leaving angry red marks.

'Guys!' Rat shouted, bursting through the door with a ketchup moustache and a tabloid newspaper in his hands. 'I was having breakfast downstairs when someone spotted this in the paper. You've got to check it out. Lauren's gonna go ape-shit when she sees it.'

Rat threw the newspaper down on James' bed. The front page was all about Bradford being arrested and the riot in the Strand, but Rat turned five pages in to a full-colour picture of a girl covered in mud, standing in a puddle beside a wrecked Fiat.

Fortunately it's illegal to identify underage criminals so Lauren's face had been blurred, but you could still see that it was her, and they hadn't pixelated her hand flicking off the photographer.

'*Picture exclusive*,' James read exuberantly. '*KIDS IN TWO-MILLION-POUND RAMPAGE: A knife-wielding hoodie gang, high on drugs and aged as young as ten, caused over two million pounds' worth of damage at an air traffic control centre due to be opened by the Queen in less than three weeks' time . . .*'

Kevin tutted. 'Two million, my arse. We had instructions to make it look good but not wreck anything expensive. And how could they possibly know whether we were on drugs?'

'That's not the best bit,' Rat said. 'Read the caption under the photograph.'

James cracked up as soon as he read it: '*Happy Chavmas – girl hooligan greets our photographer with a two-fingered salute, shortly before being arrested by military police*.'

'Oh that's priceless,' James snorted. 'I'm having a copy of that on my wall!'

The three boys all laughed as Kevin read the rest of the article aloud and James wheeled his chair back to his desk and gathered up the towel covered in hair.

'I'd better have a shower,' James said. 'I've got clippings all down my neck.'

'Don't forget it's football down by the lake later,' Rat said. 'So don't put your best threads on.'

'I dunno if I'll be playing,' James said, as he lifted up his T-shirt to display the huge purple bruise on his back.

'That *must* hurt,' Kevin winced.

'Bloody telling me,' James said. 'I swear, the only thing

worse than an angry woman, is an angry woman who's got a big stick to whack you with.'

*

Two hours later, Lauren emerged from the girls' toilet and into a corridor streamed with tinsel and cut-out snowmen made by little kids. She'd originally been sentenced to help out in the junior block as a punishment, but she'd enjoyed it and still went over there to lend a hand occasionally.

'Happy Chavmas, Lauren,' a gap-toothed boy chanted, as four little red shirts surrounded her.

Lauren bunched her fist in the little lad's face. 'You're going the right way about losing more teeth, Kurt,' she warned, before gently squishing the end of his nose.

The quartet followed her as she hobbled down the hallway towards a classroom, her ankle heavily strapped from the night before.

'Have you seen our presents, Lauren?' one boy asked.

'We *know* she has,' another one said. 'Tell us, *pleeeeease*.'

'I don't know what you're talking about,' Lauren said firmly.

'We're not idiots,' a girl said. 'We saw all the rolls of wrapping paper going in there.'

'At least give us a clue,' another demanded.

'Aren't you all in the nativity play?' Lauren said. 'Why don't you go and practise your lines?'

'We know our lines,' they all chanted.

Lauren had reached the door of a classroom and she knocked on the glass panel, which had been covered in gold paper to stop the red shirts peeking inside.

Kevin's little sister Megan wrapped herself around Lauren's

waist. 'I *have* to know what presents I'm getting. Please, please, please!'

But Megan jumped back when a carer called Pete Bovis opened the door. 'Scram, you lot,' he said firmly. 'I told you to leave Lauren and the other helpers alone. If I see you bugging any of them again, I'll deduct one present from each of you.'

Lauren scrambled into the classroom without opening the door far enough to let the kids see what was inside.

'They're persistent,' Lauren smiled, as Pete put the bolt back on the classroom door.

The room was usually used to teach some of the littlest kids on campus. There was a mass of well used ride-on toys, an indoor sand and water play area with a tank filled with toy boats and water-wheels, and a carpeted reading corner stocked with picture books. Presently, one wall was stacked high with boxes of toys and gifts, which were wrapped and labelled at tables in the middle before being moved to the far side.

Two carers and three qualified CHERUB agents sat at the tables, working through a giant computer printout which listed the presents each red shirt would receive. Some were standard presents for everyone, while others were individually tailored based upon the age and taste of the recipient.

The four girl helpers had volunteered to get out of more onerous pre-Christmas chores, like cleaning corridors or working in the laundry, but they'd quickly come to realise that wrapping more than a thousand presents for seventy-odd red shirts was a lot less fun than it sounded.

'OK,' Lauren sighed, as she squatted on a tiny chair

designed for a four-year-old and read the next name off her list. 'Robert Cross, age eight, main presents – laptop, Manchester United kit, *Gunslinger Four* for X-box. Did anyone see the Sports World bag with all the footy kits in?'

One of the carers looked around. 'I had it a minute ago . . .'

'It's bleedin' outrageous the amount of stuff kids get these days,' Lauren sneered, putting on an over-the-top cockney accent as she grabbed a sheet of silver paper to start wrapping the football kit. 'When I was eight, all I got was an orange, an apple, and possibly a walnut – if I was *extremely* lucky.'

'Oh I'm sure,' Pete smiled, as the rest of the room laughed. 'What with your mum running the biggest shoplifting racket in North London and all . . .'

15. MUD

CHERUB campus grew out of a disused village school that now forms part of the junior block. Over time campus became a secure compound enclosing a small village and several surrounding farms. Cherubs now have access to modern sports facilities and all-weather pitches, but in the early days the only grass pitch was marked out in a neighbour's field, beside what is now the campus lake.

During wintertime the lake would flood the pitch and the studded boots of young CHERUB boys – there were no girls in those days – would churn it into a bog. As campus grew, new pitches were built on higher land and the banks of the lake were reinforced to stop the annual flood, but the tradition of playing a football match in a mud bowl on the Saturday before Christmas had remained.

To create the pitch, water was pumped from the lake to the top of a mild slope and left to run over the grass back to the lake. The campus gardeners then drove tractors over the turf and within half a day a rectangular area would become a sea of huge puddles and ankle-deep mud.

Pitch markings were impossible, but a set of ancient

wooden goal posts marked the ends of the playing area. The matches were always played after dark, so a set of portable floodlights, which frequently broke down, were put in each corner.

There were two marquees, one where players got hosed down before running to the changing rooms by the athletics track for a hot shower. The other contained a barbecue serving burgers and hot dogs and a large PA system set up to pump out loud rock music.

It was only five in the afternoon, but the sky was black and a mean wind blew across the lake. Almost everyone on campus, from the youngest red shirts to black shirts like James, had turned out. They were all well wrapped, wearing football boots or old trainers plus gloves, hats, thick tracksuits and hoodies or sweatshirts. Retired cherubs who were visiting for Christmas and dozens of staff gathered around tables, picking off bottles of beer and glasses of champagne.

James found himself in a crowd close to the edge of the pitch, where a bunch of red shirts were already running around kicking mud at each other. As he peered about, searching for mates, a hand tapped on his shoulder from behind.

'Kyle,' James said exuberantly, as he eyed his best friend. 'When'd you get back, man? Why didn't you come see me?'

'I just drove up from Cambridge,' Kyle said. 'I hoped I'd get here by two, grab a late lunch and catch up with everyone, but the traffic's shit at this time of year.'

'My man!' James grinned, as Kyle handed him a bottle of Kronenberg from the adults' table.

'Just keep it out of sight,' Kyle warned.

'So how's university?'

'Good,' Kyle nodded. 'It's really sociable and there's a really big gay scene. It's tempting just to go out and party every night, but money's pretty tight.'

'Last time you said you were looking for a job.'

Kyle nodded. 'I've started doing door security at a gay bar. It's good money, although you have to deal with your fair share of tossers.'

'Thought you'd be too small to land a job as a bouncer,' James smiled.

'Couple of big yobs in rugby shirts came into the bar one night and began mouthing off about faggots and queers. They started pushing this dude around. I ended up inviting them outside and knocked 'em cold with a metal dustbin lid.'

James laughed. 'Good to see the old combat training still coming in handy.'

'Anyhow, the next time I went in for a drink the landlord offered me a job. I get a tenner an hour in readies and all the booze I can drink!'

'Sounds good,' James smiled, before downing three gulps of his beer and burping loudly.

'Are you playing in a match?' Kyle asked.

James shook his head. 'I got my back done in by a cop last night. Doc says I might wreck it completely if I start rolling around in the mud.'

'I thought about your mission when I saw the riot on the news last night,' Kyle said. 'So how's everything else?'

'Not bad,' James shrugged. 'Dana's being weird for

some reason, but that's women for you.'

'Happy Chavmas!' Kyle said, as he saw Lauren hobbling towards them on her dodgy ankle.

Most people would have got a mouthful, but Lauren liked Kyle and hadn't seen him for ages so she gave him a hug and a quick peck on the cheek.

'How's it going?' Kyle asked, but before Lauren could answer the rock music stopped and a cringe-inducing squeal came through the PA system.

Chairwoman Zara Asker stood by the barbecue tent with a microphone in one hand and her baby daughter Tiffany held in the other.

'Can I have some quiet please,' Zara said, as the microphone squealed again and Tiffany shielded her ears with her little hands. 'The classrooms are closed until the new year, it's Saturday night and I'm proud to announce that on CHERUB campus, Christmas starts here!'

A huge cheer and applause ripped through the crowd as James looked down in time to see Zara's four-year-old son Joshua grabbing his leg. He had Meatball on a lead and Lauren crouched down and started making a fuss of the little beagle.

'Look at you all muddy,' Lauren cooed. 'You'll moan later when Zara puts you in the bath.'

'Just a few warnings before we kick off,' Zara announced. 'It's *very* cold and wet out here. I can live with a few of you getting injured, but I'm going to be very cross with anyone who gets chills or hypothermia. The matches last fifteen minutes, and when you've finished I expect *every* player to take a hot shower and change into clean, dry clothes.

'One of the privileges of being Chairwoman is that I get to look at all the requests to settle scores and pick who plays who. I'm pleased to announce that this year's first match will be Red-Shirt Boys versus Red-Shirt Girls.'

The crowd roared as more than thirty little kids piled on to the pitch. Some waded tentatively into the mud, while others ran on to the pitch at full pelt and dived forward into freezing mud slides.

James laughed at a little guy who'd clattered into his elder sister and started a slanging match, while the referee floated the ball in the giant puddle that passed for the centre circle and the crowd broke into chants of *Come on boys* and *Come on girls*.

'I'm starving,' Kyle said. 'Couldn't face motorway services. Anyone fancy getting a burger while there's no queue?'

'I'm up for it if you sneak me another beer,' James grinned.

As the game kicked off, James, Lauren, Joshua and Meatball followed Kyle towards the barbecue tent, Meatball getting excited at the smell of frying meat. James waited for burgers and hot dogs to cook while Kyle went to the drinks table to grab cans of Pepsi and bottles of beer.

By the time they'd queued and stood around the tent eating their barbecue the first match between the red shirts was over. The boys had won, but the mud-soaked girls were in uproar and claimed that a sexist male ref had given the boys an outrageous last-minute penalty.

Zara announced that the second match would be between kids who lived on the sixth floor of the main building and kids from the eighth. James shouted for the sixth floor as his neighbours piled on to the pitch, including his ex Kerry

Chang, plus friends Bruce, Shakeel, Andy, Rat and Kevin.

'Eighth floor, kick some arse!' Lauren shouted, as Bethany and loads of her other friends ran on to the other half of the pitch.

The floors in the main building were all mixed up in terms of age and sex, so newly qualified ten-year-olds were on the pitch alongside burly sixteen- and seventeen-year-olds. In a serious match this might have led to injuries, but the mud-bowl matches were played in a spirit of fun and it wasn't unusual to see kids sitting on each other or players hurling mud pies into the crowd.

With the red shirts all running off for the showers and two-thirds of the older kids forming giant teams on the pitch, the crowd was much thinner and mainly consisted of staff, kids who lived on the seventh floor and kids like James and Lauren who were carrying an injury.

James looked across at a lonely figure standing on the touchline near the other end of the pitch.

'I spy with my little eye something beginning with J.'

'Oh cool,' Lauren grinned. 'I've got to wind him up about getting bit on the arse.'

Kyle hadn't caught up on all the campus news and burst out laughing. 'What was that?'

Lauren explained Jake's encounter with the RAF guard dog as they all headed towards him, except for Joshua, who eyed his mum feeding Tiffany a Malteser and raced across to grab his share.

'How's your butt?' Lauren laughed, as she walked up behind Jake.

'You useless bloody tit,' James shouted towards the

pitch, as Shakeel missed an open goal.

Jake turned to Lauren and shook his head. 'Don't start, OK? I've had it up to here with people taking the piss and I swear, if anyone else starts I'm gonna flip out.'

'Bit tetchy are we?' Lauren grinned.

Kyle tried to sound more sympathetic. 'Is it still painful?'

'Twelve stitches in my *arse*,' Jake tutted. 'What do you think?'

James burst out laughing. 'You should get one of those rubber rings to sit on.'

'Give us a peek,' Lauren jeered, as she grabbed the back of Jake's tracksuit bottoms and yanked them down.

'Leave *off*,' Jake said furiously. 'You think it's funny? Get some massive guard dog to tear a hole in *your* arse and we'll see who's laughing.'

Lauren tutted. 'Don't cry, Jakey-poos.'

Kyle shook his head disapprovingly. 'Give the poor kid a break, Lauren.'

'It's always the same,' Lauren sighed, as she backed off. 'The ones who are first to dish out stick can't take it when it's their turn.'

Jake turned to Lauren and smiled. 'I tell you what,' he said. 'Why don't you tell your brother about his love life going down the shitter?'

Lauren's heart bolted, but she tried acting like she didn't know what Jake was talking about. 'You what?' she said contemptuously.

Jake pulled his phone out of his pocket. 'Take a look, James. Your sister made Kevin delete the original, but luckily I kept a copy.'

'Jake, you're *such* an arsehole,' Lauren steamed, as her brother zoomed in to look at the screen of Jake's phone.

The picture was small and looked bleary in the darkness, but James only took a couple of seconds to recognise the motorbike poster over his bed and the fact that Dana had Michael Hendry on top of her.

'When was this taken?' James demanded furiously.

'Yesterday,' Jake smiled. 'Ask your sister, she knows more about this than I do.'

James glowered at Lauren. '*You* knew about this?'

Lauren put out her hands defensively. 'James, you were on a mission. I was going to tell you, but I didn't want to ruin your Christmas.'

'You knew I was doing my head in trying to work out why Dana's been acting so weird,' James spluttered. 'You're my sister, Lauren. How can you let this go on under my nose?'

'Lauren's a bitch,' Jake noted, but he jolted when James turned angrily towards him.

'One more cute word out of your mouth, Jake, and I'll punch you into new year.'

Kyle was struggling to keep up with events, but he placed a reassuring hand on James' shoulder. 'Come on mate, calm down.'

'Did you know?' James said accusingly.

Kyle smiled. 'James, I haven't been on campus since July! Take a deep breath and count to ten.'

'You want me to be calm,' James shouted. 'Half of campus seems to know that Dana's getting boffed by Michael Hendry and my own sister's been lying through her teeth . . .'

'I *wasn't* lying,' Lauren said. 'I knew you'd find out and I was going to tell you, but I was hoping Dana would beat me to it and I deleted the photo because I didn't want you to find out like this.'

James was angry, but he believed Lauren had meant to protect his feelings. It was Dana he was really mad at.

'Where is she, the cheating skank?'

'I haven't seen her,' Lauren said. 'You know she doesn't like joining in. She's probably in her room reading a book.'

James turned towards the pitch and saw Michael Hendry playing on the wing for the eighth floor.

'Gimme that phone,' he shouted, as he snatched the handset from Jake.

'James, calm down,' Kyle said firmly. He grabbed James' arm, but James snatched it free.

'If anyone else tells me to calm down . . .' James growled.

Jake smirked as James charged on to the muddy pitch. Lauren was hobbling, but she was furious and grabbed Jake by the hood of his jacket.

'You stirring piece of shit,' she shouted.

'Kiss my arse,' Jake said, as he tried to wriggle free, but Lauren slapped him hard across the cheek.

Jake stumbled and fell to the ground.

'My stitches,' he groaned as he writhed in the mud, clutching his bum.

Lauren loomed over him with her hands on her hips. 'You're *such* a baby,' she sneered. 'I barely tapped you.'

16. BIG

James never intended to walk into the mud bowl and got handicapped by rapidly flooding trainers and a pain shooting up his bruised back whenever one of his legs skidded in the mud. A bunch of younger kids were chasing the ball around near the goal at the top of the slope, but Michael Hendry hung back in a gloomy area near the middle of the pitch, his tracksuit bottoms plastered in thick mud and banging his gloved hands together to keep warm.

James held out Jake's phone as he approached Michael from behind. He was furious, but his appetite for violence waned as he got close: Michael was taller, with massive arms, a massive chest, and James' combat training counted for nothing because Michael had been through exactly the same. The one thing James did have was the element of surprise.

'Yo, shit-face,' James shouted.

Michael knew he'd been rumbled as he turned to face James, but before he could act Jake's phone smashed against the side of his temple. The plastic facia cracked with the force of the blow and James followed up with two hard slugs to the stomach. The punches would have floored most men, but Michael absorbed the blows, grabbed James by the scruff of his hoodie and stomped his ankle with the metal spikes of a size-twelve rugby boot.

'You wanna mess with me?' Michael boomed.

James howled as he collapsed into the thick mud, but despite the pain in his back and ankle he grabbed Michael's ankle, swept it through the mud and raised it into the air as he sprang to his feet. Michael tried kicking free as James held his leg in the air and began painfully twisting his foot.

By this time all the players had seen what was going on. Several were running over to break up the fight and the referee was frantically blowing his whistle.

'You backstabber,' James yelled, as he wrenched Michael's foot around.

The pain made Michael's upright leg buckle and he collapsed forwards into the mud, taking James with him. Michael got on top and hit James with an explosive punch in the back of the head. Freezing water soaked through James' clothes. As he thrashed about trying to break free, Michael landed another brutal punch.

Surprise had been James' only advantage over a stronger opponent and he would have got the crap beaten out of him but for Bruce Norris wading in to save him. Bruce stunned Michael with a studded kick in the back, before wrapping his arm around Michael's massive neck and dragging him backwards.

Bruce was extremely strong for his size, but he still needed Shakeel and Rat's help to drag Michael away. James was stunned from the two head punches, but he was still conscious and Michael's girlfriend Gabrielle hauled James out of the mud, while ex-girlfriend Kerry restrained him by pulling his arm up tight behind his back.

'For Christ's sake, James,' Kerry said, as James groaned with pain. 'It's a game. You said you weren't even playing because of your back.'

James and Michael were both trying to break free when the referee arrived and rather pointlessly waved his red card at both of them.

'You think I care about this stupid match,' James growled, as he looked back over his shoulder and eyeballed Gabrielle. 'Look at Jake's phone,' he gasped. 'See what your precious boyfriend's been getting up to with Dana.'

Gabrielle's eyes lit up and the certainty in her expression made James realise that she already suspected that something untoward had been going on.

'Gab, don't!' Kerry said anxiously, as she tightened her arm lock on James.

'You said you were working on an art history project!' Gabrielle screamed, as she let go of James and stormed towards Michael. 'Is that why you spent all that time in Dana's room? You dirty, cheating son of a . . .'

Gabrielle was tall and thin and would have been no match for Michael in an open fight. But Michael was still being held by Bruce and Shakeel. The referee tried to block, but Gabrielle dodged around him and smashed the base of her palm against Michael's nose.

'I'll kill you,' Gabrielle screamed bitterly, as Michael's nose exploded with blood.

As the referee grabbed Gabrielle to prevent a second attack, her entire body wilted.

'I thought you loved me, Michael,' Gabrielle sobbed as she collapsed into the arms of the bewildered referee.

Kerry wanted to be with her best friend, but she was still restraining James. 'Behave yourself, or else,' she snarled before letting him go.

James was still hurting, but Gabrielle's desperate crying pricked his anger. He'd had a few girlfriends and there were times when he thought he'd loved Dana, but nobody expected their relationship to last for ever and most people were surprised they'd lasted as long as they had.

Michael and Gabrielle's relationship had been way more intense. He was Gabrielle's first love and they'd done everything together for so long that people rarely mentioned one without the other.

James was pissed at Dana for cheating on him. His head hurt, his back ached and his sock oozed blood where Michael's studs had ripped his skin, but he'd just witnessed Gabrielle's heart break and that put his own hurt into stark perspective.

'You OK?' Kyle said, squelching up behind James as Gabrielle sobbed helplessly in Kerry's arms.

'Head's killing me, ankle might need stitches,' James said sourly. 'Sorry.'

Kyle smiled. 'What are you sorry for?'

'This,' James shrugged. 'First time back on campus in five months and you've got all my crap to put up with.'

'I missed your crap,' Kyle said wryly. 'Your idiocy is a constant reminder of how smart and rational I am.'

James had missed Kyle's sense of humour and couldn't help laughing, even though he was in all kinds of pain.

'Put your arm round my back,' Kyle said. 'I'll get one of the golf buggies and drive you over to the medical unit.'

*

Two hours later Lauren walked along the sixth-floor corridor and knocked on James' door.

'You OK?' she asked, as she peered around the door and saw James lying on his bed in a dressing gown. He had a bandage on one ankle and a square plaster stuck on his almost bald head, which covered a nasty cut from one of Michael's rings.

The room was dark, except for a chink of light coming through the bathroom door. Lauren sat on the corner of the bed.

'Been better, been worse,' James said, as he threw down a motorbike magazine he hadn't been reading anyway and sat up so that he could see his sister.

'You said yourself you thought something was going wrong,' Lauren said soothingly. 'It hadn't been right for a while.'

'I actually feel quite mellow about breaking up,' James said. 'What pissed me off was everyone knowing about it behind my back. Including you . . .'

'I would have told you if it dragged on,' Lauren said. 'I haven't got any loyalty to cheesy bloody Dana.'

'Nice boobs though,' James sighed. 'And she was the first girl I slept with, so I guess she's one I'll always remember.'

Lauren smirked. 'Didn't you sleep with that other girl on your anti-gang mission?'

James laughed. 'OK, I'll rephrase it: Dana was the first girl I had sex with apart from two minutes of complete terror in a bathtub with a girl I never spoke to again.'

Lauren giggled. 'Only you, James . . .'

'It's Gabrielle I feel sorry for,' James said. 'She was still crying her eyes out in Kerry's room when I got back.'

'What did Zara say?'

'She came over to the medical unit, made me and Michael shake hands like a couple of five-year-olds – good news is that Gab *totally* mashed his nose. She's letting all three of us off as long as there's no more bad blood between us, but *I've* got to pay for Jake's busted phone.'

'How much?'

'A hundred and fifty,' James moaned. 'That's all my Christmas money, plus a fiver a week out of my pocket money until the end of March.'

'Bummer,' Lauren said, changing the subject in an attempt to cheer him up. 'The last mud-bowl match was *so* funny: training instructors versus black shirts. Bruce scored a hat-trick, so Mr Pike and Miss Smoke grabbed hold of him and threw him in the lake at the end.'

'Sounds fun.'

'And the chefs served hot punch and mince pies in the tent so everyone could warm up afterwards. It had a bit of rum in it, so we were only allowed one each. You know what I was thinking?'

'What?' James asked warily.

'There's this big training exercise in America coming up. Seeing as your mission ended early, you might be able to sign up.'

'Why would I volunteer for extra training?'

Lauren shook her head. 'It's in this place called Fort Reagan in America. It's not exercise and stuff. It's gonna be this massive war game up against American troops doing urban warfare training. We pretend to be insurgents, Mac's gonna be the supreme leader of the bad guys and we get a mini-holiday in Las Vegas before it starts.'

'Sounds pretty good, I guess,' James said. 'So you're sure there's no rock-breaking or hiking with heavy packs?'

Lauren shook her head firmly. 'It's not CHERUB training. It's run by the US Army and British Special Forces. They want CHERUB in the mix to give their forces a different challenge.'

'I could look into it, I guess,' James nodded.

'You could do with a break after the last few months,' Lauren smiled. 'And there's a lot of kids clamouring for places, but with your record on missions I'm sure you'd make the cut.'

'I heard Bruce talking about going,' James said. 'Maybe I'll speak to Mac next time he's on campus.'

'Cool,' Lauren said, as there was another knock at the door.

'So, you showed your face,' James said acidly, as Dana appeared in the doorway holding a large cardboard box.

Dana flipped James' light on without asking and put the box down on the little sofa by the door.

'For what it's worth, James, I wanted to be straight with you,' Dana said. 'But Michael wanted to let Gabrielle down gradually. Then she started getting suspicious and she backed him into a corner and made him deny everything.'

Lauren snorted. 'Sounds more like Michael wanted to have his oats and eat them.'

Dana snorted back. 'In case you haven't noticed, Lauren, your brother's not exactly up for any fidelity awards.'

'I only cheated on you once and I confessed straight away,'

James said, slightly bitter as he hopped off the bed and limped around to inspect the contents of the box. It was a mix of his CDs, bits of clothing, school books and other junk that had gravitated to Dana's room over their thirteen-month relationship.

Dana's voice firmed up. 'Let's not pretend we had something we didn't. I'm a weirdo who you only went out with because I've got big tits. You're a good looking guy who knows it and can't say no to anything in a skirt.'

James was bitter about what had happened and part of him wanted to end things with a screaming row where they threw stuff at each other; but his ankle and back hurt, plus he didn't have the energy.

'Take whatever,' he said, pointing casually towards the bathroom. 'Most of your stuff's in there.'

Lauren could see James was stressed and while Dana picked up her junk in the bathroom – plus a few bits of clothing and the copy of *Lord of the Rings* James had never got around to finishing – she stood beside James with a hand resting loyally on his towelling-covered shoulder.

'Have a nice life,' James said half sarcastically, as Dana lifted her hand and headed out, holding the box which was now filled with her own stuff.

'You too,' Dana said, closing the door behind her.

'It's just a shame it all had to happen right before Christmas,' Lauren said.

'My arse it is,' James smiled. 'First thing tomorrow I'm off to the shops and I'm getting a thirty-six ninety-nine refund on her Christmas present.'

17. PRESENTS

It was Christmas day, 6.58 in the morning and Meryl Spencer stood outside the assembly hall in the main building being crushed to death by hysterical red shirts.

'Everybody stand back,' Meryl roared. 'If there's *any* more pushing and shoving you can all go back to bed until eight o'clock.'

Several kids groaned, but you could see that all the red shirts knew it was an idle threat. Most of them had got up in a hurry and had made the frosty journey from their rooms in the junior block dressed in odd combinations of carpet slippers and pyjamas, covered with outdoor jackets and the occasional woolly hat.

Despite not taking the time to get dressed, most red shirts had been up for an hour or more and one pair were even caught trying to break through the fire doors outside the assembly hall at 4 a.m.

'They make me feel old,' Kyle smiled. 'Ten years ago I would have been down there waiting for my prezzies too. Every minute seemed to last an hour.'

James stood next to him, along with a bunch of other

teens who probably could have settled for a couple of hours' lie-in and opening their presents over a late breakfast; but they'd all got out of bed to see the little kids going crazy. Kids of ten and eleven like Kevin Sumner and Jake Parker were in between: young enough to be excited, but trying to act cool and not let it show.

'BAAAACK!' Meryl screamed, as one of the junior-block carers grabbed a near hysterical boy out of the crowd.

'Don't you dare hit her,' the carer said, as she grabbed the boy's wrist. 'Now you can hold my hand and I'll let you in last.'

A cheer erupted as Chairwoman Zara Asker and a bunch of other staff arrived. A plastic clock on the wall above Meryl's head ticked over to 6.59 and everyone started counting the seconds.

'Fifty-nine, fifty-eight, fifty-seven . . .'

'AAAAARGGGGHHH!' a red-shirt girl called Coral shouted. 'I can't stand it. I'm so excited!'

Kevin's seven-year-old sister Megan grabbed his arm and used him as a battering ram to get to the front of the crowd.

'For god's sake, Megs,' Kevin moaned, feeling horribly self-conscious as he was surrounded by smaller kids. 'Does a few seconds really make that much difference?'

'Sixteen, fifteen, fourteen . . .'

On ten, Meryl turned around and placed a key in the large double doorway. She turned it on three and pushed the doors open on the stroke of zero. Meryl had won an Olympic sprint medal, but couldn't ever recall moving as fast as the seventy red shirts storming the assembly hall.

The red shirts' gift piles were arranged in rows in the

centre of the wooden floor and organised alphabetically by surname. While six- to nine-year-olds ploughed into their gifts, ignoring stockings and little parcels and going for the biggest presents at the bottom of the pile, some of the youngest red shirts who hadn't quite mastered the alphabet were helped out by a couple of bleary-eyed carers who'd been up since four, setting out all the piles of presents.

By the time James and co. got into the hall the centre of the room looked like a piranha feeding frenzy, with red shirts taking the place of the fish and chunks of flesh replaced by flying tufts of wrapping paper.

Amidst the rustling and the odd jingle from an electronic toy came shouts of *Oh wow I got the light sabre/racing car/ Barbie* or whatever and the distressed howls of one small lad who'd been accidentally kicked in the face by the eight-year-old girl attacking the pile of gifts next to him.

James and the other qualified agents had stacks arranged on tables running along the edge of the room. Their presents were smaller than the little kids' toys, but every kid on campus got exactly the same amount spent on them. The only differences were in the number of presents received from friends.

As an A for Adams, James had the second pile of gifts, with Lauren's haul next to him.

'Looks like we've all got new laptops for our rooms,' Lauren smiled, as James opened a tall cylindrical present from Meryl that looked uncannily like a bottle of booze, but turned out to be a fancy chrome toilet brush and packet of disinfectant cubes.

'Haaaah!' Lauren laughed. 'It looks like she saw the state of your old toilet bowl!'

'That wasn't filth,' James grinned. 'That was my skid-mark hall of fame.'

Most red shirts had now opened their main presents and had started popping the indoor fireworks in their stockings while cramming down squares of Dairy Milk. James pulled a stripy package of Paul Smith aftershave off the top of his stocking before burrowing down and pulling out an indoor firework shaped like a champagne bottle.

Lauren was opening a pair of animal-friendly New Balance running shoes as James popped it next to her ear.

'Git,' Lauren yelled, digging James in the ribs as yellow streamers floated down on to her head. 'You damn nigh blew up my eardrum.'

'Happy Christmas,' James said, as he pulled his sister into a hug. 'Who needs a girlfriend when I've got a sister like you?'

'If you say so,' Lauren giggled. 'But if you start getting frisky there's gonna be trouble.'

'James, my man!' Bruce shouted, as he punched the air wearing a huge chrome knuckleduster with an obscenely vicious array of spikes, barbs and blades. 'Best present ever, mate. You could kill people in so many different ways with this!'

'I thought of you as soon as I saw the dodgy eBay auction,' James smiled, as he pulled more little gifts out of his felt stocking, including fancy silk boxers and a bag of gourmet jellybeans.

Unlike the little kids who were in it for the goodies, present opening was more of a social occasion for older kids like James. He was content to savour his presents and wandered over to see how Kerry was going.

'Happy Christmas,' James said.

'You too,' Kerry replied, before giving him a hug.

She hadn't showered because it was early. The back of her neck smelled like fresh Kerry sweat and the tang made him insanely jealous of Bruce.

'Poor Kyle,' Kerry said, as he wandered by. 'All grown up and no official presents!'

James had started a trend by hugging Lauren and Kerry and everyone else was soon doing it. He even hugged people like Bethany who he didn't like.

James still hadn't opened all of his loot, but he spotted Mac helping some of the younger red shirts load their haul of presents into giant bin liners so that they could carry them back to their rooms and play.

'Mac,' James smiled. 'I've been looking all over for you the last couple of days.'

'Really,' Mac smiled back, crouching down and scooping pieces from a six-year-old's K'nex set back into their box. 'Fahim and I have been staying with my son down in London. I came back to campus to catch up with some paperwork last night and I thought I'd stay overnight and see the chaos.'

'How's Fahim doing?' James asked.

'Good,' Mac nodded. 'He's the same age as my youngest grandkids and they really seem to hit it off.'

'And you?'

'Been married a *loooooong* time,' he said sadly. 'It's never going to be the same without her, but it's harder on my son. He lost a mother, a wife and two children.'

Mac's eyes were glazing over, but the little red-shirt

boy stared impatiently with hands on hips. 'My K'nex!' he demanded.

'Sorry, mate!' Mac smiled, as he began scooping up the last of the pieces. 'Are you sure you'll be able to carry that whole bag back to your room in one go?'

'For sure,' the boy nodded. 'I'll put it on one of the electric buggies.'

'So,' James said, as the red shirt dragged his presents towards the back of the hall. 'I wanted to ask if there were any spots left on this training exercise in America.'

'Oh that,' Mac said. 'It does look like fun, but why are you asking me?'

'Lauren said you were in charge.'

'I dealt with some of the sign-ups,' Mac nodded. 'But only because I know most of the agents better than Mr Kazakov. He was the one who got the invitation to do red teaming.'

'Red what?' James asked.

Mac tutted. 'Lauren's *supposed* to be going on this exercise but she either hasn't read her briefing yet, or hasn't bothered telling you. The Americans run war games at various centres around the world. Fort Reagan is the newest. It's specifically designed to train soldiers in dealing with modern, open-ended urban combat situations like the wars in Iraq or Somalia.

'Kazakov has donkey's years' experience fighting with the Russians in Afghanistan, then with training NATO special forces and advising on tactical operations in the Balkans and Baghdad. The Yanks invited him to lead the team in one of their most sophisticated war games ever and they still use cold war language. So the bad guys are always known as the reds, and running the red team is called . . .'

'Red teaming,' James nodded. 'I get it. So I need to speak to Kazakov?'

'Yes,' Mac said. 'I think you're in luck, because he was looking for more experienced agents like you, but Zara was reluctant to release too many in case they were needed for missions.'

James looked around the room. 'I haven't seen Kazakov this morning.'

Mac burst out laughing. 'The man has a heart of granite! Could you see our Mr Kazakov getting up early to go all gooey-eyed over the red shirts opening their presents?'

'I suppose not,' James smiled.

'He got back when basic training ended last week,' Mac said. 'If you're interested in the exercise, I'd suggest you pay him a visit upstairs in the staff quarters ASAP.'

18. KAZAKOV

James had been at CHERUB for over four years, but it was only the second time he'd ventured into the staff quarters on the fifth floor of the main building. The corridor needed a lick of paint and the carpet was tired, but the mostly young and single staff who lived here had got competitive with their Christmas decorations. The space outside each room was festooned with tinsel, flashing lights, ceiling decorations and tacky plastic snowmen.

The exception was room eighteen at the far end of the hallway, where the walls were bare and music from *Swan Lake* boomed through the closed doorway.

'Mr Kazakov,' James shouted, as he banged on the door. 'Are you in there?'

James realised Mr Kazakov had to be in his room, unless he was in the habit of going out while leaving his CDs playing at full blast. He tried the door handle and peered into an airy space, with white walls, balcony doors and a trendy wooden floor.

'Mr Kazakov,' James shouted again, as he stepped into a lobby area. 'Sir?'

The staff quarters were bigger than the kids' rooms on the floors above, with a separate bedroom and living space complete with its own compact kitchen.

James leaned into Kazakov's main room and saw him sprawled out over a recliner chair. A pair of expensive floor-standing loudspeakers blasted out Tchaikovsky's most famous ballet, while Kazakov conducted the non-existent orchestra with a Berol marker pen.

'Hello,' James shouted, edging towards Kazakov before gently tapping him on the shoulder.

Kazakov looked around, startled, before pulling up his legs, doing a spectacular head over heels roll and somehow grabbing James around the neck. Before James could react, Kazakov swept his legs away and pinned him to the floor with the tip of a Soviet army dagger poised between his eyeballs. Its handle was gnarled and the blade had worn away after two decades of regular sharpening.

'Bloody hell,' James gasped. 'Let me go!'

'I've killed three Afghans and stabbed a big-breasted Serbian mugger with this knife,' Kazakov growled, as *Swan Lake* reached a booming climax. 'I don't like people sneaking up on me.'

'I didn't mean to startle you,' James shouted nervously. 'I knocked, I shouted, but your music's so bloody loud.'

Kazakov rolled off James and tucked the knife back into a leather sheath on his belt as he stood up. The burly Ukrainian straightened his combat trousers and vest before grabbing the remote and turning off his music.

'Merry Christmas, Mr Adams,' Kazakov laughed. 'You should train more for speed. You have the reflexes of an old lady.'

James grunted as he used the kitchen worktop to lever himself up. Kazakov was at least the tenth CHERUB instructor to comment on his slow reflexes, but even a special programme of speed training devised by Miss Takada hadn't done much to help.

'My brother was slow,' Kazakov said, as he pointed towards a shelf of photographs. 'It got him killed.'

James looked at Kazakov in black and white. He wore Russian Army uniform and stood beside an identically dressed and similar-looking soldier. Neither could be more than twenty years old.

'Helicopter got hit by the Taliban as we were taking off,' Kazakov explained. 'I bailed; my brother left it another half second and got burned up by the exploding fuel.'

'I'm sorry,' James said awkwardly as his eyes were drawn to the next picture. It had been retouched in bright colours, as was the fashion in the old Soviet Union, and showed a slightly older Kazakov in a dress uniform with a line of medals, a stick-thin wife in a tutu and ballet shoes and a boy aged three or four in a slightly odd-looking sailor suit.

'Was that your wife?' James gasped. 'She's absolutely *stunning*.'

Kazakov furrowed his brow, before reaching up and slamming the frame face down so that James couldn't see it.

'Marriage is a difficult thing for a soldier,' Kazakov said bitterly. 'She remarried, my parents are dead, my brother is dead. My son is twenty-four and alive as far as I know. But I wouldn't know where he is, or even what he looks like.'

Kazakov simmered silently as James scrambled for something appropriate to say.

'You're a good man, James,' Kazakov said. 'You can come to America if you like.'

James smiled. 'What makes you think that's what I was gonna ask?'

'A young man is much like a cat,' Kazakov smiled ruefully. 'He wants food, sex and fun. The food in the canteen downstairs is better than I have here, I *very* much hope you didn't come to my room looking for sex, and the only fun I have to offer is a place on my red team. So am I right?'

'Of course you're right,' James laughed.

'With the blond hair and blue eyes you really do remind me of my brother,' Kazakov said fondly. 'Do you want to see where we're going?'

James actually wanted to get back to his friends, but he was stung by the accusation of selfishness and knew it would do no harm to keep on the training instructor's good side.

'Here you see the compound,' Kazakov said, leading James towards a kitchen worktop covered with scribbles, Post-its and random scraps of paper. The biggest was a collage of satellite photos which comprised a dozen inkjet prints stuck together with Sellotape.

James was astonished by what he saw. He'd been impressed by the SAS training compound a few kilometres from campus, but it would have been the size of a postcard on Kazakov's metre-long map of Fort Reagan.

'A quarter million acres of Nevada desert,' Kazakov explained grandly.

James studied the outlines of dozens of apartment blocks, more than a thousand houses, shopping areas and town squares, and the whole shebang fringed with golden desert.

Some areas were set out in broad avenues like an American suburb, while others had tight pedestrian alleyways and Middle-Eastern style homes built around courtyards, or lines of shacks to represent the accommodation in a third-world shanty town.

In the far corner of Fort Reagan was a military barracks with dozens of tents and permanent buildings, a full-sized air strip and a vast car park filled with the green outlines of everything from Hummers up to Abrams battle tanks.

James saw construction equipment and lots of newly planted trees. 'It all looks brand new,' he noted.

Kazakov nodded. 'Opened last year. It cost six point three billion dollars to build. It's the second biggest military training facility in the world, designed to give American soldiers a taste of what they can expect in urban warfare.

'Each exercise uses up to two thousand troops and ten thousand civilians – mostly college students and the unemployed, bussed in and paid eighty bucks a day. An exercise lasts between ten days and three weeks and costs upwards of a hundred million dollars to stage.'

'And we'll be playing the bad guys?'

'Exactly,' Kazakov smiled. 'They've already run a few exercises using teams of American officers and Special Forces to play out the role of insurgents. But what they really need is people from outside of the American military who can challenge their standard battle tactics during an exercise. The British are sending some troops to train at Fort Reagan with the Americans for the first time and when the question of a red-team commander came up, they threw my name into the ring.'

'Is that a golf course?' James gasped, as he tapped the greenest section of the satellite map.

'Certainly is,' Kazakov grinned. 'You won't find many of those in downtown Baghdad or Mogadishu, but those generals need to get eighteen holes in once in a while.'

James sensed the cynicism in Kazakov's voice and laughed. 'You're not big on the Americans, are you?'

'Ignorant scum!' Kazakov spluttered. 'They trained the Taliban that killed my brother and supplied the missile that shot our chopper down. Me and the co-pilot got out. Sixteen others, including my whole unit, got fried.'

James was confused. 'I thought the Taliban were the dudes with the beards the Americans are fighting against?'

'In 2007, they are,' Kazakov nodded. 'But in the eighties the CIA trained the Taliban and supplied them with weapons to fight against the Soviet Union. Same with Saddam Hussein: America supplied all the weapons for when he invaded Iran. American technology was also used to produce Saddam's chemical weapons which he used to gas the Kurds.'

James smiled uneasily. 'Politicians are a lot like five-year-olds. You know: one day they're best friends and five minutes later they're rolling around in the sandpit biting chunks out of each other.'

'Good analogy,' Kazakov said. 'I've got my strategy: ten CHERUB agents, thirty Special Forces officers and a hundred sympathisers amongst the civilian population. I'm planning to have those American generals on their knees, begging to surrender, within forty-eight hours.'

James was surprised at Kazakov's vehemence. 'It's just a

training exercise, though,' he pointed out. 'And the Americans *are* our allies.'

'Screw that,' Kazakov said, as he pounded on his kitchen worktop. 'I'll teach those pompous Yanks with their war games and their military academies a thing or two about climbing down in the gutter and fighting a proper street battle.'

James was slightly perturbed by Kazakov's attitude. It didn't sound much like the holiday in Vegas followed by an enjoyable training exercise that Lauren had sold him on.

'So when do we fly out?' James asked.

'New Year's Day,' Kazakov said. 'I'll send all of you an itinerary later in the day.'

'Well,' James said, glancing at his watch as he backed up to the door. 'I'm meeting up with the gang down in the dining-hall for some breakfast. You have a good Christmas; I expect I'll see you downstairs for Christmas lunch.'

'Perhaps,' Kazakov said darkly. 'But Christmas isn't really my thing, and there's still much to plan.'

19. ROYAL

James sat in the front row of a twenty-six seater coach and yawned as they pulled through the gates of the military airbase ten kilometres from campus. He'd been up until half-past two seeing in the new year and felt half dead because he'd drunk a couple of beers and had to get up early to wash and dry a bundle of dirty laundry so that he had enough clothes for a two-week trip.

The hydraulic coach door hissed open and an RAF security officer climbed aboard. 'Travel documents please.'

Staff members Mac, Meryl and Kazakov along with agents James, Lauren, Rat, Kevin, Jake, Bruce, Andy, Kerry and Gabrielle all held out their passports. Bethany went into a panic until she found hers in an obscure pocket at the side of her backpack.

'I've got export licences for weapons, explosives and drugs too,' Mac explained, as he held out a stack of paperwork.

'Haven't seen you come through here in a while,' the officer said, as he inspected each sheet before stamping them clumsily, with only a springy foam headrest to rest them on.

'You neither,' Mac smiled. 'I'm semi-retired now.'

'Ready to roll,' the guard said, handing the papers back to Mac before stepping up and giving Instructor Pike – who wasn't travelling on the exercise but had volunteered to drive the coach – instructions on which taxiways to use to reach their plane.

Large groups of CHERUB agents often used RAF planes, which offered an experience way more varied than the predictable rows of seats on a commercial jet. Your ride could turn out to be anything from a tiny unpressurised military transport plane to one of the clapped-out Tristar airliners used to ferry troops to bases in the Middle East.

Service was usually basic, with rock hard seats, boil in the bag army rations and no entertainment. But James was delighted to step out into crisp early afternoon sun and see that their ride bore the distinctive navy and white livery of the Royal Flight, a branch of the RAF which specialised in ferrying around royalty, heads of state and other important guests.

The VIP service extended to white-gloved RAF stewards, who lined up to say good morning as everyone stepped off the coach. RAF crew hurriedly transferred bags and Kazakov's haul of special equipment from coach to plane as a Typhoon fighter blasted off from the main runway half a kilometre away.

'Sweet as!' James gasped, as he reached the top of the steps and peered inside the plane.

It was a luxury variant of an Airbus used by regular airlines, but instead of a hundred and fifty cramped seats there were two-dozen giant leather chairs which reclined into flat beds.

The centre of the plane had a lounge area with red leather

chairs and Union Jack carpet that was either cheeky or revolting depending upon your taste. The rear of the plane had a private suite, complete with a mini office, toilet and shower, and a full-width double bed. Jake charged in and bagsied the bed, but was promptly hauled out by the chief steward, who told him sniffily that it was off limits to anyone who didn't answer to Your Royal Highness or Mr President.

'Plane looks brand new,' James noted, as his leather armchair creaked. He was immediately handed a platter of freshly sliced fruit, a hot Union Jack towel and a newspaper that looked like it had been ironed.

'It *is* new,' a stewardess nodded. 'The aircraft isn't officially commissioned until the Prince of Wales goes on a tour Down Under later in the month, but we're doing a few shakedown flights to make sure everything's working properly.'

'So we're getting the full royal treatment?' James smiled, as he pressed a button to electrically recline his seat.

'Upright until after takeoff,' the stewardess warned. 'Do take a look at the menu. We'll be serving a light lunch as soon as we're in level flight.'

Jake tugged at the head steward's lapel. 'I demand Beluga caviar and the finest wines available to man!' he shouted, before clapping his hands and shouting, 'Chop chop.'

The stewards didn't look impressed, but James thought it was pretty funny. He looked across the aisle to where Meryl Spencer was sitting and was surprised to see that the plane was already taxiing towards the runway.

'Beats three hours in the Heathrow departure lounge,' Meryl said.

*

The flight to Las Vegas would take nine and a half hours. Three hours in, James and the other agents had gravitated to the communal area in the centre of the plane. Meryl was expertly dealing cards and teaching everyone to play blackjack.

'How come you're so good at this?' Lauren asked, as Meryl flicked cards across a polished conference table.

'Celebrity casino host, Las Vegas, 1998 to er . . . about three months later in 1998.'

'What's a casino host when he's out shopping?' Rat asked.

'All the big casinos compete to lure wealthy players,' Meryl explained. 'After I retired from athletics I got offered half a million dollars to spend six months working at one of the big Vegas casinos. You do a bit of wining and dining with the big gamblers, occasionally deal a few hands at the tables, compere casino events, plus photo opportunities with Mr and Mrs Nobody from Arkansas. But most of all, you're expected to spend a lot of hours walking the casino floors in fishnets and a stupid little dress that was never meant for a fourteen-stone six-foot-two-inch Kenyan sprinter.'

'Half a million for six months,' James whistled. 'I'd wear fishnets for that.'

'I thought you wore them anyway,' Rat grinned.

'Couldn't hack the job,' Meryl explained. 'Dumbest decision I ever made. Luckily I was so hopeless they paid off my contract just before I quit.'

The kids all laughed as Meryl started a new hand, dealing each player two cards.

'Hit me,' Jake said.

Lauren groaned. 'Jake, the dealer's showing a six, you have seventeen. You'll go over twenty-one and bust out.'

'Hit,' Jake repeated firmly.

Meryl dealt Jake a four, giving him twenty-one and making it impossible for the dealer to beat him.

'Blackjack,' Jake grinned, before poking his tongue out at Lauren. 'Told you.'

'But it was still the wrong decision,' Rat explained. 'The probability was that you'd get dealt a card higher than a four and then you'd bust.'

'You're saying that because Lauren's your girlfriend,' Jake sneered.

'I'm saying it because it's based upon probability,' Rat said patiently. 'You might get lucky once in a while but over the longer term the dealer will kick your butt and you'll lose all your money.'

'If you're so smart, how come I've got more pennies than you?' Jake shouted.

Andy laughed. 'Because you're a jammy little git.'

Mac was trying to rest in one of the armchairs closest to the communal area and he sat up sharply. 'Hey,' he yelled. 'Andy, watch your language. The rest of you, do us a favour and keep the noise down.'

'Sorry Mac,' Meryl said.

She dealt everyone the cards until they busted or stuck, then revealed her own second card, and drew an extra one.

'Dealer stands on nineteen,' Meryl smiled, as she scooped up pennies from everyone except Jake and Bethany before explaining more about the game as she dealt the next round of cards.

'The interesting thing about blackjack is that the casino's edge is very small. If you know how to learn the basic strategy you have a much better chance of winning than in almost any other casino game. Pro players use a technique called card counting, which actually skews the odds in favour of the player.'

'Teach us that then,' Andy said eagerly.

Mac had given up on trying to rest and sat up. 'You can practise all you like, but you can't gamble in Vegas until you're twenty-one,' he noted.

'Even if you could, you can't just walk into a casino off the street and start card counting,' Meryl smiled. 'The principle is quite simple, but you need a good head for maths to master it. Each card two through five that the dealer dishes out scores one; ten through ace scores minus one. The higher the count gets, the more the odds of winning swing away from the casino dealer and into the gambler's favour.'

'That doesn't sound too hard,' Andy said. '*You're* supposed to be a maths whiz, James.'

James was intrigued. 'So all I have to do is try keeping count of the cards dealt out? And there are only fifty-two cards in a deck.'

Meryl smiled. 'That'd be nice, James, but to make counting difficult the casinos use up to eight decks on each table and a pro blackjack dealer moves a lot faster than I do. If anyone starts winning heavily, they'll shuffle the cards or replace the decks, meaning you'll have to start your count again from scratch.

'Also, if the casino bosses think you're counting they'll strip-search you, photograph you and dump your arse on the sidewalk. Then they'll circulate your photo to every other casino in town and you won't get near a table unless you put on a disguise or something.'

'So you've got to count all the cards in your head and not show any sign that you're doing it,' Lauren smiled. 'Can your big brain handle that, James?'

'You never know until you've tried,' James answered. 'I'd have to learn more about exactly how it all works though. Mac, is the Internet working on your laptop?'

'For a small fee,' Mac grinned.

'I'll let you swap seats,' James teased. 'I'm up front of the plane away from all this racket and you get to look up that posh stewardess' uniform when she bends over in the galley.'

Mac laughed, but Kerry flicked James' ear and called him a sexist pig.

'Sounds like a deal,' Mac said, as he climbed out of his seat. 'Just promise not to try accessing my secure e-mails. MI5's technical department set it up so that it destroys the entire hard drive if you enter the wrong password three times.'

The kids all laughed.

'It's not funny,' Mac said, half-jokingly. 'I've already wiped the damned thing twice. You have to send the whole caboodle back to MI5 in London to have the software reinstalled, and the second time I did it some twenty-something boffin had the cheek to write a report to the Intelligence Minister suggesting that I might be a security risk because of my age.'

'Well, you are getting on a bit,' Jake pointed out tactlessly.

'Maybe I am, Jake,' Mac said, smiling and wagging his finger, 'but I still have high enough security clearance to hack the report of your next fitness exam, so watch your cheek unless you fancy one of Mr Kazakov's four-week intensive fitness programmes.'

'Oh *please*, Mac,' Lauren begged. 'Make Jake suffer and you'll be my bestest friend for ever!'

'Get stuffed,' Jake said. 'And sorry Mac, I didn't mean to be rude.'

Everyone laughed at Jake's nervous apology.

'He's crapping it now,' Rat said.

James looked at Meryl. 'OK, dealer,' he said. 'I'm cashing out my pennies to go and learn how to cheat Vegas.'

'Keep playing,' Jake moaned. 'What's the point quitting? It's not like any of us can even play for money in a real casino.'

'This game's getting old,' James shrugged. 'And I'm curious about the maths behind this card-counting thing. For all I know I might have a lucrative future as a casino shark.'

'You like your maths, don't you James?' Lauren smirked, before putting her hand over her mouth. 'Cough, splutter, *major* geek, cough!'

Mac headed down the aisle as James settled on to his warm leather armchair and opened up a tiny Dell laptop.

'OK,' Meryl said, as she prepared to deal out another round of cards. 'Gamblers place your bets. Maximum five pennies per hand.'

20. STRIP

The time shift meant they reached Vegas at two in the afternoon. Landing in a large plane with a royal crest and the Union Jack flag on the side got the bevy of limo drivers and casino hosts who hang around McCarren Airport's private jet terminal seriously excited.

Meryl put her arm around Mac's waist as they stepped through US immigration and into the main terminal.

'Everyone act like you're stinking rich,' Meryl smiled. 'You'll be amazed where the slightest sniff of money can get you in this town.'

Meryl stopped walking and deliberately looked a little baffled. Within half a second she was approached by a beefy man with a dark tan who looked like he was dressed for golf.

'Happy New Year and welcome to Las Vegas,' he beamed, with a chemically bleached smile.

'We haven't booked accommodation,' Meryl explained, 'but I'm told Caesar's Palace is nice.'

'Caesar's has a great tradition, but I'm Julio Sweet, VIP host at the Reef Casino Resort. I can offer you a limousine to take you right there and a top-floor suite with compliments of the management.'

Meryl smiled graciously and tried to sound surprised. 'Complimentary?' she said. 'Oh that's very decent of you, but I have all ten of my adopted children and our Russian bodyguard.'

'We have more than five thousand rooms,' the bleached smile beamed. 'I'm sure we'll fit you in.'

Offering free hotel rooms to people who turned up on flash private jets was a calculated risk for the Reef casino: the costs of a few nights' accommodation, free limo rides and free food were insignificant compared to the hundreds of thousands – or even millions – of dollars that a wealthy person might lose at the hotel's casino during their stay.

A female host from another casino circled enviously and pounced the instant Julio pulled out his phone to call for a limo.

'Can I offer you my card?' she asked. 'Just call my number *any* time, day or night, at Casino Taipei and we'll compliment you a full dining package at any of our restaurants, treatments at the most luxurious spa in Las Vegas and of course any other special services we can arrange for you or the children.'

James whispered in Rat's ear, 'Do you reckon they'd set us up with hookers?'

Rat laughed, so Lauren thumped him. '*Don't* laugh,' she hissed. 'James is randy enough without you encouraging him.'

The man from the Reef was scowling at his rival host, while frantically tapping instructions into his PDA and trying to herd Meryl and the rest of the party towards an exit.

'We'll have two limousines here for your party within five

minutes and a minivan to collect your luggage.'

'Oh, you're so kind,' Meryl smiled, keeping up the pretence that it was all a big surprise.

'That's a very beautiful aeroplane you came in on,' the host said. 'If you don't mind my asking, does it belong to the British royal family?'

'Her Majesty is a distant cousin,' Mac lied, making his Scottish accent sound as posh as possible while struggling to keep a straight face. 'She regularly uses our skiing lodge in the Swiss Alps, and when we decided to make a last-minute trip she kindly let us use the Royal Flight.'

'*Faaaaantastic*,' Julio Sweet beamed. 'You're so lucky to know the Queen. We have billionaires and film stars coming through this terminal to play in Las Vegas, but I don't believe we've ever had royal guests before.'

Mac saw the funny side of pulling such a blatant con, but he couldn't help but feel slightly embarrassed. 'I'm a *very* distant cousin,' he emphasised. 'And it's something we prefer not to flaunt.'

'Absolutely,' Julio said exuberantly. 'Everyone on the Reef VIP team can cater to your needs in the utmost privacy.'

Two limousines and a van with Reef Casino logos on it pulled up on the road outside the terminal.

'And how long do you intend staying?' Julio asked.

'Two nights,' Meryl said. 'If that's OK?'

*

The complimentary suites were on top of the thirty-five floor Reef Casino Resort, overlooking the southern end of the Vegas Strip. Meryl, Kazakov and Mac had been given a huge three-bedroom suite with floor to ceiling marble, while the ten kids were split between three smaller but no less luxurious suites down the hall.

James ended up sharing a suite with Jake and Kevin, but with two bedrooms, each containing two king-sized beds, two massive bathrooms and a lounge with an eighty-inch plasma screen, this was no great hardship.

It was five in the afternoon by the time everyone had freshened up and changed clothes. The three boys pigged out on room service and had a massive battle with M&Ms from the mini-bar. By that time it was dark and Julio set up a pair of limousines to take the thirteen-strong group on a tour of the spectacularly lit casinos on the Strip. But it was 5 a.m. British time. Everyone was sleepy and Jake and Kevin were having real problems keeping their eyes open.

James was jet-lagged and woke at half-five the next morning. He took a solo stroll around the casino. Vegas had been crammed with new year revellers two days earlier, but was now mostly home to hardcore gamblers who'd yet to go to bed and cleaning staff buffing tiles with giant polishing machines.

James wasn't allowed to gamble, but as a hotel guest he was allowed on the casino floor so long as he didn't linger in front of a table or slot machine. He'd expected to find men in bow ties sitting at roulette tables like in a James Bond movie, but the reality was a vast airless space filled with several thousand bleeping slot machines. The cocktail waitresses flitting between the rows of machines were supposed to look sexy, but a night walking the casino's floors in high heels meant their smiles were fake and their overdone make-up was melting under the bright lights.

Beyond the casino floor was an indoor strip of more than a dozen restaurants and an upscale shopping mall with a sign out front boasting *Four million square feet of retail paradise!* But the only places open at six on a Tuesday morning were the twenty-four-hour buffet and a hotel gift shop.

James wandered into the gift shop for no particular reason and spent a couple of minutes studying the racks of tacky Vegas paperweights, snowstorm models of the Vegas Strip and plastic Elvis Presley statues that sang *Viva Las Vegas* when you reached around the back and pressed a button. The clerk had heard Elvis a million times and looked up from her copy of *People* magazine, defying James to press the button again.

At the back of the store there was a rack of books. It was mostly souvenir guides and fold-out tourist maps, but there was half a shelf dedicated to books on gambling. James' eye was drawn to a slim volume called *The Ultimate Blackjack Manual.*

He picked it up and spent a few minutes flicking through the pages. He was surprised that a book sold in a casino would contain several chapters detailing card-counting strategies, but the information was openly available on the web and he figured the casino would rather make a buck selling it to you than leave it to someone else.

'That's seven eighty-three with tax,' the assistant said, as James handed her the book. 'Got ex-casino card decks for fifty cents if you want one.'

James realised that he'd need a deck of cards to work through some of the examples in the book and nodded. 'And a pack of menthol gum,' he added.

'Ten dollars and seventy-three.'

James hadn't noticed how attractive the assistant was until he looked down at her tanned legs behind the counter. He made sure there was nobody else in store before deciding to take his first ever shot at an adult woman.

'So what time do you get off?' James asked, using a line he'd heard in about a million movies.

She smiled. 'What's it to you when I get off?'

'I dunno,' James said stupidly. 'We could meet up, go somewhere . . . or something.'

The girl burst out laughing. 'Sure, we'll go to McDonalds. I'll buy you a Happy Meal.'

James felt like he'd been shot. 'I'm older than I look,' he said.

'How old?'

James flushed bright red as he swept his change into his pocket. 'Eighteen,' he lied.

'Months or years?' the girl giggled. 'I think you should stick to girls at your school. Although ten out of ten for trying and the English accent's pretty cute!'

*

Kevin and Jake had been indoctrinated by the hotel's promotional TV channel and wanted to go to the Reef's amusement arcade and aquarium, so Meryl took them while James and the rest of the older kids headed out to see the sights. Almost everything in Las Vegas is on Las Vegas Boulevard, which everyone calls the Strip.

The Reef was at the southern end and after a big room-service breakfast the eight older cherubs spent most of the day cruising north. The Nevada desert is one of the hottest places on earth, but January is wintertime and the kids were comfortable walking in sweatshirts and jeans.

A six-kilometre journey along walkways, escalators and travelators took them through massive casinos complete with pyramids, fake Eiffel towers, Venetian canals and roadside shows including spectacular fountains and a cheesy medieval battle.

All the kids had money from Christmas and things are quite a bit cheaper in the States so they cruised several giant malls. James bought some cargo shorts and a polo shirt in Abercrombie and Fitch, but he had less to spend than the others because most of his Christmas money had gone on replacing the mobile phone he'd wrapped around Michael Hendry's head.

They tried a couple of paid attractions, but after a crappy 3D Pharaoh ride and an embarrassingly naff indoor rollercoaster they gave up and concentrated on shopping and sights. By the time they reached the northernmost part of the Strip they all had aching legs, so Kerry found the location of the nearest multiplex and they squeezed into one of the limos that wait outside every casino and went to see a film that hadn't reached the UK yet.

It was gone 8 p.m. when they got back to the VIP suites at the Reef and Julio the host had arranged for them to have their evening meal on the rooftop terrace outside the adults' suite.

After the aquarium Meryl had taken the two younger boys on a tour and had lunch with some friends she'd made in the area during her short stint as a casino host. The kids had to keep up the pretence of being Mac's adopted children, but

Meryl now became Mac's *ex*-wife because he'd spent a large part of the day in the casino and returned sloshed with a forty-something Texan woman dressed in tight jeans and fancy cowboy boots.

'I lost seven Gs at the baccarat,' Mac grinned. 'But I bagged a beautiful lady as compensation.'

James had never seen Mac drunk before, but after losing his wife and two grandkids six months earlier he figured the old man deserved a chance to go crazy, and Mac could afford to drop twenty thousand dollars at a casino.

Nobody knew exactly how rich Mac was, but he'd sold shares in a computer company he'd founded for several million pounds before taking the chairman's job at CHERUB and rumour had it that he'd enhanced his fortune since then by investing in technology companies over the twenty-five years that followed.

The kids were in a good mood and mucked around noisily as they ate dinner, but Mac and Meryl had both had a few drinks and didn't particularly care. They were starting dessert when Kazakov stumbled in, accompanied by genial casino host Julio Sweet and a burly casino security guard. Kazakov's face was berry red and his shirt had a horrible grey stain where he'd toppled an overstuffed ashtray.

'Hello, hello,' Meryl smiled. 'Where the hell have you been all day? I haven't seen you since breakfast.'

'There was an altercation downstairs in the casino,' the security guard said rigidly. James noticed that he had dark glasses and an earpiece like FBI guys always do in the movies. 'We've asked this gentleman not to return to the casino floor for the remainder of his stay.'

'Yankee pigs!' Kazakov growled. 'I was up four thousand dollars. I bet on black six times and six times it comes up red. I swear the game was rigged!'

Kazakov was a large man who probably could have taken out the security guard and half the room with it if he'd wanted to, so a tense silence settled over the long dining table, until Mac suddenly banged his fist on the table and roared with laughter.

'You should have listened to Meryl,' Mac grinned. 'Roulette's a mug's game.'

'Six bastard times,' Kazakov said. 'I was up four thousand. Five minutes later I'm down three thousand. Boom!'

'That's gambling for you,' Meryl said. 'I'm pretty upset too. I lost eight bucks playing the five-cent slot machines.'

Mac stumbled over the terrace and pulled five hundred-dollar chips out of his blazer pocket. 'Enough to drown your sorrows with,' he said, before pulling a bewildered Kazakov into a hug. 'Pull up a chair, have some dinner and forget all about it.'

Julio snatched Kazakov's chips and hastily changed them up for five one-hundred-dollar bills so that Kazakov wasn't tempted to head back down to the tables.

'Get me a steak,' Kazakov said. 'The biggest, bloodiest steak in town and a bottle of vodka to drown my sorrows.'

The casino host's job is to make their clients gamble as much as possible, and it was a mark of Julio's skill that he'd successfully persuaded Mac and Kazakov to lose ten thousand dollars when they'd arrived intending to gamble less than a tenth of that amount.

Julio followed Mac back to the dining table and tucked

him back in at his place. 'Perhaps after dessert I can take you back to the VIP tables? You mentioned your taste for Scottish single malt whisky and we have a really spectacular selection behind the bar, including a fifty-year-old Springbank. I believe there are less than one hundred bottles still in existence.'

Julio was desperate to get Mac back to a baccarat table. The host had taken a huge risk by giving four of the casino's best suites to people who arrived on a very fancy plane but had no track record as gamblers. The ten grand Mac and Kazakov had lost would barely cover the cost of renting four luxury suites and that was before adding all the complimentary meals, room service and limo rides they'd been taking.

'You're only in Vegas until morning,' Julio swooned, as he placed a clean napkin over Mac's lap. 'A busy man like yourself, it might be a long time before you get to play again and I'm sure your new lady friend would enjoy some more time at the tables.'

'I'd *love* to play some more,' the Texan said, before kissing Mac's earlobe.

'Let me finish my dessert,' Mac said.

All of the older cherubs were concerned for Mac's wellbeing.

'Daddy,' Kerry said firmly. 'You've got an early start tomorrow. Perhaps you should stay here in the room and chill out with us.'

Julio shot Kerry daggers as Mac finished his dessert and headed inside with the Texan's arm around his back.

'I hope he's all right,' James said warily.

Bruce shrugged. 'Let the old guy enjoy himself, I say.'

Meryl checked over her shoulder to make sure that Mac, Julio and the Texan were all well out of earshot. 'Mac's a big boy,' she smiled. 'I'll let him have his fun, but I'll go down and fish him out of the casino if it looks like Julio's getting the better of him.'

21. BUS

James headed back to his room after dinner, but Kevin and Jake were charging around like lunatics. They flicked each other with towels and had the TV in the lounge turned up way too loud. James yelled at them to pack it in, but they ignored him and he eventually sought refuge in the girls' room across the hall.

Kerry opened the door, dressed in a hotel robe and slippers.

'What you up to?' James asked.

'Watching *Ugly Betty*,' Kerry explained, as James stepped into the plush suite.

James looked around and couldn't see anyone else. 'Where've they all gone?'

'Bethany and Andy went downstairs to the arcade. Lauren's doing something or other with Rat and Gabrielle has a headache and went to bed early.'

'How's Gab doing?' James asked, as he followed Kerry back to the sofa.

'What do you think?' Kerry said, a touch of acid in her voice as she turned down the TV. 'Michael basically ripped her heart out.'

James pointed to the door. 'I can go do something else if I'm interrupting your show.'

'Nah, sit down,' Kerry smiled. 'They're about ten episodes ahead over here and I haven't got a clue what's going on.'

They sat together on a huge leather sofa in front of the TV and Kerry moved a big box of chocolates off the table so that it nestled between them. Kerry's legs looked amazingly smooth and James wondered if she was naked beneath the robe.

'So how's it going with you and Bruce these days?'

'He's a good guy,' Kerry smiled. 'Did you see the necklace he got me for Christmas? It was *so* beautiful. It must have cost a bomb.'

'Last time I asked you said there wasn't much of a spark between you,' James said, as he dug into the box to take out a chocolate. 'You said you might break up with him.'

'Bruce is totally different to you,' Kerry said teasingly. 'He's a gentleman.'

'He's one of my best friends,' James nodded. 'Although he's so obsessed with martial arts and stuff it's kind of boring. Sometimes it's all he goes on about.'

James pulled a crescent-shaped chocolate out of the box, but Kerry slapped his wrist. 'Don't scoff all the orange creams. They're my best ones.'

'Why don't you come and get it?' James said, poking out his tongue and balancing the chocolate on the tip before leaning across and sliding his hand into Kerry's lap.

Kerry punched him hard in the ribs.

'Owww,' James gasped, as Kerry stood up. 'You made me bite my tongue.'

'What planet are you on, James?' Kerry growled, as she pushed James away with her foot.

'I'm only messing,' James said.

'I cried for days after you dumped me for Dana. Now she dumps you, and a week later you expect me to throw myself at you like nothing ever happened?'

'Sorry,' James said, realising that the enticing thought of Kerry being naked under the robe had made him move *way* too fast.

'You're disgusting,' Kerry shuddered. 'Bruce is supposed to be one of *your* best friends and he has more respect for me in his little *fingernail* than you have in your whole body.'

'Kerry, you know I still have feelings for you. I got carried away and I'm really, really–'

'Just leave,' Kerry growled. 'Forget it happened, but *don't* try it on like that again.'

*

After two days of private planes and luxury suites came the harsh reality of a 5.30 a.m. checkout and a four-hour drive to the Fort Reagan training compound in one of the remotest areas of the Nevada Desert. The Reef concierge took Mac aside and gave him a tacky plastic VIP card which would enable him to earn casino points on a future visit, plus a two-for-one coupon at any of the restaurants.

The tone was polite, but the implication crystal clear: you didn't gamble enough to justify all the freebies we gave you and if you come back you can pay for your own damned room. There was also a conspicuous absence of help with the luggage and all the kids had to make several runs up and down in the lift to get Kazakov's stash of equipment down to their pick-up point.

Their ride was a shabby green bus, with UNITED STATES ARMY stencilled along each side. The driver was a heavy-set black man, who saluted Kazakov before issuing everyone with hospital style identity bracelets that included a microchip and a tiny photograph. Once fixed on, the plastic bands could only be removed with scissors.

The bus was large and everyone was still sleepy, so the cherubs spread out and kept quiet as they cruised through the Vegas suburbs and into the open desert as the sun broke the horizon.

James ended up near the back of the bus with a rather sorry-looking Mac sitting opposite. He kept coughing, so James passed over the bottle of mineral water from his day pack.

'Cheers,' Mac said, keeping his voice down because Jake was dozing in the row of seats in front. 'So what did you make of Vegas?'

'Very cool,' James said. 'I'm definitely going back when I'm older. How did it go at the tables after dinner?'

Mac had always been a big man on campus. He seemed different dressed in a crumpled shirt, with stubble and a hangover.

'Dropped another eight hundred bucks,' Mac smiled. 'Which was nowhere near enough to keep Julio happy.'

'And your lady friend?' James asked boldly, half expecting Mac to revert to being an authority figure and telling him to mind his business.

'She was totally in cahoots with Julio,' Mac said. 'I was staggering back to my room just after one this morning and she says: "Julio says you ain't gambled enough for a freebie, so it's six hundred dollars if you want to sleep with me".'

James laughed loud enough to make Jake open one eye. 'Did you pay her?' he gasped.

'What kind of person do you think I am?' Mac said incredulously. 'I told her I'd rather have a nice cup of tea and sent her packing.'

*

By 8 a.m. they were on an Interstate eighty miles outside of Las Vegas. There were strips of fast-food joints and shops every few miles, but they had to stop at a particular one which Kazakov had already phoned to order thirty kegs of beer.

'I don't know what Kazakov's plan involves,' Mac grinned, as they stepped off the bus into a parking lot and stretched their legs.

'I'm not even sure that I want to,' James smiled. 'The part with the beer kegs looks like fun though.'

Kazakov, the bus driver and a guy who'd come in especially early to open up his liquor store loaded the kegs into the base of the coach as the cherubs headed towards a twenty-four-hour diner. Inside it was about eighty per cent full and the sweat-glazed hostess had to split the party of twelve between two tables, with a bunch of uniformed US soldiers at the table in between.

James ordered something called a Cake and Steak Grand Slam, which was a giant platter of just about everything on the menu, including a large T-bone steak and side stack of pancakes in a swimming pool of maple syrup.

Kazakov arrived at the table before the food, but their driver spotted some colleagues from Fort Reagan and went to sit with them.

'You all going up to the Fort?' the waitress asked, as she doled out the breakfasts. 'Looks like there's another big exercise starting there this morning.'

Her name badge said she was called Natasiya and Kazakov gave her a smile.

'What's a nice Ukrainian like you doing way out here in the desert?' he asked.

'Paying the bills and raising my kids, same as every other waitress,' she smiled. 'Most people think I'm Russian.'

'English speakers can't tell,' Kazakov tutted. 'I get the same thing in Britain. Some people even think I'm Polish.'

James had twice as much food as anyone else and Bruce shouted over the US soldiers at the table in between, 'You gonna eat all that, fat boy?'

James knew he'd never get through it, so he let Lauren and Rat take one of his pancakes and Kevin had two rashers of crispy bacon to go with his French toast.

'You sure you don't want some, Bruce?' James shouted. 'Put some meat on them skinny bones?'

'Might be skinny but I could kick your butt any day,' Bruce shouted back.

A female soldier at the next table turned angrily to James. 'Would you two mind?' she drawled. 'Can I eat my breakfast without you boys yellin' in my ear?'

'Sorry,' James smiled, before turning back and starting to cut his steak.

A corporal sitting directly behind Kazakov stood up with

an empty maple syrup jug and rudely ordered the waitress to give him a refill.

'Goddamn service here sucks,' the soldier complained, as he sat down. 'That Russian ain't getting no tip out of me. Reckon she learned her waitressing skills in the Gulag.'

Kazakov slammed his coffee down and swivelled around to face the corporal. 'Why don't you shut your mouth and learn some manners?'

The corporal bared his brite-white twenty-something teeth at Kazakov as Natasiya arrived with a jug of hot syrup. 'Maybe you should mind your business, old man.'

Kazakov shook his head and turned back to his breakfast. 'Typical Americans,' he muttered loudly. 'Ignorant, loud and *stupid*.'

The burly corporal bolted out of his seat and tapped Kazakov on the shoulder. 'I happen to take offence at foreign people coming to my country and talking like that.'

Meryl smiled. 'Why don't we *all* stop mouthing off and have a nice breakfast?'

Kazakov ignored her and spoke loudly so that everyone in the diner could hear. 'In my country we love your American flag. We cut the soft fabric into little rectangles and then we wipe our asses on it.'

James and Rat struggled not to laugh as soldiers and civilians at the surrounding tables jeered with outrage.

The corporal's eyes bulged as he leaned towards Kazakov. 'You wanna take this outside?'

'Anytime, cowboy,' Kazakov grinned, as he stood up.

The corporal looked surprised by Kazakov's bulk. He'd started an argument on the basis of Kazakov's grey head in the row of seats behind, but now found himself nose to nose with a physique and scarred face that looked like it had won several wars all by itself.

'Change your mind, cowboy?' Kazakov sneered. 'Guess I'm bigger than the girls on your high school wrestling team.'

The restaurant went quiet as people stopped eating and turned to watch the testosterone fuelled drama. James glanced around and didn't like the fact that at least six other booths were filled with soldiers and none of them looked like they were about to add Kazakov to their Christmas card list.

'Not worth fighting over, boss,' James said to Kazakov, as he tugged on the Ukrainian's shirt.

The female soldier was doing a similar job trying to settle down her buddy and the giant bus driver had come across from his table to urge calm.

After a few seconds where it could have gone either way, Kazakov and the corporal settled back into their seats. But then every eye in the restaurant turned towards the distinctive ratcheting sound of a shotgun chamber being loaded.

A tough-looking female chef had stepped out of the kitchen and had both barrels aimed at Kazakov's head.

'Ma'am, there's no need for that,' Mac said anxiously.

'No need?' she said incredulously. 'I got two sons and a daughter in the armed forces, mister, and you can get your anti-American ass the hell out of my restaurant.'

Diners cheered and clapped as Kazakov stood up and backed away from his table.

'And the rest of yous,' she added, waving the gun at James and the others.

Mac pointed at Kevin and Jake. 'We just brought the children in for some breakfast.'

The chef looked at the two boys before yelling at one of the waitresses. 'Natasiya, make this order to *go*.'

The Ukrainian waitress rushed over with a heap of cardboard cups and polystyrene food boxes. It wasn't ideal, but Mac nodded appreciatively at the gun wielding cook as James and the rest of the party hurriedly scraped food from plates into boxes and poured drinks from glasses into cardboard cups.

'Thank you ma'am,' Mac said, as he reached inside his jacket.

'Keep your damned hands where I can see 'em,' the cook screamed, stepping forward so that the barrels were right in Mac's face.

'Cool it!' Mac gasped. 'I'm reaching for my wallet.'

By this time, Kazakov and the rest of the CHERUB party were on their way to the door with their hastily boxed food.

'Showed you, asshole,' one soldier shouted. 'Got your ass kicked by a girl!'

James' face burned with embarrassment as they moved through the automatic exit door, pausing only to grab serviettes, straws and plastic cutlery. Kazakov bristled as a chunk of corn bread hit him in the back of the head, but Meryl jabbed him in the back and told him to keep moving.

'American cocks,' Kazakov shouted, turning around and flicking off the diners as he made it out into the morning sun.

Mac was last out of the diner, and everyone turned on Kazakov as they hurried back towards the coach.

'I don't care who you people are or what your rank is,' the driver shouted. 'You pull another stunt like that and you can get off my bus and walk.'

'Are you out of your bloody mind?' Mac shouted. 'Picking a fight with thirty soldiers! We're lucky we only had a gun pointed at us.'

'Ignorant American scum!' Kazakov screamed. 'Their missile killed my baby brother and their crooked casino robbed my three thousand dollars.'

Meryl groaned as she climbed aboard the bus. 'You're a big boy, Kazakov. You shouldn't gamble what you can't afford to lose.'

James crashed in a seat behind Bruce. He grabbed the steak out of his box and tore off a massive chunk with his teeth.

'Shame it didn't kick off,' Bruce smiled. 'I haven't been in a decent fight for months.'

'Psycho,' James grinned. 'Steak's *bloody* good though. Maybe we can stop in again on the way back . . .'

22. FORT

If the bronze bust of America's fortieth president on the front gate had been replaced with Mickey Mouse, the entrance to Fort Reagan could easily have passed off as a theme park. The army bus joined a queue of traffic at the entry gate to a massive parking lot which was losing a battle with encroaching sand. James' eye followed the perimeter fence until it vanished over the horizon.

Military personnel arrived in buses and got waved through an express line, while the civilian traffic had to bide its time as soldiers checked their paperwork, searched trunks and inspected the underside of cars with mirrors held on the end of long stalks.

The vehicles were mostly cheap starter cars and the passengers inside were usually young. Most were college students looking to pick up eighty dollars a day, but to enhance the realism of the eight-thousand strong civilian population the US army had also recruited older couples, kids' soccer teams, a blind hiking club and two disabled basketball squads.

'The Americans don't do things by halves, do they?' Bruce smiled.

Everyone was impressed by the scale of the operation as they peered through the windows of the army bus at lines of parked cars and boisterous college students carrying backpacks and beer coolers towards the main entrance.

Mac and Kazakov stayed aboard the bus as it passed through the military entrance. Meryl led the kids with their wheelie bags on a kilometre-long walk towards the entry plaza. The corrugated metal building was the size of an outlet store, with a thousand strong queue snaking through lines of barriers outside the main entrance.

Soldiers with megaphones were shouting orders. 'Have your identity documents, legal documents, social security and medical history forms ready for inspection.'

The queue was horribly slow and James heard the message thirty times as he inched forward with his eyes fixed on the bodies of high-spirited college girls who all wore matching jackets with *USC Soccer* written across the back.

While they waited the queue almost doubled in length. Jake and Kevin swung on the barriers until Meryl yelled at them, while an old couple fussed over sunglasses and double-checked their luggage to make sure they had the right medication.

Things moved more efficiently once they got inside. There were counters numbered A through W, like customs at an airport, and a soldier told everyone what queue to join.

'Welcome to Reaganistan,' a female soldier told Meryl, as the CHERUB party reached the yellow line at the head of queue R. 'Papers please.'

Meryl had a whole bunch of passports and forms at the ready, but they all got waved through because they'd already been issued with their identity bracelets. It was the same story at the next set of counters where everyone else lined up to get their picture taken.

After passing through the processing building in less than ten minutes, they followed a red line to a second building called Equipment and Briefing.

'Pack contains safety goggles, emergency alert alarm and food supplies for your first three meals,' a soldier announced, before repeating the same sentence for the people behind.

At the next station everyone had the chips in their identity bracelets scanned, before a laser printer churned out individual accommodation assignments, along with a map of Fort Reagan and a set of directions. At the final stop, everyone was handed a Fort Reagan safety manual and, most importantly, a zip-lock bag containing five hundred Reaganistan dollars and an apartment key.

The notes came in denominations of one, five, ten and twenty dollars and had a bizarre design which mixed the US Army logo and pictures of weapons with lots of Arabic-style script and a picture of a nondescript man in a turban.

James pulled out a twenty and read the disclaimer on the back of each note aloud. 'This note remains the property of the United States Government. It is designed to purchase food, meals and other essential items within the confines of Fort Reagan military training compound and has no value as currency. You must surrender all notes when leaving Fort Reagan and failure to do so may result in federal imprisonment and a fine of up to fifty thousand dollars.'

'Guess they don't want them going on eBay,' Lauren smiled.

A long corridor led to a carpeted waiting area which already contained more than a hundred people. An LCD screen on the wall told them that the *Next showing of the Fort Reagan introductory film and safety briefing begins in 14 minutes.*

After riding on the bus and then spending an hour queuing and being processed, everyone needed the toilet, which was OK for the boys but the girls all had to join an enormous queue and they barely made it back before sets of automatic doors opened and people started heading into a large auditorium.

Three hundred people crammed on to backless benches before the lights went down and the automatic doors closed.

'I want popcorn,' James giggled, as the screen lit up with an aerial shot of Fort Reagan and a cheesy voiceover.

'*The twentieth century saw the largest and bloodiest military conflicts in the history of mankind, but as the third millennium dawned a new kind of warfare emerged around the world.*'

The screen cut to pictures of smiling American troops driving Hummers through the streets of Baghdad, and soldiers walking up a hillside in white United Nations helmets, waving to friendly peasant women.

'*These twenty-first century battles don't take place on the high seas, on marked battlefields, or even in the air, but in densely populated urban environments. Instead of battling tanks or artillery fire, the American soldier of today is likely to find himself fighting insurgents and terrorists using roadside detonations, car bombs, hostage taking, extortion and kidnapping. The military must learn to fight not just in open battle, but against a ruthless enemy who uses the civilian population as his or her shield.*

'*In order to train for these situations, the Defence Department realised that soldiers needed a twenty-first-century training facility in which to train for twenty-first-century warfare. Built at a cost of over four billion dollars, Fort Reagan is the result.*

'By coming here to Fort Reagan, you'll be playing a vital role in training American troops and helping to save real American lives in the battlefield. Every aspect of our training exercises is meticulously planned and designed for utmost realism, but individual safety remains paramount. So please relax and pay attention as we guide you through safety procedure at Fort Reagan – the world's foremost urban warfare training facility.'

*

After a safety briefing filled with advice ranging from always carrying your safety goggles and putting them on if you see people shooting simulated ammunition, to being told not to run on staircases and to 'stand well clear of moving vehicles' the crowd was moved into a thousand-seat outdoor grandstand, where they waited for another half hour before two army officers stepped on to the sand-covered stage and began speaking a touch self-consciously.

'Citizens of Reaganistan, thank you so much for attending this town meeting. I am United States General Shirley. I am the commander of the one-thousand-five-hundred strong American-British taskforce that has been sent to restore peace in your small country.

'The role of our taskforce is to support the democratically elected government of President Mongo and help to eliminate the terrorist Reaganista movement. In particular we are searching for the Reaganista leader known as Sheikh McAfferty.'

All the cherubs smiled as the screen behind the general

showed a blurry twenty-year-old picture of Mac.

'McAfferty is believed to be responsible for more than one hundred terrorist acts over the past three months. Our task is to arrest McAfferty and his lieutenants, seize their supplies of weapons and ammunition and bring a halt to their terrorist action.'

The general paused. A few members of the crowd clapped and there were even a couple of shouts of '*USA!*'

'Unfortunately, ten per cent of the civilian population supports and sympathises with these insurgents. No doubt this includes some of you sitting here listening to me now. We also believe that they have up to one hundred expert military personnel, trained by a foreign power.

'Over the next two weeks, my men will be conducting patrols and searches of your town, fighting terrorists and trying to stop the violence. We apologise in advance for any inconvenience caused.'

James looked at the other cherubs and shook his head. 'How cheesy is this?' he grinned.

'Somewhere between mature cheddar and stilton,' Rat nodded.

The general continued speaking. 'If any of you have any questions or–'

James flew about a metre into the air and hundreds in the audience screamed as a huge bang and a ball of flame blew up behind the seats. A bloody-faced actress came bounding down the grandstand steps, holding a baby and crying her eyes out as a second blast erupted off to one side and an emergency siren started to wail.

The general spoke again. 'Ladies and gentlemen, it appears

we are under terrorist attack! Please remain calm and return to your homes in an orderly fashion.'

The audience realised it was a special effect designed to set up the atmosphere of conflict, but it had given everyone a scare and the crowd was wary – half expecting more bangs as they hurried out of the grandstands with their luggage and their twenty-four-hour food supplies.

'Cheesy, eh?' Lauren grinned, as she jostled down the grandstand steps behind James. 'You looked like you were gonna shit yourself.'

There were no more bangs, but a smoke machine had been turned on under the grandstand and another in the street outside, forcing the crowd to scatter before they could pull out their maps and work out where they were heading. It was all designed to make the civilians uncomfortable and it seemed to have worked.

The grandstand had a newly built tarmac road, but leading off it was a maze of oddly sized white buildings and narrow alleyways designed to mimic the layout of an ancient city.

Meryl led the ten kids a few hundred metres away from the smoke before pausing to look at her map.

'It's under two kilometres to our accommodation,' she said. 'According to this there's supposed to be a bus service that circles the compound.'

'Wasn't there a bus stop back the way we came?' Kevin asked.

'I think that was the massive queue we walked past,' Bethany said. 'We'll probably be better off walking.'

23. HOME

Like most real developing-world towns, Fort Reagan had few street signs, and to confuse troops the maps everyone was issued with contained many inaccuracies. Of course, this also confused civilians and Meryl and the ten cherubs ended up doing several detours before they finally found their homes for the next two weeks.

Fort Reagan had sections designed to mimic different real-world cities, so the accommodation varied from low concrete sheds made to resemble shanty towns, to large private houses and high rise blocks. Meryl's party had four apartments on the fourth floor of a drab concrete block. Kazakov and Mac had been allotted a pair of detached houses in the next street.

The apartment interiors had been designed to minimise the chances of anything getting broken by the bored and frequently drunk college students who usually occupied them. They had bare concrete walls, white tiled floors and bathrooms with indestructible steel fittings like you'd expect to see in a prison cell. The kitchens had a few cheap utensils, plastic plates, plus a fridge and rather sorry-looking cooker and washing machine.

'Depressing,' James said to Rat, as they unpacked their clothes in a cramped bedroom with two single beds covered with army issue blankets and a sign on the wall saying that the United States Army reserved the right to charge for property damage.

'I like the bare concrete walls and the vague whiff of plumbing,' Rat smirked.

'Aye aye,' James said, staring out of the window and seeing a college girl standing in the opposite block. She was reaching back to put her long hair into a clip and her raised arms accentuated her breasts. 'Oh for a face full of those beautiful watermelons.'

The thought of watermelons sent Rat charging towards the window, but he was slightly disappointed. 'Nice,' he said. 'But they're mangos at best. You were doing better than that with Dana.'

James turned sharply towards Rat. 'Don't talk about *her*.'

Rat didn't answer because the college girl had spotted them ogling her and was flicking them off and mouthing something that ended with the word *perverts*.

'Aww, come on baby,' James shouted. 'Give us a flash.'

Rat collapsed on the bed laughing as the girl opened her window and yelled at James. 'I'll get my boyfriend over there and he'll kick both your asses.'

'I'll pay five Reaganistan dollars per nipple,' James shouted, as the girl furiously slammed her window shut and pulled down her roller blind.

Rat thought this was hilarious, and he was still lying on the bed convulsing half a minute later when Lauren walked in.

'What's so funny?' she asked.

'Nothing,' Rat snorted. 'Just observing James' ultra-smooth technique with the ladies.'

Lauren waved a hand in front of her face. 'It's probably better if I don't know . . . Meryl had a phone call from Kazakov. He's calling a strategy meeting in fifteen minutes, he says we've got to get ourselves organised before the Americans start searching.'

James stepped out into the hallway and was surprised to find a heavily built Englishman peering out of the living-room window. He was only average height, but he was almost as wide as tall and he definitely wasn't the kind of guy you'd want to mess with.

'Have you met the sarge?' Lauren asked. 'He's on the level, he's worked with CHERUB before.'

'Sergeant Cork, SAS,' the big man said, raising one eyebrow as he gave James and Rat crunching handshakes. 'We'll have sixteen of my boys helping out Kazakov with the day to day running of the insurgency.'

'Cool,' James said. 'And what's so exciting about our balcony?'

'Looks like you can clamber on to the roof from that window ledge. We'll be able to set up a lookout and see any army patrols coming all the way down from their base.'

'Sounds a bit much,' James said.

'Not if we want to keep our weapons for more than a day or two,' the sarge smiled. 'I'll pencil you in for a midnight to four a.m. watch, shall I?'

'Not bloody likely,' James grinned. 'Besides, if you start using kids as lookouts the Yanks will suspect us. Better to use one of your boys.'

To minimise suspicion they walked to Kazakov's house in small groups. James went with Rat and Lauren. At the end of their street was one of the two dozen cafés run by soldiers which would sell you a meal for two Reaganistan dollars. Despite his giant breakfast James stopped off for a burger while Lauren and Rat bought cans of drink and samosas.

As they stepped out with their food a pair of patrolling soldiers offered them a polite good afternoon and said that there was a hundred Reaganistan dollars for anyone who gave them accurate information about weapons or insurgents.

'There are a few shops in the town centre that sell PSP games and stuff,' one soldier added. 'So it's worth your while if you hear anything.'

'Thanks,' Lauren said brightly, as the soldier looked away. But her tone changed once they were out of earshot. 'Everyone in town is gonna snitch on us if they go around doing that.'

'At least the veggie samosas are good,' Rat said, before looking up towards a faint buzzing sound in the sky overhead.

The pilotless white drone had a reflective dome built into its belly, which bristled with surveillance equipment.

'No expense spared,' James said warily, as he looked up. 'Those things have laser guidance systems controlled by the remote pilot. They fire an invisible beam down at the target. The missile detects the beam and it hits the target dead on.'

'Can't blow buildings up on a training exercise,' Rat said. 'But that thing would certainly spot one of Sarge's rooftop lookouts in two seconds flat.'

*

Kazakov's house was luxurious on the outside, with a mowed lawn and neatly trimmed hedge, but apart from the rooms being bigger it was fitted out in exactly the same spartan style as the apartment where the kids were staying.

The eleven CHERUB agents, plus Meryl and the SAS sergeant gathered in a basement room which couldn't be looked into either from the paved street or from the apartment block directly behind it.

'I've split insurgent operations into three cells,' Kazakov explained. 'The sarge and I are the only contact points between them. Cell one is already working to create a secure environment for Mac. Cell two consists of the majority of the SAS team, who will be working with our eight hundred civilian sympathisers.'

'We just got offered money to snitch on the way over here,' Lauren said. 'How do we know we can trust them?'

'You can't be totally sure,' Kazakov said. 'But the insurgents are on an extra twenty dollars a day and they won't get that if they switch sides. Plus, I've been given my own supply of Reaganistan dollars so we can do some bribery of our own if the right opportunity arises.'

'Gimme, gimme, gimme,' Jake shouted. 'I'll shoot all the Yanks you like if you give me enough for an X-box game.'

'Shut up,' Bethany tutted. 'This is serious.'

Kazakov continued. 'Cell two's job is to keep supplies of weapons and ammunition secure, harass and shoot at American patrols with simulated ammunition, plant paint bombs and smoke grenades and generally make life difficult for the Americans.

'Cell three comprises the people in this room and our job is to implement my special strategy.'

'What's that?' Jake asked.

Kazakov smiled. 'The Americans are expecting us to be ducking and weaving. So our plan is to go all out and attack their base and force a victory.'

James looked aghast. 'Well I count fourteen people in this room and there *are* supposed to be fifteen hundred American troops.'

'I can count,' Kazakov said. 'But the Americans have rigged the ratios so that they can make their training exercises look good. Conventional military wisdom is that you need one soldier for every ten civilians to successfully crush an insurgency. In Iraq, the American forces peaked at one soldier for every one hundred civilians and that's why they kept getting their asses kicked.

'On this exercise there are eight thousand civilians and one thousand troops. That's one soldier for every eight civilians. That's enough troops to roadblock every street and search every home on a daily basis. If we play the way they're expecting us to, we'll be lucky if we can keep an insurgency going for a week, never mind put up a fight for the entire two-week exercise.

'Luckily I've had a couple of months to plan and I've had access to reports on all the training exercises at Fort Reagan since it opened eighteen months back. The first part of my plan was successfully implemented while you lot were having your safety briefing.'

Kazakov pulled a small receiver unit out of his pocket. 'The base commander, General O'Halloran, kindly took me on a tour of the military headquarters while you lot were going through induction. Sarge and I managed to place a video transmitter in the room.'

Sergeant Cork smiled. 'We'll know what they're up to at all times. I've got the boys in cell one taking turns to monitor the signal twenty-four hours a day.'

The CHERUB agents all smiled at this, but they failed to see how one listening device – no matter how well placed – could give them the edge over a thousand trained US troops.

'We can't do much while the Americans are watching our every move,' Kazakov continued. 'Drones like the one James and Lauren saw on the way over here can be left to glide over an area in virtual silence for ten to twelve hours and watch every move we make. As soon as it gets dark, we've got to take them out.'

24. DRONE

It was dark by six. Fort Reagan felt like a holiday camp, as college-age civilians hung out around the food joints and tiny supermarkets on chilly street corners, eating junk food, talking trash and flirting.

There was no alcohol on sale and you weren't supposed to bring any in, but the searches on entry concentrated on X-rays for knives and weapons and it seemed like half the population was getting loaded on vodka smuggled inside mineral water bottles.

The gainfully employed didn't have two weeks to take part in military training, so the population divided starkly between college kids and pensioners. Inevitably this caused friction over loud music and people running up and down the corridors between apartments, hurling water and flour at each other.

The soldiers were ever present. If James looked out of an apartment window he could guarantee that at least one soldier would be in view. Sometimes they were knocking on doors or conducting good natured searches in the street, but as in a real engagement the US Army had been ordered to start gently by winning over the civilians.

This mainly took the form of soldiers chatting up college girls and letting old men hold their rifles and talk about old wars. James leaned anxiously out of the living-room window when he heard some shooting, only to see that a couple of soldiers had a team of boy scouts standing at the bottom of a drained swimming pool, shooting simulated ammunition cartridges at Pepsi cans.

For all the realism of the buildings and the weapons at Fort Reagan, James saw a major flaw: the civilians were ninety per cent white and a hundred per cent English speaking. With no language barrier or cultural differences the situation bore more resemblance to freshers' week on a university campus than a war zone in the third world, while facing the threat of compacted chalk and coloured paint instead of death left a distinct lack of menace in the air.

James set his watch alarm for 6.30 p.m. and headed down to the lobby with Rat and Jake after it went off. They met up with Bethany and Lauren before heading out into the darkness. Fort Reagan had been open less than two years, but the streetlights were deliberately gloomy and the pavements were laid unevenly.

A couple of turns took them away from the noise around the fast-food joint and into a narrow alleyway which had been daubed with graffiti and filled with battered rubbish cans to give a sense of atmosphere.

Torches shone in their faces as they reached the end. Men's voices and the clank of military hardware sent a chill down James' back.

'What you kids doing out in the dark?' an army officer barked.

'Exploring,' James shrugged, playing up the role of surly teen. 'There's sod all else to do.'

As the three soldiers closed around the kids, one pulled a rustling paper bag out of his flak jacket. 'Peanut brittle, or marshmallow?' he asked.

The kids all dug into the bag.

'Thank you sir,' Rat said, feigning good manners as he bit into a piece of toffee.

'I wouldn't stray too far from home in case you get lost,' the officer said. 'And it's best to put your goggles on if you're walking in the dark. The simulated ammunition we're using here only stings if it hits your body, but it could damage an eye from close range.'

The five cherubs nodded obediently as they pulled up their goggles and moved off. James checked back over his shoulder a couple of times, but there was no sign that the soldiers were following as they turned a corner and moved quickly down a metal staircase into the basement of a building designed to resemble a shop.

The homes, plus small shops and restaurants run by the army, were fitted out, but even the United States military budget didn't extend to paying for the hundred thousand civilians you'd need to fill the whole of Fort Reagan, so many of the buildings were bare concrete shells.

There was electric light in the basement, but nobody had bothered sinking the wiring into the walls so strands of loosely tacked cable ran between low-energy bulbs. A nearby water pipe was leaking and mildew sprouted in a puddle at the far end of the room.

'Sarge, Kazakov,' James smiled, as he stepped in.

'How are we doing?'

'Good,' Kazakov whispered. 'Kerry and Gabrielle are already up there scouting the area. Apparently there's between six and eight soldiers working the landing strip. Engineers and techies, no sign of any guards.'

'Here's your kits,' the sarge said, pointing to a stash of guns and ammunition. 'Compact machine guns, paint bombs, stun grenades, smoke grenades – don't get those mixed up – plus gas masks and walkie-talkies. I assume you can all handle that stuff?'

'Course,' Jake said, as he unzipped his pack and stuffed ammo clips into it before attaching grenades to the belt of his jeans.

'The patrols are everywhere,' Sarge explained. 'We've got to assume that we'll be stopped and searched somewhere between here and the landing strip. Bethany, I'll carry your equipment, you can walk twenty metres ahead. If a patrol stops you, scream like they startled you and we'll come from behind and ambush them.'

'Are we planning to cheat if we get shot?' Lauren asked. 'You know, try washing the paint off or something?'

'No,' Kazakov said firmly. 'We want to win, but if you cheat in a war game the whole thing becomes pointless.'

'Besides,' Sarge added, 'to discourage dishonesty the paint will foam and spread if you try washing it off with soap and water. If you get shot, spend your regulation fifteen minutes lying dead, then head straight to the cleaning station where they have the proper chemicals.'

'You're only dead for twenty-four hours, anyway,' Rat noted. 'And I heard one of the college kids who's been here before saying that the food's better up at the army base.'

'Might as well get shot then,' Bethany grinned, but Kazakov glowered at her.

'If I see *anyone* slacking off, they can expect a nice twenty-kilometre speed hike with a heavy pack when they get back to campus,' Kazakov growled. 'Is that clear?'

'I was only joking,' Bethany gasped anxiously.

'How far is the airfield?' James asked.

'Two kilometres,' Kazakov said. 'But we're taking an indirect route through the back alleyways so it ends up more like three.'

As they started heading up the stairs, Sarge pointed at a sealed plastic bag filled with granulated powder. 'James, you need that as well.'

'What the hell is *Phenolphthalein Suspension*?' James asked, reading the label and feeling slightly alarmed by several hazard symbols as he crammed the giant bag inside his backpack.

'It's a special treat for all my American friends,' Kazakov said, before smiling cryptically.

Sarge explained. 'While the others deal with the airbase, you and I are going to sneak inside American HQ and dump the contents of that bag into their water supply.'

'Laxative,' Kazakov said, before roaring with laughter. 'They'll be shitting like there's no tomorrow.'

*

The tiny jet engine inside the drone cut out as it landed on the short airstrip and rolled silently for a couple of hundred metres before crashing into a green net stretched across the runway. Two technicians ran out and wheeled the craft a few metres backwards before one bent forwards to open a fuelling hatch. Neither man realised that he was being watched through binoculars from scrubland less than twenty metres away.

'That is a nice butt,' Kerry said. 'The one thing I don't like about Bruce is his bony arse.'

Gabrielle lay flat on her chest as the two men wheeled the drone back towards its hangar. 'James has a nice butt,' she said.

'I still can't believe that ignoramus,' Kerry snorted. 'Thinking he can dump me for Dana and then have me back as soon as he fancies it.'

'Men are all pigs,' Gabrielle sighed. 'You might as well go for the cute ones, because at least you'll have some fun.'

Kerry smirked as Kazakov's voice sounded in her earpiece. 'We're in position. Tell me what you're seeing, girls.'

Kerry flipped her microphone down over her mouth and took a quick confirming glance through her binoculars. 'Two on the runway, one female technician inside the hangar, plus two *possibly* three remote pilots inside, controlling the drones. Best time to move is when they open the main doors to push the drone in and that should be within the next minute or so.'

'Bruce, are you in position?' Kazakov asked through his mouthpiece.

'Roger,' Bruce said.

'No shooting, Bruce, we need those uniforms without paint stains. OK, Kerry, all teams authorised to move on your mark.'

Kerry waited until the engineers had wheeled the drone

all the way back to the hangar and pressed the button to roll up the electric shutter.

'Mark,' Kerry said.

Kerry and Gabrielle watched as Bruce and Andy sprang out of the undergrowth on the opposite side of the landing strip. Bruce's silhouette moved impossibly fast, booting one of the unarmed technicians in the stomach and Karate chopping him behind the neck as he crumpled, then throwing a roundhouse kick to floor the other guard before Andy had even arrived on the scene.

The six strong party of Sarge, Kazakov, James, Rat, Lauren and Bethany pulled down their hoods, then charged in from further afield as Bruce and Andy dragged the two bewildered army engineers under the hangar door.

The hangar was designed to handle helicopters, but its brilliantly lit interior was empty except for four drones lined up against the left hand wall. The female technician knelt over one of the drones, surrounded by circuit boards and her toolkit. By the time she looked up and saw that her colleagues had been floored, Bethany Parker was less than two metres away.

Bethany took the safety off on her machine gun and aimed it at the kneeling technician's face from point blank range.

'You wanna go blind?' Bethany shouted. 'Who else is in the building?'

The technician smiled. 'Kiss my ass, limey.'

Bethany didn't know what limey meant, but it sounded like an insult so she kicked the technician in the guts.

'Try again,' Bethany growled, smiling sarcastically as the technician clutched her stomach. 'Who else?'

While Bethany grilled the woman, Andy helped James and Sarge strip the two male technicians of their uniform and identity badges. Kazakov, Lauren and Kerry ran to the back of the hangar and passed into a corridor which led to the control room. Gabrielle acted as a lookout near the hangar door, while Jake and Bruce concentrated on destroying the drones.

'I'm not saying one goddamn word,' the female technician shouted, before panicking as it dawned that the boys were about to trash the drones.

Kazakov had been in touch with one of his former SAS colleagues and managed to get hold of blueprints for a near identical drone used by the British. Explosives and potentially dangerous weapons like knives and stun guns weren't allowed inside Fort Reagan, but he believed that lifting the drone's main access panel and blowing up a paint grenade inside would pretty much wreck all the sensitive electronics.

The female technician lunged towards Jake and Bruce. 'You're not allowed to do that,' she screamed. 'Do you know how much these things cost?'

Bethany was sick of the technician's big mouth and let rip with the machine gun. Twenty rounds fired off in less than two seconds. The technician screamed out and crashed back against the wall as fluorescent pink paint poured down her uniform.

By this time the two male technicians had been stripped. James was horrified to see that the technician whose trousers came close to fitting him wasn't wearing underpants.

'Dirty git!' James complained, as he inspected the trousers.

'I hope he didn't leave you any little brown presents,'

Andy smirked, as James swapped trainers and jeans for the technician's horribly warm trousers and sweaty boots.

James hurriedly buttoned the technician's combat jacket over his sweatshirt and read the name on the soldier's ID card. As he pulled a camouflaged cap down over his eyes, he hoped the guards on the gate of the main army compound didn't wonder why First Lieutenant Juan-Carlo Lopez was a sixteen-year-old with blond hair and blue eyes.

'Ready, James?' Sarge asked, buttoning up the other technician's jacket.

'Yes, Sarge,' James said, before clicking his boots and saluting ridiculously.

The pair were barely out into the night when the first paint grenade exploded. Kazakov wasn't an aeronautical engineer, so had no idea that in order to conserve fuel and reduce noise the drones had a carbon fibre skin less than two millimetres thick. He'd expected the paint to explode inside the drones and foul up the electronics, but the blast actually broke the drone into two halves.

Shards of carbon fibre clattered dangerously in all directions across the hangar, accompanied by a shower of bright pink paint that reached up to the ceiling. It was a minor miracle that none of the cherubs got hit by enough of it to be considered dead.

Rat and Andy cracked up laughing, until they realised that the drone had been fully fuelled and petrol was now running all over the floor.

Lauren and Kerry had just burst into the control room from where the drones were piloted and the noise of the explosion made them dive for cover. The two controllers sat at large flat-panel screens which showed various views from the two drones presently circling over Fort Reagan.

One controller had a pistol strapped around his waist and when he saw the two girls he ripped it out and shot Kerry in the chest. As the force of the simulated round knocked her back into Mr Kazakov, Lauren let rip with her machine gun, showering the far wall and the two controllers in pink paint.

'Down on the ground, you're dead,' Kazakov shouted, pressing his giant Russian army boot on the waist of a startled controller who'd been knocked out of her swivel chair by Lauren's bullets. Kerry was coughing and the clouds of paint left a sickly tang of oil in the air.

Kazakov and Lauren each studied one of the paint-spattered screens before looking at the controls, which consisted of a standard keyboard, a joystick and a thrust handle.

'You can't touch those,' one of the controllers shouted.

'If you don't play dead like you're supposed to, I'm gonna kick your arse,' Kazakov warned.

Lauren experimented by gently nudging the joystick, making the on-screen view veer to the right and indicating that she was in direct control of the drone. She could see one edge of the dimly illuminated base through the main camera in the nose and she turned the drone towards it as a second and third paint blast erupted in the hangar next door.

The explosions of paint inside the second and third parked drones caused a spark or burst of static which ignited the spilled petrol from the first. The flames rushed out in a multi-pronged star, chasing trickles of petrol across the floor. Within a second a klaxon sounded and all the cherubs and technicians, except for Jake, had made it out into the darkness.

From the rear of the hangar Jake made his way through the door towards the control room. 'We're on fire, guys,' he shouted, pausing briefly to inspect the paint-spattered walls before giving Lauren a tug.

'Just a sec,' Lauren said. 'I didn't know you cared.'

She wasn't panicking because she was less than two metres from a fire door and the two 'dead' controllers were already on their way out. Lauren didn't want to risk injuring someone by having the drone crash over Fort Reagan, so she pointed it towards the desert and set it on a gentle downwards trajectory.

'Should crash somewhere out in the desert in a minute or two,' Lauren explained.

Kazakov wasn't quite so adept with the controls and took slightly longer to set his drone on a similar course. After making it outside last he pressed the transmit button and spoke into his headset. 'Are we all safe?'

'If you have Jake, Kerry and Lauren we're safe,' Rat confirmed.

Out front, Rat was startled by a powerful blast of carbon dioxide powder exploding from walls in the hangar. Aircraft are filled with huge amounts of explosive jet fuel and this newly built facility was equipped with a fire suppression system that could blast all of the flame-feeding oxygen out of the building, killing even the most serious fire in a matter of seconds.

Rat jogged around to the side of the building and met up with Kazakov and the rest of their party. The ringing alarm and the clouds of white carbon dioxide powder billowing into the sky would undoubtedly attract a large contingent from the army headquarters less than half a kilometre away.

'They'll be here any second,' Kazakov said. 'We'd better run – except for you, Kerry. Head up to the cleaning centre, but keep your mouth shut. I want you back at the apartment, fed and refreshed, in twenty-four hours.'

25. WATER

James looked back over his shoulder at the plume of carbon dioxide powder spewing out of the hangar door. Disorganised troops ran from the army headquarters a hundred metres ahead as Sarge spoke to Kazakov on his walkie-talkie.

'What did Kazakov say?' James asked, as they walked briskly towards the army HQ.

'He thinks it's his birthday,' Sarge smiled. 'You and me have to carry on as before.'

'Weren't we supposed to get inside the base *before* all hell broke loose?' James asked.

Sarge grinned. 'You've been trained to improvise, haven't you?'

James didn't answer because they were almost up to the army-base perimeter. A male and female private guarded an open mesh gate. Everyone had to show their IDs and with a dozen other soldiers in plain view starting a fight wasn't an option.

'Message for the general,' Sarge said in an American accent, flashing the ID he'd found in his jacket pocket.

The dark-skinned guard didn't even look at it. 'What's that shit up there, dude?'

'Drone caught fire,' Sarge shrugged. 'I think some dumbass engineer sparked a fuel tank.'

'Anyone hurt?'

'Don't think so.'

'General's gonna be *mightily* pissed!' the guard laughed. 'Glad I'm not in your shoes, brother.'

James flashed Juan-Carlo Lopez's ID at the female guard for about half a second before chasing after Sarge. The guard shouted *hey*, as if she wanted to take a better look, but James kept moving and she didn't come after him.

The army compound was permanent, but like everything else inside Fort Reagan it was meant to replicate a war zone. The buildings were a mixture of prefabs made from bolted aluminium sections and heavy-duty tents with vinyl floors, electric light and air conditioning.

The pair ran fifty metres into the camp and cut up a wooden boarded path between two long tents where the soldiers bunked. Sarge squatted down and lit up a paper map with a small Maglite. Desert moths flickered in the cone of light.

'What are we looking for?' James asked.

'Hundred and fifty metres that way,' Sarge said, pointing north. 'Only permanent building on site. It provides water and power for the whole army base.'

The army was rapidly catching up with events. As Sarge headed off a siren whooped three times and orders were barked over a PA system.

'*Enemy action reported. All off-duty patrol units assemble in front of the vehicle compound immediately.*'

Soldiers were resting in the long tents on either side of

James and the announcement caused a lot of cursing. He could hear equipment being thrown around and lots of comments along the lines of *what stupid bullshit exercise are they gonna put us through now.* James enjoyed the sense of mischief as his boots followed Sarge's across the wooden boards.

After the tents came a tarmac lot covered with US Army Hummers and armoured personnel carriers. As a concession to civilian safety, the front and rear of each vehicle was painted fluorescent yellow and the driver's doors all had notices on saying that the vehicles were mechanically restricted to fifteen miles an hour.

Troops were running on to the lot and jumping into open-topped Hummers, before pulling into a queue of traffic leading towards a double width vehicle gate.

'You get your asses out there,' a furious officer was shouting. 'Drive to your sectors and grill every asshole you see. I want these insurgent sons of bitches brought back here for interrogation. We have the manpower and I want this organisation crushed by sunrise.'

'I think we've spoiled his evening,' James said, smirking at Sarge as they crossed to the far side of the parking lot.

The facilities building was a concrete shed with a tin roof. On one side was a half buried tank filled with oil for the generator. On the other a whole bunch of water pipes and high voltage electricity cables fed up a rocky slope towards the rest of the base.

The deserted stretch of tarmac leading down to the building was brightly lit and easily visible from the vehicle gate, so Sarge cut down a steeply sloping footpath carved into the rocks. The only illumination came from distant car headlamps and James gave himself a fright as his shoulder brushed a rock, causing a lizard to scuttle away.

'I'll cover you,' Sarge said, pulling his rifle into a firing position and giving James a shove towards the shed.

All James could hear was his own breathing as he dived across the single lane of tarmac in front of the building. The heavy steel door groaned and he stepped into a dark passageway.

'Hello?' James said, trying to sound innocent in case he had company.

The generator buzzed behind a door with a million yellow warning stickers on it and the burnt smell in the air reminded him of the time he'd melted a circuit board in science class.

Once he was confident that he was alone, James walked down the hallway, which opened into a double height space. This contained a huge drum-shaped water tank with a six-rung inspection ladder up the side.

He grabbed his radio. 'Looks clear, Sarge.'

By the time Sarge arrived, James had the bag of Phenolphthalein out of his backpack and was ready to slit it open with his multitool.

'Don't,' Sarge gasped. 'Swallow three specks of that powder and in eighteen hours' time you'll be blasting off like the space shuttle.'

Sarge threw James rubber gloves and a paint-sprayer's mask before clambering up the side of the tank. He flipped up the inspection hatch as James slit the bag and passed it up to him.

Sarge dumped the drug into the giant tank as James went

into the SAS man's backpack for the second load.

'Piece of cake,' Sarge grinned as he came down the ladder.

They put the empty drug packets inside a large zip-lock bag, then dumped their gloves and masks inside before sealing it up and dumping it in a large bin nearby. Sarge handed James a bottle of alcohol cleanser.

'Use plenty,' Sarge ordered. 'Do your hands, then your nose and mouth. When you get back to the apartment, ditch the uniform by sealing it in a bin liner then take a hot shower. Until then, don't eat or drink anything you've touched and don't put your fingers anywhere near your mouth.'

James was stunned by the degree of caution. 'How toxic is this stuff?'

'It's military grade, designed for special ops,' Sarge explained, squeezing his eyes shut as he slathered his face in the gel. 'The drug is encased in microscopic plastic caplets that start leaking the drug twenty hours after they first contact water. It takes a thirtieth of a gram to induce severe stomach cramps and diarrhoea.'

'Not nice,' James said, glancing at his watch as he slung his pack over his shoulder and headed towards the exit. 'So in theory, in twenty and a half hours from now every American on this base is going to get a severe dose of the shits?'

'That's what Kazakov's hoping,' Sarge laughed.

26. ESCAPE

Mission accomplished, James and Sarge headed back up the rocky path towards the main part of the base. The last of the Hummers stood in a short queue near the gate, waiting for orders on which area they were expected to patrol.

The voice of the officer organising the patrols still ripped across the near deserted parking lot. 'I want information. I want to see asses kicked! You're my boys – now get out there.'

'We were supposed to be in and out before they discovered we'd attacked the drones,' James complained. 'How the hell are we gonna get back to base with five hundred guys searching for us?'

Sarge shrugged. 'If there's five hundred guys searching for us out there, can't be many left in here.'

He stepped inside the first of the sixty-metre-long accommodation tents, and shouted, 'Anyone seen Corporal Smith?'

If the tent had turned out to be full of men he could easily have backed out claiming it was all a mistake. But as Sarge expected, every man and woman had been sent out on patrol. James followed him inside and you could tell from the scattered clothes and miniature TVs flickering in the gloom that everyone had cleared out in a hurry.

The tent was divided into bays, with four beds to each side of a bay. Every fourth bay was a lounge area, with a big TV and either a pool or foosball table. James and Sarge only encountered one man as they passed through. He had a foot in plaster and lay on his bunk in underpants, rocking out to his iPod.

'This looks as good as any,' Sarge said when they stopped in the seventh bay, which was just over half-way between the middle and the end of the long canvas dome.

He grabbed clean uniform, towel and boots from an open locker before pointing James towards a plastic shower unit in the far corner.

'Didn't we just poison the water?' James asked warily.

'There's plenty in the pipes between here and the tank,' Sarge explained. 'It'll take a good hour or two for it to feed as far as here.'

'What if anyone comes through?'

'We'll figure it out,' Sarge said casually. 'I want a shower and clean clobber. Then we'll chill here for an hour or two and head for home when things calm down.'

James liked Sarge's plan: he wasn't comfortable with either the pungent odour of Lieutenant Lopez's aftershave, or the idea that his clothes might be contaminated with tiny caplets of the Phenolphthalein powder.

The shower was a peculiar affair. The grubby plastic basin flexed when he stepped behind the curtain and he was mystified by the lack of controls until he saw that the shower only worked when you picked up the nozzle and squeezed a trigger.

When he stepped out two minutes later, a heavily tattooed

and naked Sarge threw him a towel before stepping in after him. The uniform James put on was still someone else's, but this time the green T-shirt and sand-coloured trousers were freshly laundered. The only reasonable boots he could find were too big, so he found two pairs of clean socks and gave them a good blast from someone's deodorant before pulling them on.

'What did you see?' a woman asked.

James looked around. His brow shot up as he recognised the female guard from the gate, accompanied by a female officer. They were two bays along, talking to the man with the broken foot. James dived across the aisle towards the shower.

'Company,' James said anxiously.

'So what?'

'They're searching. It's the woman from the front gate.'

'You serious?' Sarge gasped, bursting through the shower curtain and grabbing James' damp towel off the end of a bed.

James took another peek and saw the female guard coming towards them.

'You go,' Sarge ordered, as he hopped into a pair of trousers. 'I'll catch up.'

But James was spotted as he crossed the centre aisle for his backpack. There was a sharp crack followed by a chalky pink explosion as he dived on to the ground between two beds.

Dressed only in trousers, Sarge grabbed his rifle and did a double tap: two well aimed rounds fired in quick succession. While Sarge covered, James skidded across the vinyl floor and crawled into the next bay, but three male soldiers were coming through the flaps twenty metres ahead.

The tent had zipped exits in the leisure areas and some of these were even left open to let in fresh air, but James wouldn't get to one before the guards. His only hope was the slot where a portable air conditioner protruded through the fabric.

'I bloody know her,' Sarge gasped, firing shots in both directions as James jumped up on a bed. 'That woman on the gate: she was at a NATO special forces conference in Malta last year. Must have sussed us after we rushed through.'

James hit the air conditioner with all his might. The bed grated backwards and the tent fabric billowed. Most importantly, the air conditioner broke away at the point where it was clipped to the tent fabric. James held the fabric taut with one hand and pounded repeatedly on the air conditioner.

After a dozen painful blows, the air conditioner tilted backwards off its mounting and hit the sand outside with an almighty thunk.

'Nice one,' Sarge smiled, keeping the approaching guards at bay with more covering shots as James threw his backpack through the square hole in the fabric and hauled himself up off the bed.

James got his head through, but his shoulders were a tight squeeze and Sarge had to break away from firing to give him a shove. The domed shape of the tent acted like a slide, but James' palm hurt from pounding on the air conditioner and a hard landing on the sand made it worse.

'Take both packs,' Sarge yelled, as he threw his pack through the hold.

James was disorientated and it took him a couple of seconds to realise that Sarge wasn't coming with him: if his sixteen-year-old body needed a push to get through the hole, Sarge didn't have a hope in hell.

'I'm dead,' Sarge shouted, as the shooting inside the tent finally stopped. 'Use smoke cover and get out of here.'

Hoping to buy a few seconds, James unhooked a smoke grenade from inside his pack. He pulled the pin and lobbed it through the square hole before starting to run. In basic training cherubs are taught to always be tactically aware, but James realised he'd been relying on Kazakov and Sarge to do everything. Now he had to think for himself.

The odds were stacked against. James was trapped inside a secure base on a high state of alert and everyone would be looking for him as soon as the guards inside the tent stopped breathing smoke and called out on their radios. The main gate was less than fifty metres away and James' best and probably only shot at getting out was a surprise assault.

He ran to the end of the boarded path between tents and ducked out. The gate was now closed and the guard had been doubled to four men, but despite the circumstances they still didn't look particularly alert.

James looked back over his shoulder before grabbing his rifle. The spot lamps around the perimeter gave him good light to make a shot. He laid a stun grenade and two smokers in the sand before going down on one knee, bracing the rifle stock against his shoulder and lining up the first guard in his scope.

From fifty metres, he hit the first guard dead in the centre of the back. A jerk left enabled him to take out the second with a pink explosion.

'Attack,' the third man shouted, diving for cover as James' shot sailed over his head.

James ripped the pin out of the stun grenade and lobbed it towards the gate. He hurled the first smoke grenade into the no man's land between the tent and the gate and left the second on the ground between his legs. After switching his rifle to automatic firing, James broke cover and started running towards the gate as the flash from the stun grenade turned the sky white.

The fourth guard's senses were temporarily blitzed by the stun grenade, but the third man lay on his belly firing randomly into the increasingly dense smoke cover. Other men were coming out of the tents behind and a bullet whizzing past James' left side made him realise that he hadn't pulled up his goggles after taking the first shots through the scope.

The thought of being blinded scared him, but he kept running. The smoke filled his lungs and he could hear men approaching from all directions as he closed to within five metres of the gate.

A gap in the smoke gave James a clear shot at the last remaining guard. Surging with panic, he missed. The guard took longer to aim and his shot came so close that James felt it go by. The last round in James' magazine hit the guard in the thigh.

Wild shots came from all directions, but the smoke gave James excellent cover. He grabbed the gate, realising almost too late that he had to lift a metal peg out of the ground to release it. Two bullets thunked the wire gate as he looked anxiously at the four guards. They'd almost certainly get a roasting from their commanding officer if he broke free, and one of them grabbed his ankle.

'Cheat,' James shouted, as he lashed out with his boot.

Almost without knowing it James had got the gate open far enough to make it through. The thick smoke made his eyes stream. His lungs burned and he felt like he had concrete blocks tied to his legs, but somehow he managed to pull up his goggles and sprint away from the compound.

27. REPLAY

James ran several hundred metres over the open ground outside the base, with smoke covering his back and randomly aimed paint exploding on the ground close by. Eventually he reached a maze of low-lying huts designed to resemble a shanty town.

Unlike a real-world shanty made from scrap, the sanitised Fort Reagan version comprised concrete sheds with electricity, water and sewage. The closely packed accommodation didn't afford much privacy, but in many ways it resembled the college dorms the residents were used to.

Music blasted from all directions and barefoot girls danced around a bonfire built in the area's baked earth marketplace. To give a more authentic atmosphere, food in the shanty was sold from market stalls and the engineers' unit which ran Fort Reagan even released chickens and goats into the streets for the two-week duration of each exercise. Most of them were tame and the college kids fed them corn chips.

The partying left the back streets deserted. James took several turns before ducking into an alleyway between huts and catching his breath. He looked about suspiciously, but no American troops had followed him into the area.

He pulled his radio out of his jacket. 'Kazakov,' he whispered.

'Loud and clear, James,' the Ukrainian answered. 'How's it going?'

'The goods are in place, but we had to fight our way out. Sarge got shot and I'm gonna need some backup out here to make it home.'

'Negative,' Kazakov said. 'We don't need you here and you could easily be followed in the dark. It's best to steer clear of the apartments until daylight.'

James tutted. 'So what do you expect me to do? Where am I gonna sleep?'

'Use your initiative; I've got enough on my plate. Kazakov out.'

The way Kazakov said *out* made it pretty clear that he didn't want to hear from James before morning.

'Unbelievable,' James mumbled to himself. 'After everything I've done for that Russian git.'

While James' weapons afforded some protection, the combination of youth and badly fitting US army clothing made it impossible to blend in. It was going to be a long night and he had to find somewhere to hide quickly.

*

As soon as the drones were disabled, Kazakov radioed his SAS teams. They climbed into preselected rooftop positions with sniper rifles and began taking pot shots at the American soldiers.

He led Lauren, Bethany, Rat, Gabrielle, Bruce, Jake and Andy on a rapid march away from the airfield and towards the apartments. They were heavily armed and they shot first when they eyed an army checkpoint, taking out three soldiers with bullets and paint grenades and scaring the hell out of half a dozen civilians queuing for a random search.

The soldiers struggled with conflicting demands. They'd been sent out to make friends with civilians, but suddenly faced bullets whizzing down from rooftops and paint grenades being lobbed at them from balconies.

Every soldier knew that ten per cent of the population was getting paid extra to support the insurgency and the banter between troops and civilians quickly got replaced by suspicion. It might only be a training exercise, but every soldier had a real-world incentive to do well: a good performance could lead to promotion and the higher wages that came with it, a bad one to a stagnant career or even redeployment to a less prestigious back up unit.

Within twenty minutes of the attack on the drones, General Shirley had ordered dozens of extra checkpoints to stop insurgents from moving about freely. In the most troubled areas soldiers announced curfews and told everyone to get indoors.

Many college-age civilians had been drinking and got aggressive because they didn't want to be shut up inside bland apartments at eight-thirty in the evening. They faced being stopped and searched by angry troops for the second or third time in a matter of hours and even though it wasn't for real, people got angry having to queue at a checkpoint for ten minutes just so they could walk to the next street to visit a friend or buy groceries.

Kazakov's detached house was vulnerable to a surprise

raid, so he joined the kids in the comparative anonymity of the apartment block. Sweating and breathless, everyone piled into the girls' apartment, threw down their equipment packs and sprawled over the furniture.

'How's my eyes and ears?' Kazakov asked, as Kevin came out of a back bedroom with binoculars hanging around his neck.

'Good,' Kevin smiled, although he was still upset that he hadn't been allowed on the main raid with all the others. 'A team came into this building searching door to door. I ran down to the third floor and set up a booby trap with the paint grenade like you showed me. Took out all three of them.'

'Nice work,' Kazakov nodded. 'And the SAS snipers?'

'Seems to be working out,' Kevin nodded. 'They shot up all the soldiers hanging out near the canteen and grenaded the roadblocks until they all pulled out of the area. I haven't seen any army for over half an hour.'

Meryl came through from the kitchen holding a plastic tray stacked with steaming pizza slices. 'Where's the other two?' she asked, as the kids all grabbed food.

'Kerry and Sarge are dead. James is hiding out.'

'Shall I save some food for him?' Meryl asked.

Kazakov shook his head. 'I've told him to hide out overnight in case he's being tailed.'

'He sounded really pissed off when Mr Kaz told him,' Bethany grinned.

'More pizza for us,' Jake smiled, as he grabbed a second slice.

'What about all this equipment?' Lauren asked. 'We're

sitting ducks if the army starts searching this building.'

'We sit tight,' Kazakov said firmly, as he pulled a small video receiver out of his trouser pocket. 'We keep all the weapons here. Someone will have to keep lookout on the front and rear exits. If the army shows up for some reason, we should have time to mount an ambush on the staircases before they get close.'

The apartment had a wall-mounted TV with a protective Perspex screen over it.

'This should be good,' Kazakov said, grinning like a kid with sherbet as he ran an AV lead from the receiver to the TV. He cursed the remote until he found a button that brought up a grainy colour image. It looked like the edge of a desk and a couple of blurry computer screens set at a slanted angle. A date and timecode scrolled at the bottom of the image.

'Nice camerawork, Spielberg,' Jake grinned.

'I only had a few seconds to position the device,' Kazakov said irritably. 'Shut up and listen.'

The hard disk in Kazakov's receiver could store several hundred hours of video. He set the recording to play back from a couple of minutes before they'd blown up the drones. The TV showed a pair of army boots resting on the desktop and what sounded like a game of poker being played by bored admin officers out of shot on the other side of the room.

The kids gathered around the screen, holding cans of Pepsi and stuffing the last of the pizza as the report of the raid on the aerodrome came in. The picture was fixed on the tabletop and the fuzzy screens, but audio quality was excellent.

Boots ran in and out. A soldier announced that the shit was about to hit the fan and then General Shirley came running in.

'*Gimme status*,' he shouted.

'*One of the drone pilots radioed, sir. They're under attack. The drones are being destroyed by a group of masked teenagers*.'

'*Pardon me?*'

'*The drones, General. They're used for–*'

'*I know what they're used for, Corporal! Do you think I'm some kind of asshole? Get troops up there now to investigate. If it's insurgents I want them nailed*.'

'*Drones ain't cheap*,' the corporal continued. '*Haven't you deployed a security team up at the aerodrome?*'

There was a prolonged silence.

A new voice: '*General . . . What do you want us to do?*'

'*Goddammit!*' the general raved. '*They're supposed to be acting like insurgents! They're supposed to be on the streets planting paint grenades, not coming through the front door and destroying my aerodrome. What kind of insurgency is this supposed to be?*'

'*Had a lot of incoming mortar fire on all of our bases when I was in Iraq*,' the corporal noted. '*Insurgents will attack anything if it's improperly defended*.'

'*Corporal, you are* dismissed,' General Shirley shouted. '*When I want your opinions I'll ask for them. Kazakov, that son of a bitch! There's over six million dollars of hardware up there . . .*'

A phone rang once before a woman answered. '*General, it's Sean O'Halloran, the base commander*,' she said. '*He wants to know if you're aware that explosions have been heard inside the aerodrome–*'

'*I'm busy . . . A head-on assault on my base. That Russian . . .*

OK, these are my orders. Checkpoints on every main street. Screw being Mr Nice American. Get every able-bodied soldier out of this base and cracking heads. I want weapons seized and insurgents arrested or shot.'

The woman spoke again. '*The base commander is demanding to speak with you, General. He says you're personally responsible for any hardware entrusted to your men during this exercise.'*

'*Hand me that phone,*' the general ordered. '*Commander, we're investigating the situation and I'm sure it's not as serious as it sounds.'*

As the general spoke into the phone, a new voice sounded across the room. '*General, we're receiving reports that our troops are coming under sniper fire throughout the streets of Reaganistan.'*

Kazakov paused the playback and smiled at the kids perched on the furniture around him. 'I'm not Russian – I'm bloody *Ukrainian*,' he shouted, before erupting into a booming laugh. 'I don't give out praise often, but you kids were great tonight. This time tomorrow, we'll be driving a victory parade through General Shirley's precious base.'

28. STALK

James used the darkness, a casual demeanour and his US Army uniform to bluff his way through a checkpoint on the main thoroughfare out of the shanty town while the officer running the show seemed more concerned with grilling a twenty-year-old student about his contraband camera phone than bothering with James' ID.

He ended up in a three-storey shell building less than a kilometre from the apartments. James couldn't turn on the electric lights because they'd be spotted in the darkness, so he navigated to a second-floor room by torchlight. There was a cold water tap on the wall and a toilet with hundreds of dead insects floating inside on the landing.

There was no furniture, so he sat on the sandy concrete floor as cold desert wind howled through badly fitted doors and windows. He rearranged the contents of his backpack to try and make a pillow, but it was rock hard. In any case he was too tense to sleep.

Every so often an American Hummer would drive by in the narrow street outside and he'd hear shoot-outs between regular soldiers and SAS snipers, or the dull blast of a paint grenade. Judging by the amount of fighting, the Special Forces teams were also arming insurgent sympathisers.

However hard James tried there was no way he could doze on bare concrete, and grains of sand down his back and inside his boxers were driving him bananas. He'd filled his canteen from the tap, but he was hungry and he rummaged inside his pack for something to eat. There was no food, but he did find a little hotel gift bag with the pack of cards and the *Ultimate Blackjack Manual* he'd bought the day before.

There were bulbs ablaze in some apartment blocks two streets away. James shuffled up near to the windows where the pages caught the stray light. He blew away the sand on the floor between his legs, spread his cards out and started to read.

After a couple of chapters devoted to basic blackjack strategy and some short biographies of 'Blackjack Hall of Fame' members who'd *made fortunes and were now banned from every casino in the world*, James passed on to chapters detailing the mathematics and strategies used by the most successful card counters.

Most people would have given up on seeing the first simple equation, but James' inner maths geek liked the idea that you could actually use mental arithmetic and a few relatively simple strategies to beat a casino and win millions of dollars.

As James read more he realised that card counting didn't even require you to be brilliant at maths. What it required was the ability to keep count of five things at once: the dealer's current hand, your current hand, the running count of high and low cards, the total number of cards left in the card shoe and finally – if you wanted an extra edge – a separate count of the number of aces left in the deck.

According to the book, anyone practising with a pack of cards a couple of hours a day could master basic card-counting skills within a few days. James already understood standard blackjack strategy in terms of when to stick and when to ask the dealer for an extra card. The next step was to practise the rapid dealing of blackjack hands, trying to play with perfect strategy while keeping a basic count of every card dealt.

James began to flick the cards down on the concrete between his legs, starting off slowly and building up speed as he got a feel for it. There was no rush: it was ten hours until sun-up and four and a half years until he'd be old enough to sit at a casino table.

*

'Morning, knob-head!'

James' head hurt as he opened his eyes and jerked forward. The low sun blitzed his retinas and he half expected to find the muzzle of a gun in his face. Much to his relief, his eyes eventually focused on Gabrielle's pencil thin legs in a pair of running shorts.

'What's with the cards?' she asked.

'That's my brother,' Lauren smirked. 'Always playing with himself.'

James hadn't had anything like a full night's sleep and it took him a few seconds to suss everything out: his neck ached because he'd fallen asleep sitting against a concrete wall while dealing cards. Lauren and Gabrielle were here because he'd radioed the coordinates on his GPS through to Kazakov the night before. The girls had come out to meet him because he needed a set of civilian clothes before he could move safely in daylight.

'How's things?' James asked, holding his back and groaning as he stood up.

'Kazakov's on cloud nine because the army is on the run. The drones are wiped out, General Shirley is going psycho in his command post, changing his orders every few hours, running around like a headless chicken and generally making sure that he never gets a second star on his helmet.

'The SAS have recruited and armed sixty bored college kids and wiped out more than a hundred and fifty US troops. Oh, and Andy gave Bethany a massive love bite.'

This last piece of information made James laugh. 'What a slapper! How many boys has she snogged?'

Lauren tactfully ignored the jab at her best friend and picked James' book off the floor. '*The Ultimate Blackjack Manual*,' she snorted. 'Gimme a break. You don't seriously think you can beat the casinos do you?'

'It's a proven technique,' James said, snatching his book back.

'All credit though,' Lauren grinned. 'It's the first time I've seen you with a book that doesn't have pop-ups.'

'Why, you're *so* funny this morning,' James said sarcastically, as Gabrielle handed over a set of his clothes. 'Did you have a tough time getting over here?'

'We picked our moment,' Gabrielle explained. 'The bug Kazakov placed in the army control room means we know what orders the troops are getting before they do. General Shirley gave orders to step down the checkpoints because our snipers kept picking them off and lobbing paint grenades at them.'

'The only trouble is, we couldn't get you on your radio,' Lauren complained. 'Deaf git.'

'Sorry,' James yawned. 'Earpiece must have fallen out while I was sleeping.'

'The Americans don't like it,' Lauren grinned. 'One of the General's criteria for success is minimum civilian casualties. Every time an explosion goes off at a checkpoint half a dozen civilians end up getting blasted.'

James spoke admiringly as he swapped his army kit for ripped jeans and battered Adidas running shoes. 'Kazakov's a natural born warmonger. I mean, he may be psycho but you've got to have a certain admiration for the guy.'

'He hates the Yanks *so* much,' Lauren nodded. 'I think he wishes that the weapons were real.'

*

Inevitably the Americans had uncovered some caches of weapons, brought some insurgents in for questioning and inflicted a few casualties in more than twelve hours of intense cat-and-mouse through the streets of Reaganistan.

As soon as General Shirley gave the order for his troops to retreat to base, Kazakov – who'd slept for less than an hour – gave orders for all the insurgents to change positions. Instead of meeting up at the apartments, Lauren and Gabrielle took James to Kazakov's detached house.

They stopped off at one of the small supermarkets along the way and spent fifteen Reaganistan dollars on bacon, ready-made pancake batter, orange juice, icing sugar, Nutella, aerosol cream and maple syrup so that Lauren could make breakfast.

Rat, Bethany and Andy had already arrived at the house with a cache of weapons, while Mac was being guarded by a five-man SAS team in the house next door. Gabrielle offered to help make the pancakes, but Lauren enjoyed cooking and said she didn't want anyone to see her secret recipe.

Gabrielle ended up on one of two large couches in the living-room, facing James.

'Comfy,' James yawned, as he lay on the couch and wriggled about to scratch his back. 'Sand gets everywhere.'

'It's inside the buildings and you can't keep it out because none of the doors and windows are properly fitted,' Gabrielle said, as she caught on to James' yawn. 'Had a shower at the apartment last night. Put on clean clothes, but ten minutes later I'm scratching like crazy.'

'Tell me about it,' James nodded.

'You'll tear all your skin off,' Gabrielle warned, as she stepped over to James. 'Let me do it.'

James sat up as Gabrielle came over. She laid her palm on the back of James' shirt and rubbed it up and down.

'Ooooh, that's the spot,' James purred. 'I'll shower after breakfast, if I can stay awake that long.'

'So how are you dealing with stuff?' Gabrielle asked. 'I mean, over Dana.'

This was awkward. James knew that Michael and Dana going off with each other had hurt Gabrielle more deeply than it had hurt him.

'I thought something was up,' James said. 'One day everything was fine: had a big bash for my sixteenth birthday and the next few weeks we were like a couple of randy rabbits. Then all of a sudden Dana doesn't want me touching her and she's saying it's all too much.'

Gabrielle smiled. 'I didn't get that with Michael. I think he was quite happy to have two girls on the go at once! I was on campus, so I knew he was spending time with Dana. But when I confronted him he said I was being paranoid and that they were working on some history project together.'

'Babymaking project by the sound of things,' James grinned.

'I guess it's one to chalk up to experience,' Gabrielle sighed. 'But they say your first love is the hardest to get over and I really, really loved him.'

James reached up and touched Gabrielle's arm. 'You two were so close. Us lads did awards for all the girls one time and you won *girl most likely to get married first*.'

Gabrielle laughed. 'When was this?'

'Ages ago, like summertime or something. We were on one of those boring mission safety courses and all the lads started talking about girls and making up stupid categories.'

'What did everyone else get?'

'I probably shouldn't say,' James grinned. 'Amy Collins was *sexiest retired cherub*. Kerry got *best legs* and *hardest to get into bed*.'

'I'll tell Kerry that,' Gabrielle laughed.

'Bethany won the *best younger girl* category, although I voted for her in *girl you most want to smack in the mouth*,' James continued, knowing he was probably saying more than he should but delighted that he was making Gabrielle laugh.

'Did Dana get anything?'

'*Best tits*,' James nodded. 'I was dead proud.'

'You boys are so classy,' Gabrielle snorted, laughing so hard that she had to sit on the arm of the couch next to James. 'What else?'

'We came up with loads,' James grinned. 'But it was yonks ago. I can't remember all of it.'

'You're a funny guy, James,' Gabrielle said. 'I think that's why you get away with so much.'

'You know I've always liked you,' James said coyly, before reaching up to put his arm around Gabrielle's back. 'I mean we're both–'

'No, no, noooo!' Gabrielle shrieked, jumping out of the way before laughing even harder. 'Us girls were talking about you trying to get off with Kerry the other night. Lauren and Kerry *both* said you were such a randy git that it was only a matter of time before you hit on me.'

James felt the colour drain out of his face. 'Kerry told you about that?'

'You know girls,' Gabrielle said. 'We like our gossip.'

James looked serious. 'Does Bethany know? She's got a big trap and if Bruce finds out he'll kick my head in.'

Gabrielle shook her head. 'Just me and Lauren.'

'Pancakes,' Lauren said cheerily, as she came into the room holding two plates stacked with freshly cooked pancakes mounded with cream, sugar and chocolate spread. 'What's so funny?'

Gabrielle pointed at James, before roaring with laughter again. 'Guess what he did?'

'I told you,' Lauren shrieked, as she handed James his plate and a knife and fork. 'Five minutes alone with anything vaguely female . . .'

James was embarrassed, but he was also starving hungry and the orangey smell rising from Lauren's calorie-packed pancakes made his stomach growl.

'Oh he's sulking now,' Lauren teased, as James stared down at his plate. 'Poor little lamb.'

James had made a complete tit of himself and was smart enough to know that anything he said to defend himself now would only put him deeper in the hole.

'Nice pancakes, sis,' he said, trying to ignore the giggling and hoping that they couldn't see him blushing.

'I wish I had my phone to text Kerry,' Gabrielle snorfled. 'She's going to *love* this.'

29. ICE

After a 4,000-calorie pancake breakfast and a shower, James found pillows and a duvet in a wardrobe upstairs and crashed out on a squeaky-framed bed. His body clock had barely adjusted to American time and losing a night's sleep was the last thing he'd needed.

The sun was bright and the curtains tissue-paper thin. James buried his head but still couldn't sleep. He ended up putting his earpiece back in and passing three restless hours listening to communications between the exuberant Kazakov and his various teams.

Because the checkpoints had proved so vulnerable to attack from grenades and snipers, General Shirley's latest strategy was based around snap searches: well armed convoys of open-topped Hummers would halt outside a building, troops would steam inside, force everyone to lie face down on the floor and then search for weapons, radios or any other sign that they were part of the insurgency. This strategy was effective at unearthing enemies and their weapons but the suspicion and rough handling by the soldiers didn't win many friends amongst the civilians.

'Everyone's going down the road to get burgers in a minute,' Rat said, stepping into James' room without knocking. 'You coming?'

James peeked from under the duvet and checked his watch: it was just gone noon. 'Who's everyone?'

Rat shrugged. 'Lauren, Jake, Bethany and me.'

'Gabrielle?'

'Nope,' Rat said, breaking into a smile. 'Kaz sent her out on some op with Bruce. I heard you'd made a tit of yourself. Is that why you're looking like a wet weekend?'

'Along with a few other things,' James moaned, as he threw off his duvet and grabbed his jeans.

'What have you got to be miserable about?' Rat asked.

'Where to start,' James said. 'My anti-terrorist mission went belly up, Dana dumped me, I've got a blinding headache 'cos I missed a whole night's sleep and apparently every girl on CHERUB campus thinks I'm a dickhead.'

Rat fought back the urge to smile. 'Not *all* of them.'

'I'm ice cold,' James complained, as he stuffed his feet into his trainers and looked around for the Velcro wallet with his Reaganistan dollars in it. 'Dana dumped me, Kerry doesn't want me back, Gabrielle doesn't fancy me and even the random babe I chatted up in the casino shop started taking the piss out of me . . .'

'Yeah right,' Rat said. 'You have *such* problems with the ladies. You've had a girlfriend practically since the day you arrived on campus, plus loads more on missions. Thinking about it, *that's* probably half your problem.'

'Eh?' James said.

'You know,' Rat shrugged. 'Imagine you're a prospective

girlfriend. Everyone on campus knows what you're like. You cheated on Kerry about six times then dumped her–'

'It wasn't six,' James interrupted. 'Three . . . Four tops.'

'Then you got off with Dana and slept with some random girl the first time you were out of her sight. I mean, a girl like Gabrielle knows your reputation and she's not gonna be looking at you and thinking you're great boyfriend material, is she?'

'S'pose,' James said. 'Although why I'm taking advice from someone who fancies Lauren is frankly beyond me.'

'Fine, ignore me,' Rat said smugly, as they started heading down the stairs. 'But I'm telling you, with your reputation you're gonna have to work hard if you want to get anywhere with any girl on campus.'

'I'll have to rely on good looks and charm then,' James smirked, putting on his watch as they headed into the main hallway.

'What charm?' Lauren asked from the bottom of the front staircase. 'I've stepped in turds with more charm than you.'

'Took your time, didn't you?' Jake complained, as he opened the front door. 'I'm absolutely starving.'

Jake was alarmed by the sight of three Hummers filled with soldiers pulling up outside. 'Holy shit!' he gasped, slamming the door shut.

'Don't move!' a soldier shouted over a PA system built into one of the Hummers. 'Remain calm!'

'If James hadn't taken so long we'd have been out of here already,' Bethany said.

'Jake, you're cutest,' Lauren said, instinctively taking

charge. 'Answer the door, act scared and stall 'em for as long as you can.'

The house was stuffed with guns and equipment, so there was no way to hide their links with the insurgency. In real life the threat of a dozen highly-trained US soldiers might have brought on a surrender, but as they were only facing simulated rounds the five cherubs pulled on their goggles and prepared for a rumble.

James and Rat bolted back up the staircase. Lauren and Bethany ran into the kitchen to grab their rifles as Jake cautiously opened the front door.

'Why'd you close the door?' a major in mirrored sunglasses barked. 'Who else is in there?'

Jake put on his best scared little boy act. 'I'm alone, sir. My dad's out buying cheeseburgers.'

'Don't worry, boy,' the major smiled, resting a paw on Jake's shoulder. 'We've got a job to do, but we'll be in and out in a flash.'

Three more soldiers were running up the driveway, while squads of four ran around the back of the house on either side.

'Come in then I suppose,' Jake said sheepishly.

Upstairs, James and Rat found their packs. They tooled up with grenades and clipped fresh magazines into their rifles. They had to keep low so that they couldn't be seen by the soldiers running around the back of the house.

'I'm counting twelve men,' James whispered, as he bobbed up to glance out of the window. 'I'll cover the staircase, you shoot from up here.'

Lauren and Bethany made similar preparations in the kitchen.

'You've got nothing to be scared of, son,' the major said calmly, as he nudged Jake down the hallway and through to the living-room. 'But I need you to kneel on the floor with your hands on your head.'

Three colleagues rushed in after the major with their guns raised. One followed the major into the living-room, one headed back towards the kitchen, while the third started creeping up the stairs.

'Radio,' a lieutenant said anxiously, as he spotted someone's headset on the floor.

The major glanced at it suspiciously, before eyeballing Jake and speaking in a much firmer tone. 'Does that belong to your father?'

Jake scrambled for an excuse. 'I was playing outside and found it in the street.'

'You don't say?' the leader said happily, bending over to pick it off the floor. 'We've been on the lookout for one of these so we can hear what our enemies are talking about.'

Jake was on edge, knowing that things might kick off any second. The soldiers all had guns, the other cherubs all had guns and he didn't fancy being stuck in the middle when the shooting started. His only hope was a pistol he could see holstered under the major's jacket.

The first sign of trouble was the near simultaneous blast of two paint grenades in the back garden. Lauren and Bethany had pulled pins and dropped them silently through a vent in the kitchen window, before ducking down behind the cabinets.

Four soldiers were hit by the flying paint. As two more stood dumbly and inspected their clothing to see whether they were alive or not, Lauren stood up behind the counter and took them out with well aimed blasts. Bethany spun around and shot the guard who'd come along the hallway.

Upstairs, Rat took aim through a back window and shot one soldier, but narrowly missed the last man standing as he vaulted over a hedge and made a run for it. At the same instant, James poked his rifle between the banister rails and shot the soldier coming up the stairs.

Back in the living-room, Jake made his move. He wailed like the blast had frightened him and wrapped his arms around the major's leg. By the time the big man realised Jake's real intentions, the eleven-year-old had already grabbed the major's pistol and shot him from point blank range.

At that kind of range simulated bullets pack a real punch. The major bawled a torrent of swear words as he crumpled to the floor, clutching at his thigh. Simultaneously, James jumped the entire staircase and shot through the front door, hitting a soldier standing on the front lawn.

Bethany had continued down the hallway and covered Jake's back, aiming through the living-room doorway and shooting the last of the four men who'd come through the front door.

James was startled by the shot directly behind him and launched a vicious back kick that hit Bethany hard in the stomach. Before she could scream a warning, James spun around and shot her twice in the belly.

'Ooops,' James said, as Bethany writhed on the ground clutching her guts with the top half of her body streaming with chalky pink paint. 'Sorry.'

'You idiot,' Bethany groaned. 'Do I look like a soldier to you?'

'I think we got them all,' Jake gasped, as he ran into the hallway. He saw his sister on the lawn and burst out laughing. 'Oh dear!'

'Was that deliberate, James?' Bethany growled.

'Of course it wasn't,' James smirked. 'Just a happy accident.'

Bethany was tempted to shoot James back, but Mr Kazakov would have her running punishment laps if he found that she'd deliberately shot one of his team.

'Dead girls can't talk,' Jake said, as he pointed at the paint-spattered soldier lying silently on the lawn. 'See you in twenty-four hours.'

'Jake, I just saved your butt in case you didn't notice,' Bethany growled.

Lauren came out of the kitchen and Rat jogged down the hallway to see what was occurring.

'Pretty impressive,' Rat said. 'Eleven to one kill-ratio against trained soldiers.'

'Who got away?' James asked.

'One bloke scarpered away into the bushes,' Rat explained. 'I think he legged it, but we'd better not hang around 'cos he's bound to have called for backup.'

James was the senior agent and he had to make some decisions. 'Jake, Rat, booby trap the inside of the house and the Hummers with grenades,' he ordered. 'Lauren, go inside and pack up as many weapons as you can carry. I'll update Kazakov on the radio, then I'll be in to give you a hand.'

30. TREASURE

Bethany headed towards the proccssing facility to declare herself dead. The dead soldiers walked alongside and they were understandably curious about being taken down by a group of kids with British accents and expert marksmanship.

Bethany stuck to their prescribed back story: 'Our parents are military staff who live on a British cold-weather training facility in a remote region of Canada. There's not much to do, so our parents set up a cadet group where we all learn self defence and go paintballing on weekends.'

'No kidding,' the major smiled. 'That little brother of yours had me fooled. Almost shot me in the one place a man don't wanna be shot . . .'

As his comrades laughed, Bethany smiled and felt proud of Jake for probably the first time ever.

'This man Kazakov,' the major said. 'Have you seen him? None of us knows what he looks like.'

Bethany smiled coyly. 'You've gotta work harder than that to wheedle information out of me.'

One of the soldiers was dragging behind and the major looked back at him. 'You OK, Martin?'

'My stomach,' the soldier answered grimly. 'Feels like I've got a basketball lodged in my belly.'

'Know what you're saying,' a colleague nodded. 'I got the same. Must have eaten some bad chow in the mess hall last night.'

*

Jake, Lauren, Rat and James dumped their rifles and equipment back at the apartments before heading off to buy burgers. James dozed through the early part of the afternoon. He woke to find the apartment crowded: Gabrielle and Bruce were back from a sabotage operation, along with Mac and the four SAS toughs who'd been keeping him on the move and guarding him since the beginning of the exercise.

James headed into the kitchen. Everyone crowded around the breakfast bar, listening to a walkie-talkie.

'What's up?' he asked, opening the fridge and downing several mouthfuls from a four-pint carton of orange juice.

'We're monitoring the bug in the army command office,' Mac explained. 'Looks like your little experiment with the water supply is starting to have consequences.'

James wasn't sure about Kazakov's most extreme tactic and was decidedly uncomfortable about sharing the blame. 'I was following orders,' he said defensively. 'Sarge didn't even tell me what was going on until we were inside the base.'

'Remember history class? The Nazis on trial at Nuremburg,' Lauren grinned, before adopting a German accent. 'I was only following orders.'

'And the Nazis all got hanged,' Rat added.

Dark laughter erupted around the breakfast bar. James

looked to Mac for some reliable information. 'So what's going on right now?'

'We're arming sympathisers and making efforts to ambush the snatch squads. Over eighty American soldiers have reported sick already and men from all over are returning to base with stomach cramps.'

'Sarge told me twenty hours,' James said, glancing at his watch. 'So it's probably just the beginning.'

'Kazakov's chuffed to bits,' Mac nodded. 'He reckons up to ninety per cent of the American troops will be wiped out with diarrhoea and vomiting by six this evening. He's got insurgent sympathisers posting fliers inviting the entire population to a free booze-up in the shanty town.'

'That's right next to the army base,' James said, as the full ambition of Kazakov's plan became clear in his head. 'There's a thousand American troops. But over a hundred and fifty have been shot and if ninety per cent of what's left are sick that's gonna leave less than a hundred in fighting condition . . .'

'We're talking about full-scale revolution,' Jake grinned.

A gruff-voiced Welsh SAS officer spoke admiringly. 'I don't think the Yanks knew what they were letting themselves in for when they invited Kazakov to do red teaming. He was our main tactical consultant for a decade and I don't think anyone ever bested him, either in training or on a live operation.'

The youngest of Mac's guards nodded. 'The guy's been fighting wars since before I was born. It's criminal that they didn't make him our regimental commander.'

'Why didn't they?' James asked.

'Protocol,' the Welshman explained. 'Kazakov has only ever been a consultant. It would have ruffled a lot of feathers if they'd appointed an outsider. But the man's a tactical genius.'

As if on cue, Kazakov's voice came through their walkie-talkies. 'I need bodies,' he announced. 'Thirty-three beer kegs and two hundred bottles of vodka ain't gonna shift themselves.'

*

General Shirley had started off trying to make friends, then attempted to clamp down with roadblocks after the aerodrome attack. But without the drones providing aerial surveillance the roadblocks were vulnerable to snipers and paint grenades so he'd been forced into using snatch squads.

Casualties were lighter with this tactic. Insurgents were arrested and weapons seized, but with no permanent presence on the streets Kazakov's insurgents had freedom to move around setting ambushes, blockading roads and recruiting insurgent sympathisers.

War zones in the real world suffer from high unemployment and are filled with bored youngsters. The young men and women inside Fort Reagan were the same, with one TV channel and dwindling reserves of booze.

Most of those receiving the extra twenty dollars a day to support the insurgency were happy to take a rifle and receive basic military instruction from the teams of SAS officers, if for no other reason than that it was something to do. More than a hundred and fifty men and women had been armed and given basic tactical firearms training over the space of a day and a half.

Spies in the shanty town spotted convoys of troops leaving the nearby army base and as the day wore on the SAS officers trained insurgents in more advanced techniques, such as burying paint grenades close to roads and rigging lengths of wire so they're tripped when a vehicle passes over.

Under Fort Reagan rules any vehicle hit with a spot of paint more than ten centimetres in diameter was deemed to be disabled and the crew inside had to get out on foot.

By 6 p.m. the sun was dropping below distant sand bluffs and ambushed Hummers littered the streets. More than eighty additional troops had been shot for losses of less than half that number of insurgents.

Kazakov sheltered inside a concrete hut in the shanty town, listening to the bug in General Shirley's command post. The American was suffering stomach cramps and getting increasingly irate as more and more of his troops went down with diarrhoea. He'd even called base commander O'Halloran and asked that the exercise be abandoned because of a possible health scare, but the commander gave him short shrift: you can't abandon a real war if there's an outbreak of food poisoning, so why should you abandon an exercise?

In the central square of the shanty town more than a thousand young men and women had gathered to party around a huge bonfire. The thirty kegs of beer hadn't lasted long, but Kazakov had arranged a plentiful supply of wines and spirits. Rock music blasted, barbecued steaks were served in fresh baps and he'd even brought in a few fireworks.

Almost half the crowd were either armed insurgents or unarmed sympathisers. Normally it would have been unacceptably risky to gather so many poorly trained men and women together less than half a kilometre from a US Army base, but there weren't enough healthy troops left to take any action.

The only sign of an army presence was an occasional rapid drive-by, with the driver circling the shanty town at his vehicle's maximum 15 mph speed, while two men in the back surveyed the situation with night-vision binoculars.

James and the rest of the cherubs hung out in a big group just off the main square. Young men were flirting, dancing and joining long queues for the rapidly diminishing supplies of alcohol. Many of them carried their weapons openly and a few of the drunkest even took aim at the fireworks.

'Need a slash,' James said, crushing a plastic beer cup and strolling away from the gang.

After the restful afternoon he felt brighter than he'd done all day as he cut away from the square between rows of near-identical huts. The alleyways were crammed compared to the night before when he'd passed through in his stolen officer's uniform.

He found a staircase cut into the rock, which led up to an elevated area of the shanty town. Three men urinated against the stone sides and a huge lake of piss had collected behind a nearby hut. The residents wouldn't be happy when they got home, but there was nowhere else to go so James unzipped and joined the fray.

As James strolled back to the party an attractive blonde stepped in front of him and asked if he knew anywhere she could get more to drink.

'Queues are a nightmare,' James said, eyeing the girl with

her tight fitting shorts and blue and white striped top. Her shoulders were broad and she had a big bust and nice legs; but she looked at least twenty so James figured she was out of his league.

'I've had enough,' the girl said, stumbling forwards and grabbing James by his arm. 'I'm horny.'

'That's an unusual name,' James said.

She smiled girlishly and tapped her varnished index finger on her chin. 'You can call me that if you like, but my real name's Cindi-Lou.'

'I'm James.'

'You're pretty cute, young James,' she said, stepping forwards so that her breasts almost touched James' chest. 'How about we go and do something your mommy wouldn't approve of?'

James cracked a huge involuntary smile as the girl put her hand around the back of his neck and pulled him into a kiss. After all the female-related trauma of the past few weeks it was exactly the tonic his damaged ego needed. Lust pulsed through his body as he imagined getting his hands on female flesh.

'How far's your hut?' James asked excitably, reaching across and putting his hand on Cindi's bum.

'Not far at all,' she smiled.

James noticed Bruce heading by to take a pee as Cindi grabbed his hand and started leading him off. Bruce didn't utter a word, but his expression clearly said *you jammy bastard*.

'You remind me of a guy I dated in high school,' Cindi said. 'Cute face and a nice ass. I did stuff to that guy that would make your eyes pop out!'

James had an ear-to-ear grin. His cold streak was over. He was *still* James Adams and there were at least three condoms in the back of his wallet. He could hardly believe his luck as he followed the attractive butt down a cobbled alleyway. Maybe her shoulders were a bit on the manly side, but you can't have everything . . .

They ducked through a low door into a gloomy one-room hut.

'Cosy,' James smiled.

But Cindi didn't smile back. A dark figure slammed the door shut as Cindi snatched James' wrist and twisted it hard behind his back. He struggled but she'd taken him by surprise and pulled his arm into an excruciating lock.

'You kick me and I'll break it,' Cindi screamed.

As the light came on, James' legs were kicked away and his body slammed face down on to a laminate-topped dining table. He saw two women in army uniform. The oldest one moved in swiftly and locked a set of handcuffs behind his back.

Cindi smiled as she turned James on to his back. 'I left something out,' she smiled, suddenly neither horny nor drunk. 'I'm *Sergeant* Cindi-Lou Jones, United States Army Intelligence Corps. These other two fine ladies are Corporal Land and Lieutenant Sahlin.'

James smiled and tried to sound cool. 'So I suppose a shag's now totally out of the question?'

Sahlin was the oldest and meanest looking of the three soldiers: olive skinned, with a hairy chin. She moved in and punched James in the kidneys. 'A smart mouth can land a boy in a lot of trouble.'

'We've got rules here!' James shouted indignantly. 'You can arrest and interrogate me, but you can't use force.'

Jones tugged James' trousers and boxers down with a single violent movement. 'If you don't cooperate, boy, we might just be spilling a nice hot cup of coffee down there on your intimate parts.'

'You let the mask over your face slip and we identified you from the surveillance cams on base,' Jones explained, as she pulled off her striped top, revealing a sweaty green combat vest underneath it. 'General Shirley's looking at a career nosedive if this operation doesn't start going his way. He's authorised us to bend the rules if we feel it necessary.'

'You'd better start talking,' Sahlin added. 'Intel-ops officers like me are trained in about a million different ways to hurt little boys like you without leaving a mark.'

'How come you're not on the toilet with the rest of the Yanks?' James asked.

'The intelligence officers live and eat in a separate building on the far side of the base,' Sahlin smiled. 'Seems your Mr Kazakov missed a trick for once.'

Corporal Land was the smallest of the three women. She spoke with a sweet voice like a country and western singer. 'Ya know what, girlfriends? How about we take James back to all them soldiers, release him in the middle of our base and tell our boys that he's the one what made 'em so sick.'

'For god's sake,' James shouted. 'This is a training exercise. You're not allowed to do this!'

'Yosyp Kazakov is making a lot of important people look *real* bad,' Land smiled. 'We don't like that one little bit.'

James watched as Lieutenant Sahlin pulled a sinister-looking metal probe out of her shirt pocket.

'Honey,' Corporal Land said sweetly, moving in close and dabbing James' sweating brow with a tissue. 'You'd better start telling us some things we want to hear. 'Cos when the lieutenant's little probe heats up and gets shoved where the sun don't shine, you're gonna know *all* about it.'

31. PATRIOTS

Lauren, Jake, Kevin, Rat and Gabrielle all charged forward into the packed square as Kazakov drove through the crowd, standing in the back of a captured Hummer.

'The enemy is weakened,' Kazakov bellowed. 'Soon the final attack will be upon us. Victory is in sight!'

The crowd didn't know what to make of this burly man with a weird accent and two days' worth of stubble.

'I know what you're thinking,' Kazakov said. 'You are all Americans. You love America because it's the greatest country in the world!'

The young and drunk crowd around the Hummer loved this. There were some cheers and rifle shots fired into the air.

Twenty metres back, Lauren turned to Rat and smiled. 'Now we can add "world-class bullshitter" to "tactical genius" on Kazakov's résumé.'

'I know some of you aren't comfortable with the idea of fighting American troops,' Kazakov continued, 'but what we do here this evening will help our army to fight better in future. When the bullets are metal instead of compressed chalk, when the grenades are high explosive not fluorescent paint, American troops will be better prepared.

'What we do here will save the lives of real Americans fighting against evil all around the world. It's the patriotic duty of every insurgent to ready your weapons and prepare for the final assault on the army base. Are you ready to kick some butt?'

A moderate cheer ripped through the crowd.

'Let me also remind you,' Kazakov went on, 'you have all signed two-week contracts for this training exercise. If we win this final battle, the exercise will be over and you'll all receive over eleven hundred dollars for two days' work!'

Patriotic pride had done its bit, but this appeal direct to the wallet had a much greater effect. Cheers and screams roared through the crowd.

'Are we ready to attack the base?' Kazakov shouted.

A blast of *yeses* ripped through the crowd.

'Are we ready to kick some butt?' Kazakov repeated, followed by more cheers. 'Let's get up there and storm the base!'

The frenzied crowd started surging out of the square.

'Don't forget to wear your goggles and god bless the United States of America!' Kazakov shouted.

One of the SAS men changed the music playing over the PA system to the US Marine Hymn. A Scotsman punched his fist in the air and started a chant of *USA, USA* as Kazakov's Hummer crawled through the crowd towards the edge of the square.

'Victory!' Kazakov shouted. 'Victory!'

The crowd was moving out of the square in several

different directions. Many were just here for the booze and headed for home, but the two hundred SAS men and insurgents were emboldened with drink and patriotism and began charging between the lines of huts.

Lauren reached around to grab her rifle out of her pack. 'Where have James and Bruce got to?' she asked impatiently.

'I'm right here,' Bruce answered, hurrying towards the scene and grabbing his pack from Jake. 'Ready to bust heads, Brucey style.'

'So where the hell's James?' Gabrielle asked, glancing at her watch. 'He went for a slash before you did.'

'I saw him with a piece of tail,' Bruce said. 'Hand on her butt. Looked like they were heading off to some hut in the back streets for a bit of fun.'

'You what?' Lauren gasped. 'It's the final assault!'

Rat grinned admiringly. 'Can you believe that guy? Was she hot?'

'Nice T and A,' Bruce nodded. 'Bit butch for my taste, but I wouldn't say no.'

Lauren was irritated at the way they were discussing women and scowled severely at Bruce. 'I'll be sure to mention your comments to Kerry when we meet up.'

'I'm just saying that she was hot.'

'I hate him,' Rat said, smiling enviously. 'I bet James is in some hut right now, bouncing around on top of some bimbo– OWW!'

'It's not funny,' Lauren growled. 'I'm gonna have words with James. The way he carries on he's gonna end up catching some disease and having his willy drop off . . .'

*

James was spread-eagled over the dining table, with his shorts and trousers around his ankles and his hands cuffed behind his back. He didn't doubt that an army intelligence officer knew how to inflict severe pain if she wanted to. The question was, was Lieutenant Sahlin bluffing? Had General Shirley really got so desperate that he'd authorised his staff to use torture? There were now only two women in the room with him – Corporal Land had been sent out to investigate the loud civilian cheering.

'Tell us exactly what you did inside the base.'

James turned his head to one side and grinned. 'Shouldn't a nice girl like you be home baking cakes and having babies?'

'Cute,' Sahlin said, as she pressed James' head against the table top and swept the tip of the probe across his cheek. There was a sharp hiss and James' whole body shot into spasm. His nose filled with a burning smell from the singed stubble on his cheek.

'You can't do this,' James yelled. 'I'm sixteen years old. I'm here with a British cadet group—'

'Shut your damn hole,' Sahlin ordered. 'I only touched your stubble. Now you start talking, because I've cracked tougher nuts than you, bucko. What did you do inside the base?'

James tried to think. Maybe they were bluffing and wouldn't hurt him badly, but he didn't fancy finding out for the sake of a training exercise.

'We put some drug in the water tank,' James explained.

Sahlin smiled. 'What drug?'

'Some really complicated name,' James said nervously, having genuinely forgotten. 'The packaging is probably still in the bin inside the services building. It's pretty toxic stuff, so we sealed it all into a zip-lock bag with our masks and stuff.'

'And this drug is what's causing all the tummy trouble.'

'That's why we did it,' James nodded.

'Is there an antidote?'

'Do I look like a pharmacist?' James asked.

Sahlin thought about this for a second before changing tack. 'What are Kazakov's plans?'

'Can't you work that out for yourself?' James snorted.

Sahlin used the probe to singe some of the hairs on James' bare bum.

'*Chrrrrist*,' he shouted. 'Cut that out! I'm cooperating aren't I?'

'I don't like your attitude,' Sahlin explained. 'Kazakov's plan: tell me everything you know, now!'

'Steam through the front gates while you're all doubled up on the toilet,' James smiled. 'That's the plan and you can't do squat about it.'

Sahlin looked up at the sergeant. 'Jones, call base. Get someone to go find that packaging in the services building and identify the contents. Make sure General Shirley knows we have confirmed intelligence of an all-out attack.'

James overheard as Sergeant Jones spoke into her walkie-talkie. The reply came through the loudspeaker laden with sarcasm:

'Good to hear Army Intelligence is keeping us informed. Tell Lieutenant Sahlin that if she wasn't on the ball we might not have noticed the two-hundred-strong armed mob currently trying to smash through our front gates. If it's not too much trouble, maybe you could get your butts up here and help us out.'

'Insurgent pigs,' Sahlin shouted. 'Didn't I send Land out to investigate all that cheering and shouting?'

James couldn't help laughing and earned a punch in the back for his trouble.

'Maybe they shot her,' Jones said anxiously.

'This is just great!' Sahlin sighed, before slapping James hard on his bare arse. 'Looks like you're not the only one who got caught with your pants down, bucko! We'd better shift out of here.'

Sahlin and Jones grabbed their rifles and packs.

'What about our handsome little captive?' Jones asked.

Sahlin smiled as she placed the handcuff key on the table in front of James' mouth.

'Ah come on,' James complained. 'How am I gonna get them off with my hands behind my back?'

Sahlin smiled. 'Bucko, do I look like a woman who gives a shit?'

Jones had picked up James' pack. 'He's better armed than us,' Jones noted, as she clipped grenades from James' pack to her belt. 'You want any of this, Lieutenant?'

'Pass me a paint grenade,' Sahlin said, smiling nastily as she dangled the grenade in front of James' eyes before pulling out the pin with her teeth. 'You're a real nasty piece of work, bucko. Putting that drug in the water supply. Some very good friends of mine are in a bad way.'

With that, Sahlin wedged the grenade down the back of James' T-shirt before snatching her pack off the floor.

'Nighty night, Bucko,' Sahlin smiled, flicking off the

light switch and slamming the metal door of the hut. 'Have a blast.'

'Bitch,' James shouted, as he jumped frantically to his feet in pitch darkness.

His trousers were around his ankles, his hands were cuffed behind his back and no matter how much he wriggled the grenade wouldn't budge. It would go off in under ten seconds.

32. ATTACK

Sending a posse of two hundred insurgents to the military compound's well defended front gates might seem suicidal, but Kazakov had already sent two pairs of SAS men into the base to soften things up.

As Kazakov's Hummer approached, the first team cut the power lines from the main generator, plunging the entire US base into darkness. Simultaneously, the second team triggered a sequence of jerry-rigged paint grenades taking out the three able-bodied guards on the gate.

Kazakov's Hummer charged through, smashing the gates apart before cruising on towards the front doors of the command and control building. The following pack of insurgents continued to chant *USA, USA* as they poured into the camp.

Half were untrained insurgents who'd only been given guns within the last few hours. The remainder comprised crack teams led by SAS officers and each was tasked with securing a strategic location within the base, such as the communications centre, or the hospital.

Bruce, Jake, Rat and Gabrielle moved with a small

team of insurgents led by the Welsh SAS officer they'd chatted to back at the apartment earlier that afternoon. Their target was the main weapons-storage locker, which was expected to be one of the toughest buildings on the base to secure. But a different picture emerged as the group raced through the darkness over the wooden boards between the accommodation tents.

Men could be heard groaning desperately in their beds. Others stooped in the canvas doorways looking like sweaty ghosts. None of them cared about the base being under attack and a nauseating acidic stench hung in the air.

The base's sewers had been unable to cope with more than six hundred cases of diarrhoea. Toilets had backed up and men had resorted to using everything from buckets to hastily dug holes in the sand and even their own helmets. Once used the articles were thrown outside.

'I'm gonna spew,' Gabrielle complained, zipping her combat jacket and burying her nose under the fabric.

'This is beyond nasty,' Rat said, fighting back the urge to gag.

At the rear of their group a college girl who'd never shot a gun until the previous day grabbed hold of a tent pole and retched into the sand.

'Keep moving,' the Welshman said determinedly. 'It's in your heads, black it out.'

Beyond the accommodation tents the base was desolate and the air mercifully clear. Weapons storage would normally be the most secure area on a military base, but all they found was a single private sitting by the front door. He looked so pitiful that nobody even had the heart to shoot him.

*

The grenade wouldn't kill James, but the paint inside was compressed at high pressure and triggered by an explosive chemical reaction that would scorch his back.

James jumped in the air, grabbed handfuls of his T-shirt and madly wriggled his shoulders to free the grenade. With less than five seconds left the grenade's handle finally unsnagged from the collar of his shirt and it dropped to the ground, but instead of hitting the concrete floor with a thunk, it landed softly in the seat of the trousers gathered around his feet.

'Shitting shit!' James panicked.

He now had horrible visions of the paint exploding upwards and plastic casing shooting up and whacking him in the nuts. He stepped on the heel of one trainer and banged his knee on the dining table as he freed one foot. Once the foot was clear he put his sock down on the floor and kicked hard with his other leg, which still had his trousers and shorts bundled up around them.

This flung the grenade up high. There was a white flash as it exploded in midair two metres across the cabin. The grenade contained a highly compressed liquid that expanded into several litres of pink foam the instant it hit the atmosphere.

Doors and windows rattled with the force of the blast and James crashed into the wall as the warm, hissing foam hit him at more than fifty miles an hour. It trickled down his legs, out of his hair into his eyes as he tripped over a chair leg and felt himself tumbling through the blackness towards the floor.

His temple grazed the wall, but it wasn't serious and he stayed down for a couple of seconds, catching his breath as the foam hissed.

James was less seriously hurt than he would have been if the grenade had exploded next to his skin, but he still faced the reality of being half naked in the dark with his hands cuffed behind his back. He stood cautiously and realised that he needed the light on if he was to have any hope of finding the handcuff key.

With only a vague idea of the furniture layout, James felt his way towards the door. He'd come in face first and been slammed down on the table, so he'd not seen the light switch. But he knew roughly where it was because Sahlin had turned the light off an instant before she'd headed outside.

He felt around with his back to the wall, but you can't raise your hands very high when they're cuffed behind your back so he ended up turning to face the wall and eventually felt out the light switch and turned it on using the squishy tip of his nose.

The pink dye had saturated the room, including the surface of a bare bulb mounted on the ceiling. James got his trousers up before hobbling through the pinkish-hued light and sitting on a dining chair.

He shuffled the handcuffs under his bum, straining painfully at the wrists as he squeezed his butt cheeks together and wriggled until the cuffs were around the back of his thighs. Once this was done he fed his legs through and brought his hands around to the front.

Now he just needed to find the key under the pools of foam so that he could get the cuffs off.

*

The US forces put every able-bodied man behind the defence of the command building. General Shirley and several of his most senior staff had dosed themselves up with scant supplies of anti-diarrhoea medicine and stationed half a dozen healthy guards in well defended positions around the building's perimeter.

The insurgent mob tried getting close, but more than a dozen were expertly picked off by soldiers barricaded behind sandbags. Kazakov's Hummer took a hit from a well-aimed paint grenade, but the man himself dived out in the nick of time.

Kazakov ducked behind the paint-spattered vehicle, surveying the building with binoculars while seven SAS men stood around waiting for his orders. These were some of the most able soldiers in the British Army yet they doted on Kazakov like pilgrims awaiting orders from their guru.

'We aim everything at one spot,' Kazakov decided. 'Lots of smoke, lots of paint grenades. Find planks of wood, bed sheets, anything that will shield the paint.'

'Maybe we could wait it out?' an SAS man suggested. 'No water, no electricity. They can't do anything.'

'No,' Kazakov said firmly. 'This is our time. Most of the poisoned water will have drained through the pipes when the diarrhoea broke out and the toilets were repeatedly flushed. As soon as the soldiers get clear fluid into their systems they'll start feeling better. The balance of power could swing back in their favour in less than an hour.'

It took a few minutes for everyone to prepare for the assault. A dozen smoke grenades were already starting to fume when two of the biggest SAS men approached Lauren and Kevin.

'Kazakov just had a bright idea,' one of them said. 'You two are riding piggyback.'

'You what?' Lauren asked.

'It's a single storey, we'll rush up to the side and when we get close we fling you two up on the roof. There's bound to be a skylight or a service hatch which you can climb through and cause some mischief.'

Lauren was knackered and would have settled for an early night, but Kevin was keen to prove his worth after being left out of the raid on the aerodrome.

The two soldiers gave it a few seconds for the smoke to build up before crouching down to let the kids sit on their shoulders. Kevin was no problem, but Lauren was a pretty chunky thirteen-year-old, especially with a rifle and a heavy equipment pack.

'You're a lump,' her ride groaned, as he lifted her into the air.

The insurgents came under heavy sniper fire as more than a hundred bodies rushed the command centre. The tactics of fighting with paint were different to killing with real bullets: mattresses and wood worked as shields, but the snipers aimed at the ground or aimed shots at walls knowing that there was no distinction between a direct hit and a ricochet of chalk dust.

Even in this final battle there was little sign of cheating, probably because the soldiers would be reprimanded and the civilians would lose all their pay if they were caught out.

It had been a few years since anyone had carried Kevin on

their back and he couldn't help laughing as he was borne piggyback through the chaos. Shots cut holes through the curling smoke, but the SAS man reached the side of the command centre without being hit. Kevin grabbed the guttering before standing up on the man's shoulders and pulling himself up on to the roof.

'Where's Lauren?' he shouted.

The soldier looked around, but there was no sign either of Lauren or the soldier who'd been carrying her.

'Looks like you're on your own, kid.'

The smoke made it hard to see more than a couple of metres and the flat plastic roof flexed ominously under Kevin's trainers. The building was rectangular, fifteen metres wide and thirty long. It had no windows along the sides, so the only light entered through skylights which also opened up for ventilation. Most of these were partially covered with sand and Kevin was forced to crawl over the rooftop, sweeping away the sand with his elbow before peeking down inside. The main power grid was out, but he could see emergency lighting and computer screens running off backup power inside.

Fighting spread to all sides as the insurgents closed in and the odd stray shot skimmed the rooftop as Kevin crawled cautiously. Ten metres in from the gutters, he encountered a raised aluminium dome with a ring of angled skylights around the edge.

He peered down into a large room filled with torchlight. There was a giant map of Fort Reagan on the table and desks for several dozen men, but there were only three men present. Kevin recognised General Shirley. He looked stressed, with an elbow resting on the map table and a phone in his hand.

Kevin could barely hear over the noise of battle, but General Shirley seemed to be talking to the camp commander:

'Commander, you've got to understand that we have a major health crisis on our hands. Kazakov has gone beyond the parameters of decency . . . You know I have no wish to surrender. I don't want that on my record, but I'll be covered if you call a halt to this exercise on well founded health and safety grounds . . .'

As the general squirmed, Kevin measured the gap between two ventilation slats. It was just big enough for a paint grenade. The trouble was, the general and his staff would hear it drop and have eight or nine seconds to evacuate.

Kevin took a grenade – his last – from his backpack. He pulled the pin, released the trigger and counted eight seconds on his watch before letting it drop inside. There was a chance that the grenade would shatter the windows, so he rolled away and buried his face against the domed roof.

The explosion was instantaneous and when Kevin looked down he saw that the grenade had exploded across the tabletop less than a metre from General Shirley. The two other officers in the room had also been hit.

'Christ,' the general was shouting. 'That Russian bastard!'

The general wasn't accustomed to being blown up at his desk, so he hadn't been wearing goggles and had foaming paint in both eyes. Excited by his success, Kevin lay on his back and launched a sequence of two-footed kicks, knocking the toughened glass out of its frame before sliding through the hole and dropping feet first on to the map table.

General Shirley didn't think it was possible to get any

more annoyed than he was already, but then his bleary eyes told him that he'd just been killed by an eleven-year-old boy.

'He uses children too!' Shirley shouted, sweeping away a great pile of papers from his desk and repeatedly smashing the receiver of his telephone against its base unit. 'Is there no limit to this man's depravity?'

'Keep your hair on, mate,' Kevin said chirpily as he jumped off the table. 'Oh wait, you haven't got any, have you . . .'

33. AFTERGLOW

The pink dye in the simulated bullets and paint grenades was designed to foam on contact with plain water. The final battle caused seventy further casualties, who all had to report to an office near the stadium and declare themselves dead, before heading off to the cleaning station next door.

Most had superficial hits on clothing with the odd splash of dye on bare skin. After being sprayed with a sweet smelling solution that counteracted the foaming effect victims were sent off to shower in individual cubicles. Any badly stained clothes were replaced with cheap cotton trousers and T-shirts before being taken away to be washed and dried. The dead would then get to spend twenty-four hours in a dormitory before being allowed to return to the exercise.

The exception to this smooth process was people with dye in their eyes, or people who'd taken direct hits from close range. The dye wasn't toxic, but it became a mild irritant when it dried into a chalky crust, so it had to be removed thoroughly.

The procedure was undignified and James found himself standing naked, palms resting on a tiled wall, as a lanky soldier blasted him with a jet of tepid water. A rubber-suited companion worked from closer in, using a spray gun filled with the anti-foaming agent and a long-handled scrubbing brush.

'Spread your cheeks,' she ordered, then sent a shudder down James' back as she squirted him with the icy chemical spray.

'Face forwards.'

As James turned around an announcement came over the base PA system. 'This is General Sean O'Halloran, Base Commander. As a result of successful insurgent action this exercise has now been *suspended*. Civilian personnel should return to their accommodation, military personnel should return to base. Please listen for further announcements. Message ends.'

James heard a few cheers from the insurgents who were queuing for the shower cubicles on the other side of a particle-board partition.

'All done, cookie,' the rubber-suited woman said to James, before throwing him a towel. 'Go down to the seats and wait for a visual inspection.'

James dried off quickly then grabbed his pack and a bin liner filled with his dirty clothes. He ended up sitting in a line of plastic chairs with the towel around his waist. The only other man waiting was a chunky fellow with grey body hair.

At the far end of the room, a pair of medical orderlies had a black soldier lying under bright lights, inspecting his skin to make sure all traces of the dye had been cleaned off. They paid particular attention to cleaning out his eyes with distilled water and cotton buds.

James heard his radio crackling inside his bag and pulled it out to listen to what was going on. 'Kazakov, you out there?'

'Ahh,' Kazakov answered jubilantly. 'What's this I hear about you abandoning us for a lady friend?'

The episode was embarrassing and James was in two minds about telling the truth.

'She had a sting in the tail,' James said reluctantly. 'Army Intelligence identified me from the base surveillance video. I ended up with three female intel officers holding me down and threatening all sorts of horrible and nasty things.'

Kazakov snorted and it sounded like several cherubs were laughing in the background. 'Suckered by a pretty lady! All that experience, all that training and you fall for a femme fatale: the oldest trick in the book.'

'She threatened to burn me with some probe,' James complained. '*Totally* out of order.'

'Old General Shirley started getting desperate at the end,' Kazakov laughed. 'Did you catch their names? I'll be sure to complain about their conduct in my official report.'

'Land, Sahlin and Jones,' James said. 'Sahlin was the boss. So whereabouts are you now?'

'I'm up here with the base commander, waiting for Shirley to arrive. Can't wait till he gets here and tries to wheedle his way out of this mess.'

'Isn't he there?' James asked.

'Little Kevin got him with a grenade.' Kazakov laughed some more. 'He didn't have goggles, so he's getting cleaned up.'

Up to this point, James hadn't made the link between the

uniformed general who'd briefed them in the stadium and the flabby fellow sat in the next chair along, who was now glowering at him.

'Gimme that,' General Shirley shouted, practically ripping the handset from James' hand. 'Kazakov, you cheat, don't think you're getting away with this!'

'General,' Kazakov answered warmly. 'I always enjoy duelling with a worthy adversary. Of course, when one isn't around I'm almost as happy to wipe out a turd like you.'

James fought the urge to laugh out loud.

'Six million dollars' worth of drones!' Shirley shouted. 'That's not in the playbook, Kazakov. Are you out of your mind?'

'We sent five teenagers up there,' Kazakov bragged. 'A boy scout troop! You had nothing but a couple of engineers guarding your most valuable intelligence asset.'

'And this goddamn laxative thing is degrading and depraved,' Shirley yelled. 'Sewage backed up, men excreting into their own helmets.'

Kazakov growled, which sounded kind of like a cat purring as it came through the radio at James' end. 'War is about finding your opponent's weakest link and exploiting it. There aren't any rules, General, there isn't a playbook. Without clean water, an army's dead on its feet. Didn't they teach you that at military school?'

'Kazakov, I've been involved in war games for more than thirty years and I've never seen this kind of back-handed sneakery.'

'You know what your problem is, Shirley?' Kazakov shouted back. 'When you were at West Point Academy polishing your shiny shoes and studying books, I was in Afghanistan. Minus fifteen, ankle deep in trenches filled with frozen mud and other men's filth, fighting against guerrillas who'd eat their own grandmothers if they thought it would give them an edge. War is mean and nasty. When you fight, you fight to win. There's no playbook in war, General. Forget humanitarian, forget rules of engagement and demilitarised zones and food drops. That's why you Yanks lost in Vietnam; that's why you got your asses kicked in Iraq.'

'We won the cold war,' General Shirley growled. 'We kicked your communist asses. And you talk about Afghanistan; didn't the Russians lose that war too?'

'The army didn't lose it,' Kazakov shouted. 'Politicians lost it!'

At this point a fresh voice came over the radio. 'General Shirley, this fighting is pointless,' Base Commander General O'Halloran said calmly. 'Right now we have a thousand troops, eight thousand civilians on the payroll and the world's most expensive military training facility at a standstill. I suggest that we meet at twenty-two hundred hours in my office and discuss a strategy to restart the exercise from scratch with a revised scenario.'

'I'll be there,' Shirley growled. 'But I'm not working with that Russian. I don't want my men exposed to his illegitimate tactics and I want him off this base.'

'Let's not make any hasty decisions,' General O'Halloran said.

James smiled as he heard Kazakov shouting, 'I'm not a Russian, I'm a bloody Ukrainian,' in the background.

A blast of static came across the radio. General Shirley

moved to hand it back to James but at the last minute he threw it hard at the wall, shattering the plastic case. He then stood up sharply and grabbed the bin liner containing his stained clothes.

The medical orderly turned anxiously towards him. 'General, we need to ensure that your eyes are–'

'I can see fine,' the general growled, as he stormed around to the end of the partition and pushed his way to the front of the queue for shower cubicles.

Technically Shirley was subordinate to the orders of all permanent Fort Reagan staff for the duration of the training exercise, but nobody was inclined to mess with him. Before stepping into the first available cubicle, the red-faced general turned back and recognised several of his men in the queue behind him.

'There's a kid on the other side of that partition,' Shirley said furiously. 'Cropped hair, blue eyes, no more than sixteen years old. He's the reason you've all been spending so much time on the toilet in the last few hours. Be sure to pass on your appreciation, won't you?'

James squirmed on his damp plastic seat as powerfully built soldiers thumped on the far side of the partition and threatened a variety of things ranging from arse whippings to castration and a *good old-fashioned pipe beating*.

'Dead meat,' one of them shouted as he pounded the boards so hard that the whole wall shuddered.

James had made a few enemies in his time, but having a whole battalion of soldiers on his back was a first, and he didn't like it one bit.

34. RISK

Kevin, Lauren and Rat, along with a bunch of SAS officers and some other insurgents, hung around in a reception area outside General Shirley's command room. They sat on plastic chairs, shuffling feet, yawning and being careful not to use the water in case any trace of Phenolphthalein laxative remained in the pipes.

The air outside was heavy with the smell of disinfectant. Soldiers queued up to receive rehydration medicine and anti-diarrhoea drugs helicoptered in from a hospital in Las Vegas. The least seriously affected were already well enough to resume light duties and had begun cleaning up the camp, while a crew of engineers responsible for maintaining Fort Reagan's facilities worked to unblock the sewage system and mop up any overflows.

Beyond the army base, the rumour Kazakov started that all civilians would be sent home with a full two weeks' pay had led to jubilation, only to turn into bitterness and vandalism when it was quashed.

Inside the command room Mac joined Kazakov, Base Commander O'Halloran, General Shirley and several junior officers. Messengers came and went, trying to get updates from medical staff and engineers on how soon it would be before all soldiers were back to full health and base facilities were in good enough shape for a training exercise.

It was close to midnight by the time everyone agreed that a revised mission scenario would be devised and a fresh ten-day exercise would start in forty-eight hours. But Kazakov and General Shirley were at each other's throats.

Kazakov said that Shirley was a sore loser. Shirley said that Kazakov had fought dirty and endangered the health of his men. Shirley and Base Commander O'Halloran were both one star generals, but as Base Commander O'Halloran had the final call.

O'Halloran hadn't been impressed with Shirley's command skills, nor with the fact that Kazakov's unorthodox strategies had wrecked both the drones, the expensive aerodrome in which they were housed and the sewage system.

In the end his diplomatic solution was to restart the exercise from scratch. Two of Shirley's deputies would take charge of the opposing sides, Shirley would stay on as a non-participating observer and Kazakov would be asked to leave the base.

'Bastards,' Kazakov shouted, waking Lauren and several others from a daze as he opened the doors of the command room with an explosive kick. At the last moment he doubled back and ripped the surveillance device stuck to the side of a computer monitor before waggling it under Shirley's nose.

'You see that?' Kazakov smiled. 'Another of your little mistakes. I heard every command. I knew every order before your own men did.'

Shirley looked battered. He knew there would be an investigation into the conduct of the exercise and the cost of damages. Even if it concluded that Kazakov's tactics somehow breached Fort Reagan rules, the General was still going to end up looking bad after his battalion had been defeated by a much smaller and less capable force.

'Why don't you go back to Russia where you belong?' Shirley hissed, before swinging a crazy punch.

At forty-nine, Kazakov was only a year younger than the general, but unlike the portly American he kept in shape and was fitter than most men half his age. He ducked beneath the swinging arm before giving Shirley a push that made him overbalance and topple forwards into a desk, snapping an LCD monitor from its base and sending a stack of papers to the floor.

Kazakov grabbed a plastic clipboard and swatted the panting general's bald head with it, before emptying a pot filled with pens and pencils over his head.

'Fill in your forms, General,' Kazakov glowered. 'Push your pens, but don't try pretending that you're a soldier. Real soldiers end up dead because of decisions made by buffoons like you.'

Mac and the base commander followed Kazakov out into the lobby area.

O'Halloran eyeballed Kazakov. 'Get your things and head out to the reception point. There's a black sedan car in bay three-sixteen. Reception has the key, tell me where you park it when you fly out and we'll have someone to collect it from the airport.'

Kazakov looked startled. 'Can't I stay overnight? I've barely slept in two days and we're four hours from Vegas.'

'I want the bad blood cleared,' O'Halloran said. 'There's a motel twenty miles out east.'

Mac looked at Kazakov as they began walking down a hallway towards the exit with Lauren, Kevin and Rat in tow.

'I think you'd better take James with you,' Mac said. 'Word's already out that he was the one who infiltrated the water plant and if he becomes a target I can see things escalating out of control.'

*

James woke at half-seven but the exhausted Kazakov snored on. The motel was peculiar, fitted out some time in the early eighties by someone who thought bright red plastic looked cool. The surfaces were dusty and the battery in the wall clock dead, as if they were the only people who'd stayed here in months.

James was starving and he wandered out into the morning sun. Their black Ford sedan was the only car parked outside of a room. There was desert in all directions and a two-lane highway without a car in sight.

His stomach led him to reception, which had a busted insect screen over the door and a stack of leaflets promoting visits to Area 51 and a couple of tacky local casinos.

'Is there anywhere round here you can get something to eat?' he asked.

The stringy old bird behind the counter looked up over half-framed glasses. 'Got a Burger King about twelve mile east.'

'Twelve mile,' James said, unconsciously mocking her accent. 'Nothing in walking distance?'

The woman looked up at him like he was stupid. 'You see anything in walking distance? We got a vending area out back behind room sixteen.'

James found it and stuffed in quarters until he had a bottle of no-brand lemonade and a packet of Mini Oreos for his breakfast. Back in the room he took a shower and dried off on a towel so thin you could see your skin colour from the other side. He crunched his biscuits and made a bit of extra noise as he dressed, hoping that Kazakov would wake up; but the big Ukrainian was blissed out with an open mouth and a puddle of drool on his pillow.

James was impatient to get some proper food and thought about turning on the TV, but Kazakov might get annoyed if he was woken deliberately and he wasn't the kind of man you wanted to wind up.

He felt fuller after the cookies and gassy soda, but the combo left a sickly taste in his mouth. The curtains didn't do much to stop light coming in so he sat on his bed and re-read a couple of sections of his blackjack manual before getting out the cards and practising his card-counting skills. After half an hour he got the urge to pee, but when he looked around he saw that Kazakov had one eye open, staring right at him.

'Hey,' James said awkwardly. 'How long have you been awake?'

Kazakov had done a lot of shouting over the previous two days and his voice was thinner than usual. 'Twenty minutes, maybe.'

James smiled. 'Just staring for no reason?'

'There's always a reason,' Kazakov said, as he threw off his covers and sat up. 'It's interesting what people do when they don't think they're being watched. How's it going?'

'How's what going?'

'Counting cards,' Kazakov said.

'Hard to say,' James said, 'never having sat at a real casino table and seen how fast they deal. Or tried to keep track of cards with people moving in front of you and fruit machines bleeping. Book says it's completely different to dealing out cards by yourself.'

Kazakov stood up naked and let off three pungent farts before gasping with relief.

'Shit and a shower,' Kazakov said, as James buried his face against the sleeve of his T-shirt to mask the putrid smell. 'Then we find somewhere for breakfast.'

35. SPIRIT

One thing Kazakov disliked about America – along with everything else – were the roads. He said the desert scenery was boring and the car's suspension too soft so he let James drive.

They couldn't stop for breakfast at the first diner they reached because it was the one where the owner had pulled her shotgun on the way out. Despite being starving, James didn't even bother asking Kazakov if they should stop at a McDonalds drive-through and by the time they reached a reasonable-looking diner they were half way to Vegas and it was past noon.

'Maybe I should call campus,' James suggested, as he sat facing Kazakov across a custard-yellow table top. 'Get them to sort out our flights home and stuff.'

'Could,' Kazakov said, his face so full of cheeseburger and fries that he could only manage one word at a time. 'Only . . . I've got nothing on campus scheduled until the next basic training starts in ten days. What are you so desperate to get home for?'

James shrugged. 'I thought you hated America and

everything it stood for. In fact, you said those exact words at least five times on the ride here.'

Kazakov's eyes narrowed. 'I want my three thousand dollars back.'

'Right,' James laughed. 'You don't wanna start gambling again, boss. No offence, but I saw what happened at the Reef the other night. You can't hold your drink and you're a terrible loser to boot.'

'But this card counting,' Kazakov said, raising one eyebrow. 'You said it works.'

James smiled. 'It gives you an edge, but it takes a shitload of skill. I can't get near to a table until I'm twenty-one and even if you've got an aptitude for maths, it would still take me days to teach you.'

Kazakov pulled the receiver unit he'd used to bug the Fort Reagan command centre from the pocket of his tracksuit top and thumped it down on the table.

'I know basic blackjack strategy. I wear the camera; you watch the cards and signal me when I need to bet big.'

James' first reaction was shock. 'You're tripping,' he snorted. 'I'd need a full view of the table and I'd never be able to read the cards on that titchy screen.'

'It plugs into my laptop screen. The camera itself is high resolution. I didn't know what I'd need so I brought a full surveillance kit: bugs, cameras, wide angles, telephotos, triggers, relays, signal units. It's all in the car.'

James looked around to make sure nobody was in earshot. 'Counting cards in your head is legal,' he said quietly. 'But once you start using gadgets and cameras you're cheating the casino and that's criminal. I've seen the prisons in these parts and believe me, you don't want to end up in one.'

'I'm nearly fifty years old,' Kazakov said determinedly. 'I have no home, a small government pension. I'm not wealthy like Mac. I can't afford to lose three thousand dollars.'

'Gambling's a mug's game,' James said. 'You should have known better.'

'Come *on*, James,' Kazakov begged. 'Where's your spirit of adventure? I saw the look in your eyes when you were sitting on that bed dealing cards. Concentrating so hard, counting the numbers in your head. You want to try it now, you don't want to wait for five years.'

Kazakov watched James' expression and saw that he was tempted.

'We have the best hardware,' Kazakov continued. 'You just count the cards and signal me when the odds are in our favour. Our equipment is CHERUB stock: state of the art. That camera is the size of a pin-head, the transmissions are so secure that no surveillance system could ever detect it.'

James knew he'd get kicked out of CHERUB if he was caught and possibly face criminal charges too. But Kazakov was right about the technology being better than anything regular casino cheats could buy off the shelf and everything that had happened lately left James feeling empty: the anti-terrorist mission going wrong, Dana dumping him, getting kicked out of Fort Reagan and the fact that he was sixteen and a half years old with the bulk of his CHERUB career in the rear-view mirror.

He needed a victory to get his life back on track and coming out of a casino with a big pile of dollars fitted the bill perfectly.

'Maybe we could do a trial run,' James said uneasily. 'One of the smaller casinos. All the windows on that car are blacked out so I could operate from a car park.'

'Good man,' Kazakov said, reaching across the tabletop to give James a high five. 'You know it makes sense.'

*

James wondered about himself as he drove on towards Las Vegas in the black sedan. He had a history of getting involved in half-baked schemes and winding up in trouble, but the weird thing was that he always had the appetite for another one. Being at CHERUB enabled him to channel these traits into training and missions and his appetite for risk and excitement was one of the reasons he'd been recruited in the first place. But what did it mean for his future?

When James looked at mates like Kerry and Shakeel he could see them as thirty-year-olds with a couple of kids who had their friends over for barbecues and spent weekends doing DIY. But he could never see himself that way. Maybe he'd use his maths skills to count cards or trade stocks and shares and get rich, but what if that didn't work out?

James was smart enough to worry about what he was getting into, but by the time they pulled up in a giant shopping mall parking lot to sort out the equipment he was buzzing. Having Kazakov on his side helped enormously: the Ukrainian was impulsive, but he was smart and he'd fought and won battles with enemies a lot tougher than casino security guards.

They headed into a department store and bought Kazakov some less militaristic clothes: slacks, a white shirt, a blazer and a pair of sunglasses. Most importantly they bought a scarf. If a camera is pinned to your lapel or shirt there's not much you can do covertly to change your viewpoint, but with the camera on a scarf hung loosely around your neck you can easily slide it up and down to get the best view of the table.

'There is one thing I like about America,' Kazakov grinned, as he buttoned his shirt. 'They're all so overweight you can buy my size anywhere.'

James thought America was cool and was bored of Kazakov's sniping, but he didn't say anything because he was in the back of the car linking the receiver unit up to the laptop.

'What are you seeing?' Kazakov asked.

James swung the laptop screen to face Kazakov. They'd fitted a fisheye attachment, creating an ultra-wide-angle image that was distorted around the edges.

'The resolution's superb, so I can pan and zoom and still read the cards, but you really need to sit in the middle seat at the table for me to have a decent chance of keeping count.'

Kazakov showed James the back of his watch, to which he'd stuck the vibrating signal unit. 'You'll be able to hear what I'm saying, but it's too risky for me to wear an earpiece. We'll need to work out a code.'

'It's better there than strapped to your leg,' James nodded. 'I'll send two pulses when you should up the bet. Three when you should cut it. One long pulse means I've lost the count, two long pulses means there's trouble.'

'OK,' Kazakov said. 'We'll have to work out separate signals for adjusting the camera up and down when I first arrive and during the game.'

James shook his head. 'You've got to keep the camera on the game. If it drifts, I'll have missed two or three hands by the time it's sorted and I'll have lost the count.'

'I can't sit completely still,' Kazakov said. 'It'll look suspicious.'

'You don't have to sit there stiff as a board,' James said. 'Just don't drift too far from your starting position or I won't see all the cards.'

Kazakov opened the door of the car and put his foot down on the tarmac. 'I'm gonna walk around with this thing before we hit the big time.'

'Good idea,' James said. 'Go into a café, practise sitting still without making it look like you're sitting still. I'll give you a call to let you know how it's looking from this end. Oh, and while you're in there get me a coffee and a fruit salad from that stand in the food court.'

*

Over the next two hours James and Kazakov practised their moves until they were smooth. Kazakov could walk around with the camera in his scarf, sit down and instantly adjust the camera to a position that gave a wide view over several metres in every direction.

Card counting gives you a slight edge if you keep a simple count of each card dealt and the number of cards remaining in the dealer's card shoe. But with Kazakov playing blackjack and visually checking on the number of remaining cards, James realised he could increase their chances further by keeping a separate count of the number of aces. He made calculations of the amount that Kazakov should bet by making a simple spreadsheet and running it in the right-hand corner of the laptop screen while the camera footage ran next to it.

Just before 4 p.m. James pulled into the parking lot of the Wagon Wheel Hotel and Casino. James handed over his five hundred dollars' holiday spending money and felt queasy as he drew five hundred more on his cash card. Kazakov took James' money to the casino cage and turned it into chips, along with two thousand from his credit card.

They'd parked in the most out of the way corner of the casino's open lot and James sat in the back seat watching Kazakov walking past the lines of bleeping slot machines, searching for blackjack tables.

The Wagon Wheel was known as a locals' joint. It didn't have ten thousand rooms or a model of the Sphinx in the lobby like the big casinos on the Strip, but according to James' book it did have some of the best two-deck blackjack tables in Vegas.

Playing with two decks instead of six to eight meant you had a bigger advantage when the cards were in your favour. It was also easier to see how many cards were left because the dealer held the decks in hand, rather than having them hidden inside a card shoe.

'This one?' Kazakov mumbled in Russian, as he turned to face a table.

Under Nevada law every gaming table has to clearly display all the rules and table limits. Casinos have a reputation for sneaking in extra rules that turn the odds even further in their own favour. After scanning the rules quickly, James pressed the laptop's F5 key twice to activate the vibrating receiver under Kazakov's watch and indicate that it was OK to sit down.

The centre stool was taken, so Kazakov sat one place to the left. The three other gamblers were elderly women. Kazakov played the table minimum, $10, just to get a feel for things as one of the old timers told him that she loved his accent and had a cousin who'd worked as a diplomat in Odessa. Distractions at the table are one of the most difficult things for a card counter to deal with, but Kazakov didn't have this problem because James was doing the difficult part of the job for him.

Back in the parking lot, James sat in the back seat behind the tinted glass with Kazakov's mini laptop drawing power from the cigarette lighter socket. The cards were fairly easy to watch and banter between the three women and the dealer slowed the game down.

Kazakov played solid basic blackjack strategy and won his first three hands, but James was disappointed to see lots of high cards flying across the table. The count quickly dropped to minus five, stacking the odds heavily in favour of the casino. Kazakov varied his bet between ten and twenty dollars, but the casino's edge steadily took its toll and by the time the last cards were dealt Kazakov had lost his early gains and was down eighty dollars.

A cowboy joined the table and the dealer took his break and got replaced by a woman. There were now a minimum of twelve cards to count per hand and the new dealer dropped the banter and moved faster than her predecessor. But this time the count swung in Kazakov's favour and James hit the F5 key twice, indicating to Kazakov that he should up the bet.

The odds were now in the players' favour. Kazakov upped

his bets to between thirty and fifty dollars per hand, but the cards didn't fall his way. Counting cards and upping your bet when the count is in your favour gives the player edge over the casino, but it doesn't guarantee that you'll win any particular hand and Kazakov wasn't getting the right cards.

When the dealer shuffled the decks to start again, Kazakov was down close to four hundred dollars, while the cowboy on his left had won two hundred playing a supposedly suicidal strategy of following his hunches.

James couldn't see Kazakov's face, but the instructor was fidgeting and clenching his knuckles. A pretty waitress handed a complimentary orange juice to Kazakov and a bourbon for the cowboy. Shortly afterwards the three elderly women headed off with smiles and a twenty-dollar tip for the dealer.

With just two players at the table Kazakov moved on to the centre stool so that there was space between them. He drew blackjack – a perfect twenty-one that pays odds of three for two – on the first hand bet of forty dollars. Kazakov won a couple more hands on smaller bets of ten and twenty dollars and for the second time the count swung in the players' favour.

Kazakov upped his bet to the fifty-dollar table maximum and won seven hands out of the next eight. The count dropped back into the casino's favour as more cards were dealt, but Kazakov rode his luck and by the time the dealer reached the end of their second run through the cards their losses had been wiped out and Kazakov was looking at a three-hundred-dollar profit.

'It's working,' Kazakov mumbled in Russian for James' benefit.

Over the next hour and a quarter, Kazakov kept playing and stacked up steady profits. Sometimes the count went against and Kazakov lost slightly or trod water, but when the count swung in their favour he upped his bet and the winnings piled up. His three thousand dollars of chips had turned into four thousand seven hundred and the pit boss – who was in charge of all the tables in that section of the casino – sanctioned Kazakov's request to up the table limit from fifty to a hundred dollars.

James watched as the pit boss and a colleague began to hover over the table, paying attention to Kazakov's mounting pile of chips. Blackjack dealers and senior casino staff are trained to spot card counters. Every table is viewed from above by surveillance cameras and after ninety minutes and a profit of several thousand dollars Kazakov knew someone would be in the security room paying careful attention to every move he made.

If he upped his bets every time the count moved in his favour he'd arouse suspicion and be asked to leave the casino. So Kazakov had to make the odd wrong move to throw the casino staff off the scent, but of course these deliberate mistakes all cost money.

After two and a quarter hours James began to notice the pit boss getting agitated. He changed the dealer and brought in new cards, then reduced the table limit back to fifty dollars per hand to put a cap on Kazakov's winnings.

James didn't want to push their luck on a first outing and after two and a quarter hours his eyes ached from being fixed on the tiny laptop screen. His brain was fuzzy and he needed food and a toilet break so he sent through the long signal to tell Kazakov to get out.

After tipping the dealer fifty dollars, Kazakov headed for the casino cage to cash out his chips. James rubbed his eyes and downed half a bottle of water before looking back at the screen. The cage had huge gold bars across the front and the host poured Kazakov's piles of twenty- and fifty-dollar chips into an automatic counting machine.

The total flashed up on a blue illuminated display: $8,670.

'You have a good day sir,' the teller said brightly. 'And be sure to put that money somewhere safe just as soon as you can.'

36. GOLD

James had almost shat himself, risking all of his personal savings and putting his CHERUB career on the line, but now they'd won he was buzzing. His one-third share of $8,760 was $2,920, meaning he'd almost trebled his money. Kazakov's $5,840 share meant he'd made back the $3,000 he'd lost at the Reef casino a few nights earlier.

James and Kazakov acted like best buddies as they drove the last few miles into the centre of Vegas, swapping stories about car-park security guards, evil stares from the pit boss and how James lost the count during a sneezing fit.

James turned the Ford on to the eight lanes of the Las Vegas Strip. The sun was setting behind the Stratosphere Tower at the north end of the Strip, the neon was starting to glow and an advertisement for an Elton John concert came out of a fifty-metre-high video wall.

'I hear the all-you-can-eat buffets here are pretty special,' Kazakov said.

James was shocked: hearing Kazakov complimenting something American was like turning up at your local KFC and finding the royal family tucking into a twelve-piece bargain bucket.

'Bellagio has the best buffet in Vegas,' James smiled. 'Thirty bucks a head, all you can eat. We were gonna go the other day, but Kerry and Rat didn't have enough cash left.'

The Bellagio was in the middle of the Strip, an upscale joint famous for the giant lake and fountains out front. Like all the main casinos it was vast and by the time they reached the buffet they'd walked through a vast parking structure and a casino the size of several football fields. Everything in Vegas is designed so that you have a long and tempting walk across a casino before you can get anywhere.

The marble-floored corridors and plush-carpeted playing areas thronged with pasty men in smart casual clothing. Thick glasses and greasy hair were abundant.

'What is this?' Kazakov asked, as they joined a fifty-strong line to get inside the buffet. 'Some kind of acne sufferers' convention?'

The three men ahead in the queue were spewing words about handwriting recognition software, which enabled James to make the link to some billboards he'd seen across town.

'Compufest 2008,' James grinned, as they shuffled forwards two paces. 'It's a whole massive conference for the computer industry.'

'Geekfest, more like,' Kazakov sneered. 'Give me six weeks and I'd make real men out of them.'

'They might not have the looks, but they've got the money,' James said. 'I wondered why there were so many Mercs and Bentleys in the parking lot.'

The buffet was worth the queue and James made a complete pig of himself, stuffing his plate with a dozen slices of roast meat, then going back for fish and pasta before finishing off with half a dozen miniature dessert pastries.

'So,' Kazakov said, when they were both too stuffed to eat another mouthful. 'Feel up to another session of blackjack? That fifty-dollar maximum really cut our edge. How about we try a high-stakes table?'

'You've got whipped cream on the end of your nose,' James said, as he picked his coffee cup out of its saucer. 'I looked on the Internet when we were staying at the Reef and for high stakes there are apparently two deck games with low penetration and high table limits at the Vancouver casino. It's at the south end of the Strip.'

'What are we waiting for?' Kazakov asked.

James shrugged. 'The only thing is, the Vancouver is a new casino so they'll have top-notch security systems and the higher the stakes, the more closely the table will be watched. I think we rode our luck a bit this afternoon at the Wagon Wheel. We should have taken the hint the minute the pit boss put the table limit back down to fifty.'

'OK,' Kazakov said. 'We turned three grand into nine this afternoon. If we triple our money again, we're looking at close to thirty grand.'

James smiled. 'Actually, the initial stake doesn't matter – as long as you don't hit a big losing streak and get wiped out. If you're betting five hundred dollars a hand instead of fifty, your potential winnings are ten times greater.'

'A hundred thousand dollars,' Kazakov said, pounding his fist jubilantly on his chest. 'I could go for some of that.'

'Wouldn't mind some myself,' James said. 'My share should be good for a nice Harley-Davidson.'

*

The Vancouver was one of Las Vegas' newest casinos and situated at the southernmost extreme of the Strip. Its sixty-storey hotel tower was the tallest in town and its modern white décor was aimed at a hipper crowd than the marble and heavy pattern carpets in the older casinos.

James had now seen most of the big hotel casinos and despite their elaborate attempts to differentiate with themes and attractions he found that they were all pretty much the same beneath a thin veneer: big multi-storey car parks, a few thousand hotel rooms, some swanky restaurants and a massive casino at the heart of it all.

Still bloated from the buffet, James sat in the back of the car and watched the viewpoint from Kazakov's scarf on the laptop screen. He was excited at the prospect of more winnings and confident after their success at the Wagon Wheel.

Compufest delegates were thick on the ground as Kazakov moved briskly down miles of corridors and over a spectacular glass-floored bridge that spanned the hotel's pool complex. The bridge opened out into banks of escalators that led down to the casino floor.

No part of the mega casinos was more similar than the windowless gambling floors. The slot machines and tables were all licensed by the state of Nevada and the result was near identical machines, flashing coloured lights and bleeping identical tunes and jingles.

As Kazakov passed a Nissan pick-up truck mounted on a plinth and up for grabs by suckers feeding the slot machines surrounding it, James' screen dropped out and the words *no signal* flashed up.

The picture came back a few seconds later, but the image

was heavily pixelated and the sound kept breaking up. The picture stabilised momentarily, but as Kazakov sighted the high stakes area of the casino the video signal faltered for a second time.

James feared interference from a signal jamming device inside the casino, but he opened up the onscreen control panel for the video monitoring software and saw that the signal strength was way down in the red zone. He pulled his mobile out of his pocket and called Kazakov.

'Whaddya mean no signal?' Kazakov said irritably. 'You're a kilometre away at most. We were getting six times that coverage at Fort Reagan. Are you sure you've got it set up right?'

'I'm sure,' James said. 'Fort Reagan's open country. You might not be far away, but I've got three layers full of cars parked on top of me and you're underneath a sixty-storey hotel tower.'

'Damn,' Kazakov growled. 'A signal booster would probably do the trick, but I only brought what I thought I'd need inside Fort Reagan.'

'We could try another one of the smaller casinos,' James suggested. 'Or the old casinos on Freemont Street.'

'There must be another way,' Kazakov said. 'You need to get closer. A toilet cubicle or something.'

James tutted with frustration. 'The casinos have guards and video cameras everywhere. Come back to the car, we'll drive back out to one of the smaller joints.'

'Let me think a minute,' Kazakov said. 'I'll call you back.'

James threw his mobile down on the empty seat beside him and sighed. He was the brains behind the operation, but at times Kazakov was treating him like a kid.

He watched the screen for a few more seconds, but as

Kazakov moved deeper into the casino the signal dropped out completely. Almost ten minutes passed before James' mobile rang.

'I've found your spot,' Kazakov said. 'Bring the laptop and meet me at the business centre.'

'Business centre?' James said, mystified.

James found it close to reception after a five-minute walk. The glass-fronted area contained several dozen desks, surrounded on three sides with privacy screens. There were also banks of fax machines, laser printers and a few more obscure machines like laminators and binders.

'Hey, miss,' Kazakov said, smiling to a smartly dressed receptionist standing behind a counter as James approached. 'Here's my boy. He needs a desk to get this history project done and I know if I leave him upstairs in the room, he'll be watching TV, playing Nintendo and stuffing his fat face from the mini-bar.'

The receptionist gave James a smile. 'Homework gets you down, doesn't it?' she said.

'If he wants a good college place, he needs to pull his finger out,' Kazakov growled.

'OK then,' the receptionist said cheerfully. 'The business centre is forty dollars for the first hour, twenty-five after that. Service includes desk, Internet access, printing, faxing and telephone calls. Overseas calls and colour printing are extra.'

Kazakov paid for three hours with cash. 'Do your work,' he said firmly as the receptionist led James into the business centre. 'No MSN.'

'Good luck at the tables, sir,' the receptionist said sweetly.

37. LIMITS

The receptionist smiled warmly as James picked out a desk in the farthest corner of the deserted office suite.

'Surprised it's not busier with the big computer conference in town,' James noted.

'They're all way in advance of us,' she said. 'They have their Blackberries and smart phones. I get quite a lot of jobs printing and binding contracts, but nobody uses the desks during Compufest.'

James flipped up the lid of the laptop as the receptionist walked away.

Once the computer was plugged in and booted up he opened the surveillance software. The signal strength was on nine bars out of ten. The picture was bright and the sound clear, but he almost flew up out of his seat as the receptionist put a tray with jugs of coffee and orange juice and a small plate of biscuits on the table beside him.

'Brain food,' she smiled. 'Let me know if you need any help using the printers or anything.'

'Cheers,' James said. 'I really just need to be left alone. You know, get my head down and get the homework over with.'

He felt slightly uncomfortable as he watched Kazakov on screen. The Ukrainian bought eight thousand dollars' worth of chips from the cage before heading into the high-stakes gaming area.

One of the main ways James had justified his criminal activity up to now was by the fact that while Kazakov was running the risks inside the casino he'd be in a parking lot hundreds of metres away and the chances he'd get caught were practically zero.

But now he was in the casino too, and while Kazakov only had a discreet camera and a vibrating signal device stuck to the back of his watch, James had a wireless receiver unit, a laptop loaded with surveillance software and images from a blackjack table on the eleven-inch screen right in front of him.

The high-stakes area was guarded with a velvet rope, although money was the only criterion for entry. Fixtures were more luxurious than the rest of the casino and the staff more attentive, but the slot machines and tables were identical Nevada-state-regulated stock.

As Kazakov sought out blackjack tables, James was astonished to glimpse a man with his credit card plugged into a slot machine, losing fifty dollars as fast as the spinning cherries and melons would let him. Casinos liked to call gambling gaming and portray it as a sophisticated activity for James Bond types in dinner jackets and bow ties, but in a modern casino like the Vancouver eighty per cent of the floor space and ninety per cent of the profits came from jangling slots.

High-stakes areas were usually the emptiest parts of a casino, but Compufest had brought a lot of wealthy people into town and delegates were throwing thousands of dollars across the tables and tipping good-looking waitresses fifty dollars in return for smiles and a free drink.

Kazakov realised this was ideal: casinos only cared about the bottom line and pit bosses and dealers would pay less attention to him winning while they had a dozen other punters losing money like it was going out of style. James checked the table rules and buzzed the vibrating receiver to indicate that Kazakov should take a seat.

'Evening gentlemen,' Kazakov said, taking the middle stool and planting four thousand in chips on the table.

The dealer was a beautiful Asian woman in a strapless white evening dress with the Vancouver casino logo embroidered on the back. The table had a $100 minimum and a generous $2,000 ceiling, but the computer geeks were showing off their cash, constantly betting the table maximum and making a point not to care when they lost.

For the next hour James sat in the business centre, squinting at the laptop screen and counting cards while Kazakov played with complete anonymity. The pit boss – along with half a dozen bystanders and hangers-on – had his eye on a game of baccarat across the room where an Indian businessman was betting up to a hundred thousand dollars per hand.

Kazakov's cards weren't as generous as they'd been at the Wagon Wheel and the count kept moving against him, but card counting is about playing the odds.

The odds are slightly against a regular blackjack player, guaranteeing that the casino will always win in the long run. A good card counter has a similar edge over the casino and can expect to make an average of one per cent per hand.

It doesn't sound like much, but a dealer can lay down sixty hands an hour, so on average a good card counter can double their money every ninety minutes. Even a careful card counter, who makes deliberate mistakes to throw the dealer and pit boss off the scent, can still expect to double their money for every four hours spent at the tables.

Kazakov was barely two thousand up after an hour, but then he hit a lucky streak: James signalled that the count had moved heavily in his favour at the same time as the other four players left the table. This meant that Kazakov got dealt all of the remaining cards in the deck, with odds leaning heavily in his favour.

Betting two thousand a hand, Kazakov won three in a row, then lost a hand, split a pair of aces and won with both of those hands before drawing a blackjack which pays odds of three for two.

James sat in the business centre, keeping a wary eye on the receptionist, who was running a batch of photocopying, and trying not to let his excitement show. Kazakov had won over ten thousand dollars in six minutes.

'I seem to be having a good night,' Kazakov said, lowering his sunglasses and giving the dealer a rare smile. 'Do you think it might be possible to up the table limit to five thousand per hand?'

The pit boss came over briskly and gave the dealer the briefest of nods before turning away. He had several busy tables and didn't much care that Kazakov was up more than thirty thousand dollars. A dozen other high-stakes gamblers were filling up the casino's coffers, including the

Indian baccarat player who was in the hole for over half a million dollars.

James glanced at his watch and saw he had less than forty-five minutes until his three hours in the business centre were up. Nobody else was doing business this late, and the receptionist was emptying waste baskets and switching off the copiers. James had positioned himself so that she couldn't see the laptop screen, but she was clearly waiting for him to leave so that she could shut up shop and he felt increasingly conspicuous.

Kazakov celebrated the raised table limit with a five-thousand-dollar bet on the first hand with the freshly shuffled decks. The dealer won and James stuttered as he realised that he'd just lost a year's pocket money on the turn of a playing card.

On the next hand Kazakov only bet two thousand, but lost again. Ten thousand up one minute, seven thousand lost two minutes later. James' eyes were getting bleary after watching cards for more than two hours. In his head he knew that the maths of card counting were identical whether the bet was ten dollars or a million, but his nerves struggled with Kazakov betting the price of a second-hand car on each hand.

But probability always wins out and Kazakov kept listening to James' signals to raise or cut the bet when the odds were in their favour. James got a grip on himself and Kazakov won a couple of hands. More people joined the table again, but they were betting between two and five hundred a hand, which wasn't good because it made Kazakov's larger bets the centre of attention.

The count went nowhere, but Kazakov rode his luck and came out a few thousand up. James checked his watch when the dealer shuffled and realised this would be their final run through the decks. The count moved their way and Kazakov started betting the five-thousand table limit every hand.

Kazakov won eight out of ten, including one blackjack: thirty-two and a half thousand dollars in eight heart-pumping minutes.

'I'm closing up and heading home,' the receptionist said. 'If you want your homework printed out or anything, you need to do it now.'

James was so enraptured by their sudden run of luck, that he'd not noticed the receptionist come up behind and look over his shoulder.

'Oh, right . . .' James stuttered, looking back anxiously while trying to keep one eye on the cards. 'I'm practically done. Don't worry, I can print the work in my room when I get home.'

'What have you got up there?' she asked suspiciously. 'Doesn't look like homework.'

James hastily pushed down the lid. 'It's private,' he babbled. 'Internet, web cam . . .'

This sounded horribly suspicious, but James wasn't sure how much the receptionist had seen. Had she just caught a glimpse and realised that he wasn't typing a history essay, or had she seen enough to realise that he had a camera trained on a blackjack table?

The receptionist wasn't huge and James considered knocking her out to ensure she didn't snitch. But she didn't look flustered as she backed off and walked across the carpet to switch off the last of the laser printers.

James grabbed his phone and called Kazakov. 'Cash your chips, get the car,' he whispered quickly. 'I'm probably being paranoid, but the receptionist might have seen something and I don't want to chance it.'

'Where do you want me to meet you?'

'Just get the car and get out,' James said nervously, as he looked over his shoulder and saw to his horror that the receptionist was back out front, speaking into a telephone. 'I'll tell you where to meet me once I'm sure nobody's on my tail.'

38. RAILS

James stuffed the laptop in his backpack and smiled at the receptionist as he headed briskly out of the business centre. He'd followed his training: donning a pair of sunglasses and a blue Nike baseball cap and looking down to make sure he didn't get picked up by security cameras.

'Thanks for your help, miss.'

Still on the phone, she looked up and nodded at him, her expression unreadable.

James' head spun: maybe the receptionist had barely glimpsed, or maybe she'd seen everything. Maybe she'd called casino security to grass him up, or maybe she'd called her boyfriend to tell him that she couldn't knock off early because she was waiting for some dumb kid to finish his history homework.

Whatever the truth, James couldn't risk hanging around to find out. They'd entered the casino from the parking lot at the rear and Kazakov would need a good ten minutes to go to the cage and turn his casino chips back into dollars, plus another five or six to get to the car.

Even if casino security had been informed, it would take

longer than that to watch the surveillance footage from earlier in the evening and match Kazakov to the description given by the receptionist. Even if they caught Kazakov he'd have ditched the camera and signalling device long before, making it impossible to pin anything on him.

In most hotels reception is next to the main entrance, but Las Vegas has its own rules and casinos maximise gambling opportunities rather than convenience. James stopped by a sign with arrows pointing towards theatres, parking, attractions, restaurants, health spas and various hotel towers, but there was nothing so obvious as a sign pointing the way out.

So James relied upon instinct. They'd arrived from the parking lot out back, so if he headed in the opposite direction he'd eventually reach the Strip.

He passed a line of restaurants crammed with computer-industry delegates and the odd tourist. After this came a spectacular indoor courtyard with a huge granite fountain set beneath a glass dome. Couples strolled arm in arm, a casino employee played an accordion and a couple of little kids stood on the fountain's edge throwing in coins and splashing their hands.

The next set of signs pointed left to a shopping mall and right to head back into a different section of the vast casino, but as James rounded the fountain he saw a set of sloped travelators and a sign saying *3D Cinema and the Strip*.

James looked around casually, pretending to admire the fountain. There was no sign of anyone following and he gasped a sigh of relief and decided that he'd just been paranoid. After a huge buffet meal and nearly three hours cooped up in the business centre, James spotted a toilet sign and moved in to take a badly needed piss.

It was an opulent bathroom with more than fifty urinals. There was blue neon lighting above each bowl and individual towels stacked up on stainless-steel bowls between the sinks. James soaked a cloth with warm water and used it to rub eyeballs that ached after three hours of intensely studying an eleven-inch laptop screen. He dried off with another and headed down a hallway back towards the fountain.

Three men stood at the end of the hallway: casino name tags, black suits and radios. They didn't look James' way, and he told himself not to sweat it as he looked back to see if there was a fire exit behind him. But as he passed the first two men the third stepped into his path.

'Excuse me,' he said. He was elderly, but quite tough looking and his nametag said *Joseph – Security Officer*.

'Me?' James said innocently, trying to smile as sweat beaded up on his neck.

The laptop in his backpack was loaded with evidence. They'd need Kazakov's password to log into the machine, but that wouldn't be a problem for anyone who knew what they were doing. They'd quickly find the surveillance software and although James hadn't set the video to record, there would almost certainly be several seconds of blackjack footage that would be recoverable from the computer's cache.

'If you wouldn't mind coming with us,' Joseph said gently. 'We'd like to ask you a few questions.'

'I'm sorry,' James said, scratching his head. 'What's this about? Only, I've got to meet my dad.'

Men coming in and out of the restroom looked at James

suspiciously, assuming that he was a shoplifter or pick-pocket.

'Just need you to come to my office,' the man said. 'A few questions, it's all probably a misunderstanding.'

James had to think fast. If they got him into an office with the laptop and called the cops out he'd be totally screwed. If he was lucky, CHERUB would save his butt to avoid answering embarrassing questions about his surveillance equipment, then they'd fly him back to England and Zara would kick him off campus. If he was unlucky, she'd leave him to rot as an example to any other cherubs who decided to put their training to criminal use.

Not fancying either of those options, James charged. The bigger of the two guards behind grabbed his arm, but James swung back and caught him in the face with an elbow. As the big man fell, James bolted off towards the travelators.

The long flat travelators were similar to the kind you get in airport terminals, except for the plasma screens along the sides advertising the delights of the Vancouver casino and the cheesy voiceover welcoming arrivals and urging those on their way out to come again soon.

'Move,' James shouted, as a mother wrenched her eight-year-old out of his way.

Two of the security guards were less than ten metres behind him, but the biggest one was still down on the floor seeing stars. James could have easily outrun the two middle-aged men over open ground but they were gaining because he kept having to shove people or yell at them to get out of the way.

Half-way along, the travelator left the confines of the Vancouver casino and turned into a glass-sided bridge running over shrubs and flowerbeds ten metres below. James found some space to run, but up ahead two stocky men who'd heard James' shouts turned towards him with stony faces that made it clear they wouldn't be moving out of his way.

The guards were less than five metres behind now and James realised that even if he could knock the two big men down the guards would be on top of him before he made it through.

He looked down and thought about jumping over the sides, but the lush gardens below were lined with concrete blocks and the giant searchlights that lit up the front of the casino.

Seconds before he was sandwiched between four men, James vaulted up on the moving rubber handrail and jumped a two-metre gap, landing heavily on another which took passengers in the opposite direction.

His head hit the slatted metal travelator rungs and the laptop clattered out of his backpack, which he hadn't zipped properly in his rush to leave. He grabbed the computer and began running into the crowd, against the motion of the travelator. He had a clear run of fifty metres, and despite everything gained on the security guards, but as he neared the end he hit a huge crowd of elderly women.

James took all kinds of abuse and a nasty whack from a walking stick as he ploughed through the old women, some with butts almost the full width of the travelator. When he'd cleared the old girls he found the remaining twenty metres of the travelator empty, but his relief was short-lived: it was empty because a pair of much fitter looking security guards stood at the end awaiting his arrival.

The two guards who'd chased him down the travelator were walking parallel on the other bridge. James thought about turning back, but although he couldn't see all the way to the far end through the darkness he knew there would be more casino security guards waiting for him by the time he arrived. That left only one move he could make.

After the briefest of glances to make sure that he wasn't going to land on a spiked fence or jagged rock, James swung over the travelator's glass side and dropped ten metres into the gardens below. He landed in pitch darkness, with a crunch of branches and a sharp pain as a bamboo cane jarred into his back.

He stood up, but toppled sideways, realising too late that he wasn't on the ground. His heart shot into his mouth as he stepped from the top of a low hedge into open air.

He landed in a flower bed as the security guards up above peered over the side of the travelator into shadows. Mercifully, none of them had torches, or a desire to jump over the sides themselves.

After grabbing the laptop out of a tangle of branches and shoving it back inside his pack, James kept low and moved stealthily through a jungle of bushes and shrubs. Within a minute he found himself out of the darkness and standing on the edge of a huge ornamental flower bed that was angled towards the crowd of pedestrians walking along the Strip less than thirty metres away.

The flower bed was illuminated with spotlights and the flowers – which from close range James realised were all fake – spelled out the words *Vancouver Las Vegas – Live the Dream!* below a giant Canadian flag.

James moved as close as he dared to the fence separating the gardens from the broad pavements of the Strip. Freedom was tantalisingly close, but the fence posts towered more than five metres into the air and the top portion was painted with tarry anti-climb paint.

While the security guards up on the walkways hadn't followed him, they knew where he'd gone and it would only be a matter of minutes before their colleagues came out into the gardens looking for him. He considered calling Kazakov and asking for help, but even if the training instructor had a plan there was no way he could arrive before the security guards.

All James could do was explore the gardens and hope for an exit. He set off back the way he'd come, moving along a narrow paved path set behind hedges so as to preserve the illusion of unbroken greenery as seen from the Strip.

After passing back under the twin bridges James found himself in a much wider expanse of shrubs and lawns with the starkly white hotel tower looming above him. He jolted as he heard a sound like a fire door breaking open and saw a flash of torchlight.

Then from above came a rattle and a blast of light. At first he thought it was something to do with the chase, but then he saw the approach of a four-coach monorail train, rattling across a concrete track suspended fifteen metres overhead. It was slowing down to pull into Vancouver casino's station, which was also the end of the line.

James followed the path of the overhead track through the gardens to the point where the station abutted the third floor of the hotel tower. He was delighted to find that the station's emergency exit stairs ran from between the platforms and touched down in the farthermost corner of the garden. Three torch beams shone through the bushes behind as James started to run.

He'd hoped that emergency stairs would lead to an emergency exit gate, that would in turn lead out on to the street. But on the concrete floor below the exit were arrows pointing along a broad path at the rear of the garden.

James was furious because it meant he'd already missed the emergency exit gate somewhere in the dark, and with security teams closing in he couldn't risk going back to look for it. His only option was to belt up the stairs and try catching the train before it left – assuming that security teams weren't coming from that direction too.

James straddled a gate at the bottom of the enclosed concrete staircase and raced up sixty steps, taking them two at a time. At the top was a set of glazed doors, leading on to a wide concourse where a final trickle of passengers was stepping aboard the monorail train.

At the opposite end of the platform, a set of automatic doors were rolling shut to prevent anyone else getting on to the platform. The doors of the train itself would close in a matter of seconds. James burst through the exit, setting off a squealing alarm and stepping on to the concourse as the doors started moving.

The train doors clamped his shoulders as he forced his way into a spacious compartment in the train's lead carriage. The doors bleeped and a recorded voice told him not to obstruct them. He got a few odd looks from the other three passengers in his compartment as the electric motors below the floor buzzed and the driverless train cruised silently out of the station.

James didn't realise how badly he was sweating until he sat down and felt his T-shirt stick to the plastic bench. Before even catching his breath he flipped open the laptop. The train picked up speed as it cut in front of the casino's main entrance, before dipping dramatically into the midst of a vast, open-sided structure with parked cars blurring by on either side.

'The next station for this train will be the Reef. All standing passengers please hold the handrail tightly as the train begins to slow down.'

James ignored the recorded voice as they broke back out into the night, ripples of casino lights reflecting on the curved glass windows.

As soon as the laptop came out of standby, James opened the programs menu, hoping that Kazakov's computer was loaded with the same suite of security programs as the laptops issued to CHERUB agents and mission staff.

Erasing data from a computer is surprisingly difficult. Pressing delete doesn't actually erase files, it just tells the computer that it can overwrite them when it needs the space. But even when files are overwritten, they're still not totally secure and computer forensics experts have been known to recover fragments of data that have been overwritten as many as six times.

James was relieved to find a data destruction program ready loaded on Kazakov's machine. He opened it up and expertly made seven ticks against a list of more than fifty options:

✓ Delete all data and activity logs
✓ Delete entire cache and user records
✓ Delete all personal documents
✓ Use quick and dirty mode for preliminary data destruction
✓ Use US Department of Defence Standard 5220.22-M to totally eradicate data
✓ Do not allow computer to enter sleep mode until data destruction is complete
✓ Erase this program after function is complete to remove any sign of deletion activity

James clicked start and a warning box flashed up on screen:

Basic Data erasure will take approximately 28 minutes on this machine – fragments may still be recoverable after this time.

Erasure to DOD Standard 5220.22-M involves overwriting all data 35 times and will take apx 11.3 hours. (This exceeds the predicted life of your laptop battery by 8.1 hours.)

This process is not reversible.

Start? Yes/No

James clicked yes and watched briefly as some menu screens flashed up. Once he was sure that the data wipe was running he shut the lid and let the software get on with things. Provided nobody got hold of the computer in the next twenty-eight minutes even a computer forensics expert would have trouble finding any incriminating evidence of the surveillance operation and there was no chance of them being able to recover anything as large as a cached video file.

The train lurched to the right and began slowing down for the approach to the station at the Reef casino. To James' surprise the train stopped over a road with six lanes of traffic lined up at the traffic lights directly beneath. He'd ridden the same track with Kerry and the gang when they'd spent the day touring, so he knew it wasn't part of normal service.

'What's going on?' someone asked, as James nervously slid his phone out of his pocket and thought about calling Kazakov.

A non-recorded announcement came over the train's PA system. 'Ladies and gents, I'm sorry for any inconvenience caused by this delay. Unfortunately our computer systems are reporting a minor fault with this train and one of our circuit breakers has tripped a safety system. You have no reason to be alarmed, but we're gonna have to hold the train here for a few moments while we switch out the motor and reboot the control software.'

James thought this was fishy. He'd set off an alarm when he'd charged through the emergency exit doors, and the two minutes he'd been on the train had been ample time for security to review their video footage and identify him. They couldn't announce the true reason because it might cause a panic.

James glanced desperately around the compartment as he dialled Kazakov to update him. As the mobile rang in his ear, he saw the black security camera dome in the carriage ceiling and realised that the security teams were probably watching every move. Most likely they would wait for armed police officers to arrive before letting the train roll on into the Reef station.

As James looked down from the ceiling he saw a green hammer encased in glass, and below it a set of instructions on how to use it to smash the windows in case of an emergency.

'Where you at?' James asked anxiously, when Kazakov finally answered.

'Cashing out took ages,' Kazakov moaned. 'I had to fill out a form before they'd pay my winnings. Money laundering regulations, apparently. I'm in the car, driving down ramps in the parking lot.'

'Right,' James said, putting his face up to the glass and shielding his eyes to cut out reflections. He spoke in a whisper so that the three passengers at the opposite end of the compartment didn't overhear. 'Security's all over me. I'm looking at a big Denny's restaurant on the north side of Reef Drive about five hundred metres from the junction with the Strip. That's where I'm gonna try and meet you.'

'Where are you now?' Kazakov asked.

'No time to explain,' James said. 'Just be there in five minutes' time.'

He snapped the phone shut, then used his elbow to smash the piece of glass covering the hammer.

39. RUNGS

James didn't want to be watched, so his first move was to jump high and swing the little hammer at the surveillance dome. It took two cracks to break it open, by which time one of the men sitting on the bench had jumped up.

'What the hell d'ya think you're doing?'

James tried to look menacing. 'I'm not hurting you,' he shouted. 'Sit down.'

But he was a big fellow and he wasn't going to be intimidated by a sixteen-year-old. James faced a dilemma: normally when he went on a mission and had to punch someone out it was for the greater good, but what about now? He didn't like the idea of being a guy who broke someone's nose just so that he could make a few bucks.

The guy stopped for an instant and James thought his threat had worked, but he took another step as James reached up and used the end of the hammer to rip the rotating camera out of its socket. He gave James a two-handed shove.

James was in deep shit and short of sitting down and waiting for a set of handcuffs he had no option but to lash out. He punched the big man hard in the face, then kneed him in the guts as he stumbled backwards. A final shove sent him crashing head first into the doors.

'I told you to stay out of it,' James warned, as the man's girlfriend screamed out. 'And she'd better cut that racket out as well.'

It was one of the worst moments of James' life. He was scared, he'd just battered someone whose only motivation was to stop him from vandalising a train and despite a lifelong history of making bad decisions and doing stupid things, this felt like the worst.

But that didn't mean James was in any mood to surrender and let his whole life go down the toilet. The window with the escape sign had a triangular sticker in the corner. A red dot in the centre had the words *strike here* encircling it.

James hit hard. The first blow cracked the shatterproof glass and the second turned it into a sheet of tiny pebbles. He stepped back, grabbed the overhead handrail with both hands and swung forwards. His trainers crashed through, knocking out the entire rectangle of glass and sending it hurtling down on to the road directly below.

James leaned through the hole and wasn't impressed. The single rail was completely enclosed by the body of the train, which meant there was nothing but a fifteen-metre drop on to the six lane highway below. He looked back nervously at the big man, who sat on the floor by the doors, clutching his stomach while inspecting his sunglasses to see if they were broken.

James didn't fancy his chances, but he imagined the reaction of Lauren and all his mates on campus if he got expelled, and for some reason the prospect of that humiliation seemed worse than the thought of plunging to his death.

It was too high to jump: even if he didn't break both legs on landing he'd get hit by a car two seconds later. He'd have to climb up on the roof and drop down on to the concrete plinth along which the train ran.

He'd been over sections of the height obstacle on campus that were trickier, but the thing was he had no idea if there was any way down, except at the stations where the cops would be waiting for him.

There was a grab handle designed for maintenance and cleaning crews working on the outside of the train. James took hold, stepped up on to a plastic seat and then on to the window ledge itself.

'You're gonna kill yourself!' the female passenger shouted.

'Good,' her boyfriend answered.

James was strong and had no problem twisting around to face the train and then swinging his legs up on to the roof. The train drew its current from the rail below, so there were no overhead cables to trouble him as he bolted across the curved plastic roof towards the rear of the train.

The train had an aerodynamically sloped nose at each end. James leaned over the rear of the roof to check where he was going and saw a girl of about six who was standing on the seats inside looking out. She screamed with fright and a tourist with a video camera swung around and filmed James as he slid down the glass nose and landed unsteadily on the metre-wide concrete plinth where the train met the track.

It was only now that it occurred to James that the double-ended train could run in either direction. There might be a reception party awaiting him in the Reef station, but he now realised they could just as easily run the train back towards the Vancouver, squishing him in the process.

It didn't bear thinking about. James set off. The electrified track and running gear for the train were built into the sides of the plinth, so James had a narrow but completely flat concrete path ahead of him, vanishing into the darkness.

Running was dodgy, so James walked quickly before stopping to inspect the Y-shaped pylon twenty metres behind the train. Each end of the fork supported one lane of track, but there was a conspicuous absence of footholds or rungs to climb down and even if he slithered down into the seat of the Y he'd still be too high to jump.

As he walked on, he heard an alarming rumble. At first he thought his train was coming after him, but another had pulled out of the Reef station on the second track. It was accelerating hard and touched fifty miles an hour as it whizzed past in a blur of light. The rush of air forced James to crouch down and grasp the sides of the concrete plinth.

He stood up, increasingly desperate for an encounter with either a pylon fitted with rungs or a point where the track crossed a building and he could jump down on to a rooftop. As the train on the opposite track shrank into the distance its rear lights showed him the way: a tatty billboard advertising a call-girl service was mounted under the tracks less than fifty metres away.

James cast a nervous glance backwards and jogged briskly towards the sign. The train wasn't moving, but alarmingly there were three police cruisers with flashing blue lights turning from the Strip on to Reef Drive.

The billboard was ten metres high, made from aluminium sheet and held up by three wooden trusses which were bolted to the roof of a fast-food joint directly below. It topped out a few centimetres below the monorail plinth and James rolled over the edge and lowered his foot on to the top of the aluminium.

It had to withstand desert winds, so James knew the structure would hold his weight, but he still got a fright as he clutched the aluminium bar at the top of the billboard. The whole frame flexed and the aluminium sheets boomed under his weight.

The next phase was similar to the pole slide on the height obstacle on campus, except for the added complication of having to negotiate past spotlights mounted atop the billboard. The casings were hot enough to melt skin and swarms of desert moths swirled around them.

It took James half a minute to make it three metres from the monorail track and on to the top of an angled wooden truss. He clutched the side and shuffled down the forty-five degree angle before landing gently on the flat roof of the food joint.

Away from the Strip the streets of Las Vegas are pretty deserted. As far as James could tell nobody had seen him climb down, but the police would take about a second to figure out his escape route once they arrived and shone torch beams up at the monorail track.

James kept low as he walked across the single-storey roof. When he peered over the guttering, he was pleased to find himself facing a brick wall and a deserted rear parking lot, rather than the glass-windowed restaurant packed with diners he'd have found out front.

He dropped off the roof, his nose filled with the smells of food waste and cooking oil as he jogged around to the front of the restaurant. He was actually at the rear of a cluster of fast-food joints built around a small parking lot off Reef Drive.

Customers sat at outdoor tables in the chilly night air eating burgers and fried chicken, and nobody looked James' way as he did his best to change his appearance: pulling off his baseball cap and dark sweatshirt to reveal a pale orange polo shirt beneath it.

The driveway at the front of the outdoor food court led on to Reef Drive itself. The Strip casinos were ablaze with light and in front of it were the two monorail tracks and the raised pedestrian walkway. James' train was now rolling towards the Reef station at walking pace while a pair of police cars was parked directly under the bridge. They'd shut off one side of the road because of the pane of shattered glass.

James walked past a line of tacky souvenir stores, towards the brightly lit Denny's sign, looking for a break in the traffic. He dashed in front of a tour bus, then vaulted the metal division in the road's centre before strolling across the other side, which was blocked by the cops.

Much to James' relief, Kazakov was waiting in the black Ford. James ripped off his backpack and climbed into the front passenger seat.

'What happened?' Kazakov gasped. 'You got something to do with them cops back there?'

'Drive now, talk later,' James said firmly. 'They'll figure out where I went in a minute or two and seal off this whole block.'

Kazakov pulled out of his parking space. 'If the cops are on our backs, we'd better leave town.'

'Yeah,' James nodded. 'Airport here might be a bit dodgy. We should drive to Los Angeles. There's loads of flights to Britain from there.'

Kazakov glanced at James. 'Drive through the night, get a flight early tomorrow morning. You ring the control room on campus, get them to sort some flights.'

'Right,' James nodded. 'What if they ask why we're not flying out from Vegas?'

'Christ knows,' Kazakov said. 'Tell them we fancied a road trip.'

'What about this car? It belongs to Fort Reagan.'

'General O'Halloran said to leave it at the airport,' Kazakov smiled. 'He didn't say *which* airport.'

The main Interstate between California and Nevada runs parallel to the western side of the Strip. James had been too overwhelmed to pay attention to where they were going and was surprised to feel the car accelerate. He looked out the window as Kazakov sped up an onramp and pulled on to the eight lanes of Interstate Five.

It was eleven at night. The road moved freely but the traffic was heavy and James felt a wave of relief as he relaxed into his seat, revelling in the anonymity of their black Ford. The southern end of the Las Vegas Strip was already shrinking into the distance and James realised that they'd got away with . . . *something*.

He jolted up in his seat and turned to Kazakov. 'How much?' he blurted.

'Receipt's in the glove box.' Kazakov smiled.

James popped the flap and saw a clear plastic wallet with a stack of bills inside. He unravelled the bag and looked at the receipt. *The Vancouver, $92,300, please visit again next time you're in town!*

'Not bad for one night's work,' James grinned. 'Not bad at all.'

Less than ten minutes earlier James had experienced one of the worst moments of his life. He'd taken a massive risk and still felt guilty about the man he'd beaten up in the monorail carriage, but now he was mostly elated as his head was filled with all the things that $30,766 could buy: nice clothes, days out, expensive meals, treats for girlfriends, holidays, a flash motorbike.

'Tell nobody on campus,' Kazakov said firmly. 'Spend it carefully. Don't be flash.'

'I know, boss,' James smiled. 'I'm not stupid.'

As James spoke a huge 4x4 cut in front of them, forcing Kazakov to squeeze the brake pedal. 'American idiot!' he shouted, blasting the horn before turning to glance at James. 'Make that phone call to campus,' he ordered. 'Sort the plane tickets. I can't stay in this country for another day.'

40. MORALITY

Ten days later

'Come in,' James shouted.

He'd finished afternoon lessons and was lying on his bed trying not to think about a particularly nasty essay he'd been set for his English GCSE.

Lauren came around the door. She looked tired and her hair was wet, like she'd just had a shower.

'Welcome home,' James smiled. 'Good time? How'd the rest of the exercise go?'

Lauren crashed in the swivel chair at her brother's desk. 'Not bad,' she said, kicking the carpet with her socked foot and starting to twirl slowly. 'The exercise was lame after Kazakov left. They brought in all these extra rules. Both sides were doing everything by the book, and of course the American commander had no idea what cherubs are capable of. By the sixth day Sarge got so bored that we started a mini revolt with the SAS guys and we killed our commander and started a riot.'

'Rebel,' James grinned. 'Somehow I get the impression that they won't be inviting us back to Fort Reagan any time soon.'

'They kicked us all out four days early,' Lauren said. 'And that was the best bit, because rather than coming back, we all stayed on in Vegas and hung out for a few days. Meryl still has friends out there and she got us tickets for Spamalot and a couple of other shows.'

'Shame I missed that,' James said.

Lauren's eyes were drawn towards a brightly striped shirt hanging on James' wardrobe. 'Paul Smith,' she smiled. 'That's gotta be a hundred quid, which is pretty good going for someone who's supposed to be paying off Jake Parker's phone.'

'I got lucky,' James lied. 'Me and Kazakov went to this outlet mall. It was only thirty bucks. I think they put the wrong price tag on it.'

'The day you flew home, Rat tripped on a staircase and did his ankle in,' Lauren said, continuing to turn her chair from side to side. 'They thought it might be broken, so they helicoptered him to Vegas to have it properly X-rayed.'

'Was he OK?'

'No problemo,' Lauren smirked. 'They don't let newspapers into Fort Reagan and they only have that one TV channel to make it seem more like a developing-world place. So when I ended up in a waiting room I picked up a Las Vegas paper to see what was happening in the world.'

James watched as Lauren pulled a half-page of the *Las Vegas Sun* out of her pocket and started to read. '*A teenager staged a daring escape from a monorail car after being chased out of the Vancouver casino. The boy was believed to be the accomplice of a Russian man running a card-counting scam at the high-stakes area of the Strip's newest mega-resort.*'

Lauren held up the picture of the monorail car with the smashed window. Below it were grainy surveillance photos of the two suspects. James had seen the pictures before when he'd looked up the story on the Internet to see how much the police knew.

'So what?' James said, trying not to smile.

'Aww, come on,' Lauren said. 'Credit me with *some* intelligence. If that's the best shot they got, you two made a good job of disguising yourselves and not looking up for the security cameras, but I know you. You've had that same dopey Nike Air cap since before Mum died.'

James eyed Lauren nervously. 'You didn't mention this to anyone else, did you?'

'And risk you getting kicked out of CHERUB? Of course not. I may think you're a tosser, but you're still my brother.'

'I made a lot of money,' James smiled. 'Thirty grand in one day. Once I'm twenty-one I won't need Kazakov or surveillance equipment, I can do it legally. I've ordered a couple of books from Amazon with the most advanced card-counting strategies that give you an even bigger–'

Lauren cut her brother dead and read some more from the article. '*Louisiana trawler-man, Dan Williams, intervened to prevent the teenager's escape and was floored by the powerfully-built youth in what police described as a* vicious *assault. Williams sustained two cracked ribs and was kept in hospital overnight after complaining of chest pains.*'

James looked down at his lap. 'I feel bad about *that*, obviously. But I warned the guy not to stick his nose in.'

Lauren snorted with contempt. 'You must be so proud of yourself.'

'We could go up to London next weekend,' James said, desperate to win Lauren around. 'Covent Garden, all the designer clothes shops, my treat.'

'No thanks,' Lauren said acidly. 'It leaves a bitter taste. I thought you'd grown up over the last couple of years but right now I'm back to thinking that I'm gonna end up visiting you in prison some day.'

'I know it was dumb,' James admitted. 'Very dumb, to be honest, but it happened. I'm not proud of it, but I don't exactly regret it either and you know, the money's in a shoebox behind my bath surround, if you ever need some help. Fifteen thousand quid, all in twenties.'

'Maybe you should donate it to charity or something.'

James shook his head resolutely. 'I risked my CHERUB career and my life to make that money. Besides, what's thirty thousand bucks to a ten-billion-dollar casino corporation?'

Lauren gulped air and broke into a big yawn. 'Jetlag,' she moaned. 'I'm gonna try staying awake until after dinner, then I'm going straight off to sleep.'

'I'll probably see you down there,' James said. 'I've got this essay to write on sonnets . . . What the bloody hell are sonnets anyway?'

'More top marks coming your way then,' Lauren smirked as she headed for the door. She turned back when the door was half-way open. 'Oh, there's one other thing you might be pleased to hear.'

'What's that?' James asked.

'Day before yesterday,' Lauren said, rubbing an eye as she stifled another yawn, 'Bruce and Kerry had a *massive* ruck at the hotel. It looks like they've split up.'

EPILOGUE

After a seven-week trial the leader of the Street Action Group (SAG), CHRIS BRADFORD, and former paramilitary, RICH DAVIS (AKA RICH KLINE), were both convicted of conspiracy to commit acts of terrorism.

Bradford was sentenced to fifteen years in prison. In the light of his previous terrorist convictions Davis was sentenced to life, with a judge's recommendation that he should not be released for at least thirty-five years.

An independent review concluded that the CHERUB security check team led by LAUREN ADAMS had done valuable work in uncovering slack procedures, bad training and poor design at Britain's newest air traffic control centre.

The opening of the centre was delayed by three months while the perimeter fencing was replaced with a five-metre-high wall and improved surveillance technology. The private security company was dismissed, although several staff, including JOE PRINCE, were taken on by a new contractor and redeployed to the site after extensive retraining.

Following his unimpressive performance during the training exercise at Fort Reagan, GENERAL NORMAN SHIRLEY was reassigned to duties with a non-combat unit. After three months in his new post the general took early retirement.

Each two-week mission at Fort Reagan costs over $25 million to mount and the tactics used by red team leaders are studied carefully by military planners. Although General Shirley was outraged and GENERAL SEAN O'HALLORAN was highly concerned by the destruction of his aerodrome, the US military strategic planning unit described the unorthodox and highly aggressive tactics employed by YOSYP KAZAKOV as an outstanding example of guerrilla warfare.

Kazakov was offered a highly-paid position as a full-time advisor to the US Military at The Pentagon, Washington DC, but he declined on the grounds that he enjoys his job at CHERUB and couldn't stand the idea of living in America.

The security office at the Vancouver Hotel and Casino only had the evidence of one receptionist to show for their investigation into possible fraudulent gaming by a Russian suspect. None of their electronic jamming devices or signal-detection equipment had picked up any kind of video transmission.

The casino's security boss concluded that the Vancouver's state-of-the-art revenue protection systems could only be defrauded by the kind of high-tech surveillance equipment used by security services such as MI5 or the CIA and that the chances of any such equipment being used by ordinary members of the public was negligible.

The Vancouver hotel did file a complaint about a teenage

boy causing $3,200 worth of damage to a video surveillance pod and a window on one of their monorail carriages.

Trawler-man DAN WILLIAMS sued the owners of the Vancouver hotel for damages, claiming that by stopping the monorail car with a criminal suspect on board they had negligently imprisoned him with a dangerous and potentially violent criminal, with no regard for his safety or that of the other passengers.

Williams settled out of court for $373,000. Two fellow passengers, including Williams' wife, each received payouts of $114,000.

DANA SMITH and MICHAEL HENDRY broke up after four weeks. Michael begged GABRIELLE O'BRIEN to take him back, but she told him to stick it.

JAMES ADAMS has continued to hone his blackjack skills and has told his closest friends that his ambition in life is to ride around America on a Harley-Davidson and make millions by counting cards in casinos. James points out that while using surveillance equipment to cheat casinos is illegal, counting cards in your head is not.

Summer 1940.

Hitler's army is advancing towards Paris, and millions of French civilians are on the run.

One of them is a twelve-year-old boy called Marc. His travelling companion is a British spy named Charles Henderson.

The very first CHERUB adventure is about to begin.

Henderson's Boys is a major new series from Robert Muchamore, coming 2009.

Turn the page to read an exclusive preview.

www.hendersonsboys.com

HENDERSON'S BOYS: THE ESCAPE

Charles Henderson didn't feel great about having Marc alongside him. Before joining the Espionage Research Unit he'd been a naval intelligence officer and their training course gave strict instructions never to use kids. The intelligence manual said that children were physically weak, untrustworthy, unable to handle stress and liable to panic or scream.

But Marc was the only help on offer and Henderson wasn't ungrateful for it. He'd slept less than ten hours in the past four days. He hadn't washed or eaten a proper meal and was only keeping himself going with strong black coffee and Benzedrine pills. The worst part was knowing that it wasn't over. If Henderson made it out of Hotel Etalon alive, he'd still have to break through the German and French lines and somehow get to Tours ahead of Potente, who was already on the road.

Henderson drove a small Fiat and the clock on the

dashboard told him it was just a few minutes until the eight o'clock curfew, though at this time in June there was still plenty of daylight. The roads were dead, except for the odd truck packed with German troops. Most cars had left the city crammed with refugees, and the few remaining drivers didn't want to risk being made into an example by the newly arrived Germans. Everyone had seen newspaper pictures of the corpses hanging from lampposts in Warsaw.

Marc sat in the passenger seat. The mix of adrenaline and whisky made him feel better, and regular beatings at the orphanage had left him with an unusually high pain threshold. He was worried about Henderson though. Sweat poured down the man's face, his driving was crazy and a couple of times his expression glazed over so badly that Marc thought the car was going to end up ploughing into a wall.

They cruised past Hotel Etalon at just six minutes to eight. The private road leading up to its grand lobby was lined with open-topped Kubelwagens and three of the grand Mercedes saloons used by senior German officers.

'There's four regular soldiers guarding the entrance,' Marc noted, as Henderson turned into a narrow side street and pulled up.

'I saw them,' Henderson said warily.

He stepped out of the tiny car and looked up and down the street. 'We've got to get in there before curfew or we're buggered.'

Henderson took out a duffel bag containing the partially assembled Sten gun and handed it to Marc.

'How do we get inside?' the boy asked, as the weight of the bag practically wrenched his arm from its socket.

'Every posh hotel has a staff entrance. It'll be around the back.'

'But they might be guarding that too,' Marc said. 'And if we get in, how the hell are we going to get away again when the whole city is under a curfew?'

'Good questions,' Henderson said, as they walked briskly towards the back of the hotel. 'I'll let you know the answers just as soon as I think of them.'

A left turn took them on to a concrete ramp, misted with steam curling out of the hotel kitchen and stinking of the rubbish overflowing from giant metal bins. Three kitchen staff stood in an open doorway smoking cigarettes and a bored-looking German guard sat on a step behind them.

'Act as if we do this every night of our lives,' Henderson said to Marc, as they approached the door.

'Evening, gents,' Henderson said brightly, nodding to the smokers.

They looked a touch mystified, but it was a big hotel and they didn't know everyone who worked there. The German stretched out his leg to stop them and spoke in bad French.

'My French not too good,' Henderson said, pointing jovially towards himself. 'I night porter. My son is shoe shine.'

The German didn't seem happy to have drawn guard duty on his first night in Paris and he looked up miserably and pointed into the kitchen with his thumb. 'Go ahead.'

Savage heat blasted Marc as he stepped inside. A filthy corridor took them into the hotel kitchen proper, where three men as rough as any Marc had seen leaving the Dormitory Raquel stood in front of a trough, scrubbing massive pots. Another man barged past, carrying a crate filled with empty champagne bottles.

It seemed impossible that anything could be hotter, but as they reached the centre of the kitchen Marc felt as if the sun had crash landed on his head. It seemed impossible to breathe, let alone work in such heat, but dozens of kitchen staff carted ingredients, chopped, boiled, seared and dragged heavy trays out of ovens.

Marc and Henderson caught a few odd glances, but nobody had time to stop and ask questions. When the waiters passed through the swinging doors leading into the restaurant they were able to glimpse a room filled with black uniforms. At the far end, someone was making a speech to a chorus of drunken laughter.

'It's good if they're pissed,' Henderson said, smiling as he stepped out of the kitchen into a narrow corridor with great clumps of mildew growing on the walls. 'Remember, Marc: confidence is key. Always look like you know where you're going, even if you haven't got a clue.'

Marc was scared and felt slightly woozy, but at least the corridor was merely stifling, rather than unbearable. They walked twenty metres until they came to a wooden staircase that went down to the hotel basement. A door at the bottom led them into a room containing two giant washing machines. Beyond the machines a woman worked flat out, stretching white hotel sheets over a steam-press, then taking off the flattened sheets and folding them into neat squares.

She stared oddly at Marc and Henderson. Clearly she didn't get many visitors.

'Hello,' Henderson said. 'We just started work here. I'm supposed to unblock a toilet for someone called Mannstein.'

The woman raised a single eyebrow. 'How the hell does that bring you down here?'

'I just came along the corridor.'

She looked at Marc. 'And you've brought your son to work?'

'Shoe-shine,' Marc said.

'We've never had that before,' the woman said. 'Night porter does the shoes when reception is quiet.'

'They wanted him special,' Henderson said. 'All those Germans need their boots cleaned.'

'Germans,' the woman said, as she spat on a sheet before folding it. 'I've been having a nice time these last weeks with Paris so quiet. Now they're turning everything upside down. Threw out all our guests, including residents who've lived here for years, then went down to the cellar and dragged up all the best wines and champagne. You can bet they won't be paying their bills and if I don't see my wages I'm out of here.'

'That's the breaks, I guess,' Henderson said uncertainly as he turned towards the door. 'You wouldn't know how I can find out what room Mannstein's in, would you? I don't want to go back upstairs and make myself look stupid.'

The woman tutted with contempt, but pointed towards a telephone on the wall. 'Dial zero, zero for the front desk. They'll give you his room number.'

As Henderson grabbed the phone, the laundress walked over to a clothes rail and grabbed a set of pressed overalls. 'You'd better put them on,' she said. 'If the floor manager catches you in a public area without a uniform he'll go spare.'

Then the woman looked at Marc. 'We've never had a boy shoe-shine before. The only thing I've got that will fit you is a messenger's uniform. But don't go getting polish on it because it'll never come out of white cuffs.'

'Thank you.' Marc nodded to her as he grabbed the hanger. His uniform comprised a white shirt, black trousers and a velvet waistcoat with gold buttons.

'Very fetching,' Henderson teased, as they stepped back into the corridor.

'Did you get the room number from reception?' Marc asked.

'Six-one-two,' Henderson replied. 'Now we need somewhere to put these clothes on.'

They headed back upstairs and passed a janitor's cupboard that was big enough to change in. Henderson closed the door behind them, switched on the light and unzipped the bag, taking out the compact machine gun and showing Marc how to take off the safety catch, fire and reload. On the way out, he grabbed a mop, plunger and bucket.

'Now we've got to find the lift.'

The staff area on the ground floor was a warren and it took several anxious minutes of wandering badly-lit corridors until they found themselves near the hotel's reception desk with the main elevators facing directly towards them.

Several Gestapo officers were returning to their rooms. The lift stopped at the second and fifth floors and on each the departing officers were saluted by two German infantrymen on guard duty.

'Seems they've got this place sealed up pretty tight,' Henderson said.

They were alone for the final ride to the top floor and Henderson used the opportunity to check that his silenced pistol was ready to fire.

'You sure you're OK with the machine gun?' Henderson said. 'Remember to hold it exactly how I showed you or you'll rip your shoulder off.'

The two guards stepped forwards as the lift doors opened.

'State your purpose,' one guard said, in truly awful French.

Henderson began to mumble a convoluted explanation about blocked pipes in room 612 and how the messenger boy's little arms would be needed to reach behind a sink and undo a valve. Of course, the Germans didn't understand a word.

'Blocked toilet,' the German said irritably. 'That's all you need to tell me.'

Henderson nodded apologetically as he walked off with Marc in tow. But after a few steps he realised he'd gone the wrong way and he turned around. Once they'd passed the guards again, one spoke to the other in German.

'Useless bloody French,' he sneered. 'Too much wine. It's no wonder they lost the bloody war.'

Henderson and Marc both thought it best to pretend that they hadn't understood and carried on towards Mannstein's room. Fortunately there were several turns in the corridor and two sets of fire doors.

'As soon as Mannstein opens the door I'm going to shoot him in the face,' Henderson said. 'Stand well back unless you want to get splattered in blood.'

'Right.' Marc nodded, taking a deep breath as he poised his knuckles in front of the door. Henderson dropped his bucket and mop and pulled the silenced pistol.

Marc knocked and waited.

'Who is it?' a German said.

'Messenger boy,' Marc shouted.

Henderson panicked. 'That's not Mannstein,' he gasped.

Marc didn't have time to ask what to do as a Gestapo officer opened the door. 'Message from Oburst Hinze–' he began.

But before Marc knew it, Henderson had fired his shot and a mist of the officer's blood had spattered his face. Marc was stunned as Henderson burst into the room, just in time to hear Mannstein cry out and run for the bathroom. The bolt slid across the door a second before Henderson barged into it.

'I just want to talk, Mr Mannstein,' Henderson lied. 'It's not too late. I can still get you out of France.'

Inside the bathroom, Mannstein was going frantic. Banging against the wall, stamping on the floor and screaming for help. He wasn't a fool and he knew Henderson wasn't here to talk.

'Machine gun,' Henderson shouted, pointing towards the bag.

Marc handed the gun over and Henderson stepped away from the door and let rip. The bullets shredded the door. Henderson used his fist to punch through a large hole and then aimed directly at Mannstein, who'd taken shelter by lying flat in the bath.

A second blast from the Sten gun turned him into red goo, but Mannstein's cries and the gunfire had been heard by the guards down the corridor and by several Gestapo officers in their rooms.

The first black uniform came out of the room directly across the corridor. Marc dived to the floor as the officer took aim with his pistol, but Henderson spun around and annihilated him with the machine gun.

'Shit,' Henderson howled. 'Shit, shit, shit.'

'Never mind shit,' Marc said, as he grabbed the pistol from the dead German's hand. 'What do we do?'

'What do you think we do?' Henderson said as he charged towards the door. 'Run like hell!'

CHERUB: The Recruit

So you've read *CHERUB: The General*. But how did James Adams end up at CHERUB in the first place?

CHERUB: The Recruit tells James' story from the day his mother dies. Read about his transformation from a couch potato into a skilled CHERUB agent.

Meet Lauren, Jake, Kerry and the rest of the cherubs for the first time, and learn how James foiled the biggest terrorist massacre in British history.

CHERUB: The Recruit available now from Robert Muchamore and Hodder Children's Books.

CHERUB: Class A

Keith Moore is Europe's biggest cocaine dealer. The police have been trying to get enough evidence to nail him for more than twenty years.

Now, four CHERUB agents are joining the hunt. Can a group of kids successfully infiltrate Keith Moore's organisation, when dozens of attempts by undercover police officers have failed?

James Adams has to start at the bottom, making deliveries for small-time drug dealers and getting to know the dangerous underworld they inhabit. He needs to make a big splash if he's going to win the confidence of the man at the top.

CHERUB: Maximum Security

Over the years, CHERUB has put plenty of criminals behind bars. Now, for the first time ever, they've got to break one out . . .

Under American law, kids convicted of serious crimes can be tried and sentenced as adults. Two hundred and eighty of these child criminals live in the sunbaked desert prison known as Arizona Max.

In one of the most daring CHERUB missions ever, James Adams has to go undercover inside Arizona Max, befriend an inmate and then bust him out.

CHERUB: The Killing

When a small-time crook suddenly has big money on his hands, it's only natural that the police want to know where it came from.

James' latest CHERUB mission looks routine: make friends with the bad guy's children, infiltrate his home and dig up some leads for the cops to investigate.

But the plot James begins to unravel isn't what anyone expected. And it seems like the only person who might know the truth is a reclusive eighteen-year-old boy.

There's just one problem. The boy fell from a rooftop and died more than a year earlier.

CHERUB: Divine Madness

When a team of CHERUB agents uncover a link between eco-terrorist group Help Earth and a wealthy religious cult known as The Survivors, James Adams is sent to Australia on an infiltration mission.

It's his toughest job so far. The Survivors' outback headquarters are completely isolated. It's a thousand kilometres to the nearest town and the cult's brainwashing techniques mean James is under massive pressure to conform.

This time he's not just fighting terrorists. He's got to battle to keep control of his own mind.

CHERUB: Man vs Beast

Every day thousands of animals die in laboratory experiments. Some say these experiments provide essential scientific knowledge, while others will do anything to prevent them.

CHERUB agents James and Lauren Adams are stuck in the middle.

CHERUB: Brigands M.C.

Every CHERUB agent comes from somewhere. Dante Scott still has nightmares about the death of his family, brutally killed by a biker gang.

When Dante joins James Adams on a mission to infiltrate the Brigands Motorcycle Club, he's ready to use everything he's learned to get revenge on the people who killed his family . . .

Look out for *CHERUB: Brigands M.C.*, coming soon from Robert Muchamore and Hodder Children's Books.

And don't miss the rest of the CHERUB series: *The Recruit*, *Class A*, *Maximum Security*, *The Killing*, *Divine Madness*, *Man vs Beast*, *The Fall*, *Mad Dogs* and *The Sleepwalker*.